Sugar Daddy Sweet Tooth
By: Jessica Terry

SUGAR DADDY SWEET TOOTH

First edition. September 15, 2024.

Copyright © 2024 Jessica Terry.

ISBN: 979-8990176942

Written by Jessica Terry.

I'm so grateful to my family, church family, friends, fellow authors, readers, and anyone else that has shown me even a modicum of support. It means more than I can say.

Content warning: I'm gonna make it plain; this story contains multiple people doing dishonorable things, and is not for the overly judgmental. It also contains an obese character, mentions of murder (that happens off-page), and depression.

Chapter 1

. . . .

"THEY'RE ABOUT TO START firing folks again."

Journey Garnett whipped around in her chair. Her coworker Christina had appeared behind her, hunched over and speaking in her usual hushed whisper.

"What? Where did you hear that?"

"The grapevine is hot, girl. I'm surprised *you* haven't heard it by now."

"You know I don't listen to office gossip. People say some of everything up in here."

"This isn't gossip, Journey. Some of the higher-ups confirmed it, though of course they don't want to be the ones to come out and say it. Don't want everybody panicking or whatever."

Journey's brow furrowed in concern. "Do you think it will hit *this* department? They just did some layoffs a few months ago."

"You know they're trying to tighten the purse strings around here. Word is, though, that it won't affect us. Since we deal directly with these complaining customers, we'd be last on the list. It's the behind-the-scenes departments they're cutting, mostly."

That made Journey breathe a little easier. She worked in customer service and while she didn't love her job, she certainly couldn't afford to lose it.

"I guess that's good, though I hate to hear about *anybody* losing their job like that," she mused.

"Yeah, true. But most people up in here have some kind of side hustle, anyway. And you're gonna be a big-time hair stylist, yourself. I'm still loving this dye job you did on my hair; got me feeling all glamorous and shit."

Chuckling, Journey looked at Christina's newly-dyed platinum blonde natural hair, which played well against her toasty brown skin. Between that and the short cut Journey had given her, Christina had been singing her praises ever since.

"Yeah, I noticed how you've been strutting around here like Naomi Campbell or somebody."

"Please. I have way better cheekbones." Christina hopped off her perch on Journey's desk. "Anyway, just wanted to give you the tea, since I figured you hadn't heard. And you know they don't want us spreading it and worrying everybody."

"Of course. Wouldn't want to give people a heads-up that they might be about to lose their livelihood. Better to have them blindsided."

"You know how they do. Well, let me get on back to my desk. I'll catch you later."

Journey turned back to her computer as Christina sauntered off. She couldn't help but be a little concerned, still, about the supposed layoffs. She'd been with Metro Service Group for six years and had survived multiple rounds of layoffs, but that didn't mean she felt any more secure in her position than she ever did. Everyone knew they could be out the door at any time.

She tried to put it out of her mind and continue with her day. After hearing such unpleasant news, she was more anxious than usual to get out of there and home to her son, Theo.

Before she could do that, though, she had to see her ex-husband.

"I hope he keeps his word this time," she muttered to herself as she pulled up to his home. "Dude stays in a freakin' townhouse but can't give me a couple hundred bucks a month for his son."

She knocked on the door and checked her watch. When nothing happened, she knocked harder. Several more moments of nothing passed and she was yanking out her phone when the door flung open. Dino, her ex-husband stood there shirtless and breathless.

"My bad," he said, waving her in. "I was on the phone and didn't hear you knocking."

"Uh-huh." She stepped inside but stayed close to the door. "You got what we talked about?"

He looked away from her and brushed his long locs off his shoulder. "You want something to drink or some doughnuts or something?"

"No, Dino, I don't want any doughnuts. If you could just give me the money so I can go and get Theo, I'd appreciate it."

"What's the rush?"

"I'm tired and I still have to get home and make dinner, among other things. And I'm just really not in the mood to socialize. Do you have the money or not?"

He ran a hand down his face. "Umm..."

"Dammit, Dino!"

"Look, I'm sorry! I had some unforeseen stuff come up but I *promise*, I'll be able to break you off in a day or two."

"Break me off? You're not doing me some damn favor. Theo is just as much your child as he is mine."

"I know that, J."

"And as for that promise, you told me you were going to give me this money *last* week. Let's not even talk about how behind you are."

"You don't have to keep telling me that. It's not like I'm trying to be selfish. Once this business kicks off, money won't even be an issue. I've got a conference call tonight, matter of fact."

"Oh yeah? What kind of 'business' is it this time? Selling phone service? Protein shakes? Magic lotion?"

"What, you trying to be funny?"

"Nah, I'm serious. I don't know why you keep wasting your time with all these pyramid schemes."

"It's multi-level marketing."

"It's a pyramid scheme."

"Call it what you want to, folks get straight *paid* if they work 'em right. And I've already got a string of folks ready to sign up under me."

"Yeah, that's what you said when you were doing the thing with the hair products made out of berries. You ended up with a room full of products you couldn't even give away, let alone sell."

"Why you always gotta bring up old stuff? That was two years ago."

"And yet here you are doing the same stuff. Why don't you get a real job?"

"Why, so I can be miserable working for somebody else doing something I hate like you? I wanna have my own thing."

"I wanna have my own thing, too, and I will. But in the meantime, I'm doing what I gotta do. Theo needs stuff *now*. I don't have the luxury of doing all this experimenting."

"Yeah, okay. You know, this is partly why we got divorced, because you never believed in me. I had your back when you first started doing hair. But I guess that don't go both ways."

"Whatever," Journey waved him off, turning towards the door. "I don't have time for this."

"Journey, hold up." Dino hurried over to her, covering her hand on the doorknob with his. "Look, I'm sorry, all right? I don't wanna fight with you."

"Well, you should do what you're supposed to do, then."

"I'm gonna make it up to you, I promise." He stepped close to her, leaning in to inhale her flowery perfume. "I can start right now, actually."

Journey eased back, curling her lip and frowning. "Seriously?"

"Don't act like you're never down. Is that a new nose ring? It's hot."

"Back up off me, Dino."

"And that dress is clinging in all the right places. Girl, you know you thicker than overcooked grits."

She rolled her eyes. "Bye, Dino." Pushing him away, she yanked open the door and stormed out, annoyed that she had wasted her time coming there. Even more so that he tried to get some after he flaked on her. Again.

It had been the same cycle with Dino ever since they got divorced a few years earlier; he'd get into another one of his "businesses", promise her and Theo the world, and then make himself scarce when things didn't turn out like he predicted. And he seemed to think a quick roll in the hay was supposed to make up for him not contributing financially.

Journey shook her head. She could admit there were times that she'd given in to Dino, succumbing to weak moments. But the reason she'd filed for divorce in the first place was because she could never depend on him. And she still couldn't. As usual, she'd just have to figure out how to make ends meet on her own.

She pulled up to her grandmother Olivia's house and fluffed her twistout before smoothing her hands over her cheeks, trying to erase the frown from her face. Between her job and her ex-husband, she could almost feel the stress filling up her body like juice in a glass. But she didn't want to show that in front of Theo, so she took a few deep breaths and tried to put on her game face.

Her mother's loud voice hit her before she even got to the door, and Journey rolled her eyes.

"This is gonna be a quicker visit than I thought," she mumbled, knocking on the door.

It swung open, and Journey smiled down at her seven-year-old son.

"Boy, what are you doing opening the door?" she scolded with a smile, entering the house.

"Mama O is in the kitchen and Clarice is on the phone fussin.'"

"What did I tell you about calling your grandmama by her first name?"

"Well, whenever I call her 'Grandmama' she tells me not to 'cause it makes her sound old and she don't wanna hear that."

"Lord..."

"Hey, baby," Journey's grandmother Olivia greeted as she rushed from the kitchen. "I was just finishing frosting these cakes. I told this boy I'd come get the door in a second."

"I saw it was Mama so I went ahead and answered it," Theo defended. "You always said don't answer the door for *strangers*."

Chuckling, Olivia came over to give Journey a hug and kiss on the cheek. "How was work, baby girl?"

"It was work," Journey shrugged. "Just another day of endless calls and complaints."

"It's only temporary. You'll be in business for yourself doing hair before you know it."

"I have to go to cosmetology school first. This stuff I do on the side is cool but I wanna be all the way legit with it."

"You will be. Just stay the course."

"What's Mama doing here? I could hear her from outside."

"She's back there, on the phone with Senior. They had another fight."

"I figured. That's usually the only time she comes over here."

"One of these days I'm gonna change my locks. I'm getting too old for this kind of drama."

"Please. I think you low-key like the soap opera Mama and Senior have been playing out for years. And as for all that 'old' stuff, you're in better shape than Mama is. Probably me, too."

"Girl, hush," Olivia dismissed, but she couldn't hide her pleased smile. Her firm size six frame was thanks to years of water aerobics and Pilates, and only eating meat on Sundays. Journey's size doubled her grandmother's, not that she cared.

"Theo, go get your stuff so we can go," Journey instructed. After he ran off, Journey looked at her grandmother. "Thanks again for watching him for me. I couldn't believe how much they were charging for that after-school program. I'm already ready for summer break and we're not even a week into this school year."

"You know it's no problem. The school is right down the street, anyway. No need in paying that money when I'm right here. Plus he keeps me company while I'm up in here baking and knitting folks' stuff. I can't believe how many orders for custom blankets I got after you put them on that Facebook."

"I can. They're awesome. I know I love the one you made for me."

"Who knew learning how to knit forty years ago would be putting money in my pocket today. I'm supposed to be retired."

"Yeah, but you know you don't like just sitting around, Grandmama. Trying to get you to relax is a waste of time."

"I relax plenty when I'm doing my crossword puzzles at night. I don't mind staying busy doing stuff I like doing."

"Exactly the point I'm trying to get to."

When Theo emerged with his too-large backpack in tow, Journey hurriedly kissed Olivia good-bye and started to leave, anxious to get out of there before her mother Clarice finished her latest argument with Senior. She was in no mood to hear the latest grumblings about her stepfather (who was old enough to be her grandfather), knowing Clarice would be going right back home to him in a matter of hours.

Right before she and Theo were out the door, he announced, "Oh yeah, Mama. My teacher gave me a list of stuff I'm gonna need for class. We're supposed to have it by Friday."

An immediate frown came to Journey's face, but she tried to clear it. More stuff already? She'd already had to put all of the school supplies and new clothes Theo needed for the new school year on her credit card, which was something she tried not to use except for emergencies; the last thing she needed was more debt.

Without even seeing the list, Journey knew she wouldn't have the money for whatever was on it by Friday. She wouldn't be getting paid for another week, and thanks to Dino flaking on her, she didn't have any extra.

"Okay, umm...I'll have to see what I can do, sweetie."

"But she *said* we *have* to have it on Friday."

"Well, she's just gonna have to-"

"Theo, baby, go get me my glasses from my room for me," Olivia jumped in. "They're right in there on the dresser."

"Yes, ma'am."

When he was out of the room, Olivia took some money out of her back pocket and pressed it into Journey's hand. "Here, baby. Use this."

Journey looked at her gratefully. "You don't have to do that, Grandmama. I would've figured something out."

"Hush. If you don't have it, you just don't have it. I've been there plenty of times. Get whatever the boy needs. He doesn't need to know where it came from."

Unable to resist, Journey hugged her again, breathing a sigh of relief. It was one less thing to worry about, and she appreciated that.

"It's not gonna always be like this, baby," Olivia whispered to her as Theo trotted back into the room, glasses in hand. "Just keep pushin.'"

• • • •

LATER, AFTER SHE AND Theo had dinner and he was getting ready for bed, Journey got a call from her friend Roz.

"How was the j-o-b today?" Roz asked.

"Same as always. I'm sure your day was a lot more interesting than mine."

"Did a couple of photo shoots."

"See? Told you."

"At least you know what you're gonna be doing every day. I love being a makeup artist and everything, but sometimes the freelancing can be rather unpredictable."

"Please, you've been killing it."

"And you will be, too. When are you supposed to enroll in cosmetology school?"

"Soon. But if Dino keeps leaving me hanging like he did today, I might have to push it back yet again."

"I told you to go ahead and put him on child support."

"So he can end up in jail when he can't pay it? He'll be *no* good to me, then. At least now he can help pick Theo up and keep him every other weekend. Theo was just asking about going over there a little while ago."

"I guess."

"And it sounds like they're getting ready to do more layoffs at work."

"Oh no. Do you think they'll lay *you* off?"

"The word is that our department is safe, but who knows. I'm trying not to worry about it. It's not like we haven't been through this before."

"True. It's gonna all work out, though. You're still doing hair on the side in the meantime. I saw the latest style you did, on Instagram. I never thought I'd say purple braids were cute."

"That client was right on time, too, 'cause that money went towards fixing my cracked windshield. And you have a hard time saying *any* hair is cute, since you cut all yours off."

"Oh, I love *other* people's hair; I just don't want to fool with any, myself." Roz laughed, and Journey couldn't help but join her. "Being damn near bald works for me."

"I couldn't do it. I love changing up my style too much."

"Oh, I know. You've been doing that since the fourth grade. However Ms. Clarice fixed your hair, you changed it as soon as you got to school."

"Well, that was because Mama didn't even try to make it cute. I *had* to fix it myself if I wanted to look decent and not get clowned. That's probably where my love for doing hair came from."

"I wouldn't doubt it. Oh, and don't forget, we're supposed to go and give Mom her monthly makeover tomorrow."

"I'll be there. Heading over right after work."

"Good. I'll probably get there before you do. You know Dad fired her nurse, right?"

"Another one? For what?"

"Who knows. I'm sure it's a stupid reason, especially since Mom doesn't even feel like she needs a nurse. Dad doesn't really like having another guy in the house, but Mom insists on a male nurse because she doesn't want other women around him. You know she's paranoid about someone else catching his eye."

"Just because she's overweight?"

"Girl. You can keep it real. Mom is straight obese with a capital O. Let's just call it what it is."

"Well...I didn't wanna be disrespectful."

"You're family; you know what the deal is with that. And there's nothing disrespectful about the truth."

"I guess. I've offered to try to help her get some of that weight off. But anyway, I'll see you over there tomorrow. I've got some stuff I need to finish before I go to bed and get ready to do all of this again tomorrow."

"Don't be like that, Journey. You're just paying your dues right now but before too long you're gonna be doing these shoots and stuff right along with me."

"I appreciate that encouragement, girl. 'Cause I surely can't go on like this forever."

Chapter 2

• • • •

"IT'S SO NICE OF YOU girls to come over here," Roz's mother Molly gushed as Roz and Journey got all of their supplies ready. "I'm sure you have better things you could be doing."

"Come on, Ms. Molly; you know it's no trouble," Journey insisted. "I thought of a real cute style to do on your hair today."

"What you do is always cute. Too bad it gets wasted with me just sitting around the house."

"Well, Mom, I offer to take you out somewhere but you never want to go," Roz reminded her.

"I'm too fat to fit in your little car, and we both know it."

"I wish you wouldn't say stuff like that."

"Why not? It's the truth, isn't it?"

"Well...you don't have to *stay* fat."

"Ugh. I've tried losing weight a thousand times and I always get discouraged. I admit it's my fault I'm like this. After my parents were killed, I just stopped caring. It's a wonder Clyde is still here. I know I disgust him."

"Dad isn't going anywhere."

"Only because he feels obligated to stay. Not because he *wants* to be here. We hardly even-"

"Nope! I don't know what you were about to say but I have a feeling that hearing it will make me want to burn my ears off. We get it; you and Dad have issues."

"*Issues* doesn't even begin to describe it. I know he keeps hiring these nurses just to have someone to keep me from eating everything in sight when he's not here; it's not because I need one. At least I got him to agree not to hire any more. But I know you two don't want to hear my whining." Molly brushed her blonde hair out of her face and adjusted her position on the bed. "Journey, are you seeing anyone?"

"Oh no," Journey scoffed. "Still single as a dollar bill."

"Can't imagine why. As gorgeous as you are?"

"Stop that," Journey blushed with a smile. "A relationship would be nice but I haven't even been out where I can meet anybody."

"You don't have to go out; do what I did and meet someone online," Roz suggested. "Cooper and I have the ideal arrangement; we see each other once a month."

"How is that ideal?"

"I've never wanted someone up under me all the time. By the time the next month rolls around, I'm good and ready for him. We have our weekend of togetherness, then he goes back to where he came from and I can go back to being able to fart in my own space as much as I want."

"Really, Roz?"

"What? I'm just saying."

"Yeah, well. As romantic as that arrangement sounds, I'd rather not even bother if I'm only gonna see them every once in a while. You ready, Ms. Molly?"

Molly nodded, adjusting herself again on the bed. "Sure, yeah."

Journey went to work on Molly's hair, while Roz started her makeup. Journey always liked doing this for her; they'd always gotten along great. Journey could remember when she and Roz were kids, Molly was the typical suburban housewife who made them brownies after school and hosted all the birthday parties. It was a vast difference from Journey's mother Clarice, who wasn't the warmest person to be around, and Journey started spending a lot of time at Roz's place. And since Roz's dad Clyde worked so much, it was usually just the three of them, having girl talk and doing other fun things that Journey didn't get to do at home.

"Ms. Molly, if you want me to help you work out and stuff, the offer still stands," Journey spoke up after a while. She skillfully worked the curling iron through Molly's silky tresses. "We can drop some pounds together."

"Please, you don't need to lose any weight," Molly dismissed, her eyes closed as Roz smeared a light moisturizer over her face.

"It couldn't hurt. And I don't work out much now so it'll be good for both of us. I mean, I'm no expert or anything but I'd be more than happy to try to help, if I can."

"It *would* be nice to have someone I trust. None of the trainers Clyde brought in here were a good fit for me. Some were so snide, some were condescending...like they were judging me for letting myself get like this."

"That's probably why Dad hired them. You know how he is about tough love," Roz muttered.

"Yeah, well. I get that I need some discipline but I need compassion, too."

"Compassion isn't exactly Dad's strong suit."

"You certainly don't have to remind *me*."

"Well, you just say the word, and we'll make it happen," Journey commented.

Molly smiled up at her appreciatively. "I'll certainly keep it in mind."

"I'd offer to help you with that too, Mom, but you know I barely work out, myself."

"I know, Roz. Thank goodness you have your dad's metabolism."

"I still think Journey needs to be finding a man, while she's working and doing hair and trying to be the next Jillian Michaels," Roz continued. "You haven't really had a serious relationship since Dino."

Sucking her teeth, Journey sprayed a light holding spray over the pinned curls in Molly's hair. "I guess you could say Dino kind of soured me on relationships. I'll find someone eventually but right now, I'm just focused on Theo and getting into cosmetology school, and getting rid of some of this debt I'm in."

"I wish you'd let me pay you for coming over here," Molly said.

"You're family. I don't charge family."

"Hell, *I* do," Roz chimed in as she waited for Journey to move to the side so she could resume her position in front of Molly. "Mom is the only one who gets this for free. Once you become a professional, you better start charging everybody or else every distant cousin you have will be coming around asking for the hookup."

"You probably have a point with that."

The three of them continued to talk as the friends worked on Molly. It was the only time Molly really enjoyed herself, since things between her and her husband Clyde had grown so strained. They hadn't spent much time together in months, and she knew he resented her for gaining so much weight, among other things. Just thinking about how happy they used to be compared to how they were now almost brought tears to her eyes, but she fought to keep them at bay. She'd just cry in private, like she usually did.

After a while, Clyde came home. When he entered the bedroom where the three ladies were congregated, his eyes were empty when they looked at his wife, but brightened when they landed on Journey.

"Ladies," he greeted, nodding.

"Hi, honey," Molly greeted hopefully, sitting up a little straighter.

Roz returned his nod. "Hey, Dad."

"Hey, Mr. McMillan," Journey looked up with a brief smile before returning to her task of painting Molly's nails.

"Now, Journey, how many times have I told you that you don't have to be so formal with me?" Clyde admonished with a smile. He went over and hugged his daughter, then gave Journey a familiar pat on the back, not wanting to disrupt her work. "You've known me too long for that."

"Force of habit."

"Dad, doesn't Mom look hot?" Roz asked him pointedly, noticing how he hadn't spoken to Molly directly yet. "You should take her out to dinner tonight or something. She looks too pretty to just hang out here."

Clyde eyed his wife, resisting the automatic thought that *hot* was not a word that could be used to describe Molly, no matter what Roz and Journey did to her face and hair. Maybe twenty years ago it could, but not now that she'd let herself go like she had.

He could see the way Molly was looking at him, though, as if she really wanted his approval. And he knew if he didn't say something nice, he'd never hear the end of it from Roz.

"Yeah, her face looks really nice," he finally commented obligingly. "That stuff around her eyes really brings out the blue. And I like how you did her hair, Journey."

It wasn't lost on Molly that he was complimenting Roz and Journey's skills more than he was her, and she tried to keep the dejection off her face. She didn't know why she expected anything different. As long as she looked the way she did, he simply wouldn't be interested in her.

Roz just looked at him with a slight frown and tightened jaws, annoyed that he was treating Molly so indifferently. They'd had many arguments about that in the past and she knew they'd probably have another before the night was over with.

"Um, thanks," Journey replied to him, noting the shift in the room. She was glad that she was almost done because she was ready to get out of there, all too familiar with that look Roz was shooting Clyde. "Those curls will look even sexier tomorrow, Ms. Molly. That carefree, tousled look really fits your face."

Smiling at her appreciatively, Molly gently touched her bouncy tresses. "You're such a sweetheart, Journey."

"Yes, you are," Clyde agreed, peering at her.

Blushing, Journey waved both of them off. "It's nothing. Glad to do it. All right, Ms. Molly, let's take your pictures."

"Ugh, do we have to?" Molly whined. "You know I hate pictures."

"Yes, we have to. You look too good for us not to."

"Well, I have some work to do, so I'll be in the office," Clyde announced, turning towards the door.

"So you're really gonna come home and just spend the evening holed up in your office, huh?" Roz called out as he started to leave the room. "*Way* on the other side of the house..."

"It's not a mansion, Roz. And there *is* an intercom."

"Have you had dinner yet? You and Mom can eat together."

"It's okay, Roz," Molly looked up at her daughter. "I'm sure he has a big case coming up or something. I have some salads and fruit in the mini fridge over there, anyway."

"There, see?" Clyde smiled triumphantly. "I make sure to keep that fridge stocked so she has everything she needs in here."

"No, what she *needs* is-"

"Roz!" Molly grabbed Roz's hand. "Just let it go. Please."

Pursing her lips, Roz glared at her father as he walked out, but didn't say anything else.

Molly cast a sad glance towards Clyde before looking down at her lap. "Oh shoot, I messed up this pretty polish you just put on, Journey, I'm so sorry..."

"Don't worry about it, Ms. Molly. I can fix it." Journey reached for a bottle of nail polish remover and smiled at her reassuringly. "Nothing to apologize for."

"Mom, I'll order some takeout and we'll have dinner together," Roz offered. "I'm sure you don't want to have some boring salad, anyway."

"Well, Clyde ordered those from some chef he knows, so they're pretty good," Molly replied, unable to resist defending her husband. "It's nice of him to go through all that trouble for me."

"Shelling out money for some salads in a mini fridge isn't going through any trouble. Dad has never had a problem spending money on you; he has plenty of money. How much *time* does he spend, though?"

"Roz..."

"I'm just saying. Time is way more valuable."

"You know how your father is," Molly sighed. "I know he still loves me. It's just hard for him to see me like this."

"Please stop defending him."

Journey moved faster with re-doing Molly's nail polish. This was how things usually ended up whenever Clyde came home; automatic tension. It was something Journey could never get used to and always hated being in the midst of.

A short time later, she stepped out of the room to call and check on Theo. He was spending the night at Dino's, but Journey just wanted to hear his voice. She needed a pick-me-up, as she usually did after getting a ringside seat to the McMillan family drama.

After talking to her son for a few minutes and going to the restroom, she started to head to the kitchen to get something to drink when she heard Roz and Clyde talking. Or more accurately, arguing.

"Why do you keep doing her like that, Dad?" Roz hissed. Journey could just imagine her friend standing there with a hand on her hip, which was Roz's usual stance when she was serving attitude. "Do you have any idea how that makes her feel when you act like she's not even there?"

"Roz, you don't live here anymore. You have no idea how things are when your mother and I are alone."

"Oh, so you're trying to tell me that you're loving in private, but cold-hearted in front of company?"

"Excuse me?"

"You know what I'm talking about, Dad. You didn't even speak to her when you got here. And I'm sure it wasn't lost on her that you looked more excited to see Journey than you did to see her."

"You don't know what you're talking about."

"Dad, I really wish you would get over it. So Mom gained weight. She was distraught about her parents being killed. You don't have any compassion for that?"

"I know the reason she put on all the weight. But believe me when I tell you that her appearance is not the sole issue, or even the main one. And maybe when you're married yourself one day, you'll understand that things don't always stay the same after a while. I love your mother. I haven't left her. I'm still here, providing her with everything she needs."

"Yeah, except *you*," Roz retorted snidely. "When was the last time you even hugged her? Or asked her how her day was, or how she was feeling? How about giving *her* all of your attention for a night instead of your legal briefs?"

"Look, Roz," Clyde's voice sounded tired. "There are just some matters I'm not going to discuss with you. Things always look different from the outside looking in. Molly and I have been married a long time. I promised to always be here for her, and I am. But don't try to tell me what kind of husband to be. You didn't watch your spouse sit and balloon up to damn near four hundred pounds, ignoring all of your efforts to stop her. I offered to get her counseling, therapists, whatever she needed, pleaded with her to let me be here for her, but all she wanted was more food. She shut *me* out for months. So I don't need to be judged by you or anyone else, all right?"

Feeling uncomfortable listening to their conversation, Journey headed back towards Molly's room, forgoing her intent to get something to drink. Right then, all she wanted was to get out of there.

She went to gather her things and say goodbye to Molly, and figured she'd just text Roz and let her know she'd left, since there was no telling how long she'd be in there fussing with Clyde. It was one time she was glad to be going home to an empty apartment.

Her car had other plans, though, because when she tried to start her usually-reliable Honda Civic, it didn't make a sound.

"Great," Journey muttered. "That's just great."

She had just gotten out of the car and slammed the door in frustration when Clyde poked his head outside. "Everything all right?"

"No, my car won't start. Guess the battery is dead or something."

"Did you leave your lights on?"

Peeking inside the car, Journey sighed and cursed under her breath. "Yep. That's exactly what I did. Like an idiot."

"Don't say that." Clyde strolled outside, hands in his pockets. He had removed his suit jacket and tie, and the sleeves of his blue button-down shirt were rolled to the elbows. He eyed her before nodding towards the car. "It's a simple mistake. Just pop the hood; I'll get it taken care of."

"Really? I've been meaning to get some jumper cables..."

"I have jumper cables. You can go on back in the house, if you want. I'll let you know when I'm done."

"No, that's okay; I can stay out here. Keep you company or whatever."

"Great. I'll just go get my keys and bring my truck around."

"Thank you *so* much."

Clyde nodded before wordlessly turning and going back into the house. After he pulled his Suburban around, he asked Journey casual questions about work and her son as he attached the jumper cables and they waited for them to do their job. Journey noticed how smoothly Clyde went about doing things, looking totally comfortable in his office attire fiddling underneath the hood of her car, not concerned about getting anything dirty. It was a side of him she'd never seen in all the years of knowing him.

"You're all set," he announced once Journey's engine was purring again. "I did take a peek at your oil level, though, and you should put some more in here soon."

"Can I make it another week?"

"Oh yeah, you'll be fine until then. I can get it for you, if you want. What kind do you use?"

"Oh no, Mr. McMillan-"

"What do I have to do to get you to stop calling me that?"

The question temporarily stumped Journey, though she wasn't sure why. "Uh...I don't know. I guess I just don't feel right calling you by your first name."

"Well, I wish you would think of something else. I'm not your teacher or somebody. I'd like to think you're comfortable with me by now, right?"

The truth was, Journey *wasn't* as comfortable with him as she was with Molly. She'd known them the same amount of time, but Clyde worked a lot while Molly had been a stay-at-home mother, so Journey spent way more time with Molly over the years. Over time, she grew to think of her as another mother figure. She didn't have that same comfort level with Clyde. She liked him, respected him, but there had always been that modicum of distance that she never really thought about but had gotten used to. He was just her best friend's dad who popped in between his various meetings and court cases and handed out money for them to go shopping or order pizza before disappearing again.

"Sure," she finally answered, though she sounded awkward, even to herself. She didn't know why she felt slightly uneasy all of a sudden. "Of course I do, yeah."

"Good." Clyde proceeded to unhook the cables and return them to the case he kept them in. Journey had never seen anyone have a whole briefcase for their jumper cables; they always just tossed them in their trunk and kept it moving. "You're all set."

"I really appreciate this, Mr...um, Mr. C."

He smirked at her, giving a conceding nod. "That's slightly better."

"Is there anything I can do to repay you? I don't have any cash on me right now, but-"

"Journey. Don't insult me like that."

"I'm just very appreciative. I know you said you had work to do and you probably don't have time to be messing around with my car-"

"Stop. You don't have to give me anything. I know you're grateful."

"I'm *extremely* grateful."

"That's good enough for me." Winking at her, he closed his trunk and strolled back over to her. For the first time, Journey noted how neat his salt-and-pepper beard was, and that his skin was the color of toffee. The way he looked at her seemed different than usual. Journey couldn't put her finger on how.

"Okay, well...I'm gonna get on home," she said, hating how awkward she still sounded.

"Call and let us know you made it."

"I'll text Roz when I get there."

"*Or* you can call me..."

"I...don't have your phone number, Mr. C."

"We can remedy that right now." He pulled out his wallet and retrieved a business card, handing it to her. "My cell is at the bottom."

"Oh cool...thanks." Journey slid the card into her pocket.

"If you ever need anything, don't hesitate to call me, Journey. I'm here for you just like Roz and Molly are."

"That's really sweet. I'll keep that in mind."

"I'm serious. Whatever you need. I'll do anything for you."

He was standing there, hands in his pockets, looking right at her. His eyes didn't flinch at all, conveying just how much he meant those words. Journey could imagine him fixing that glare on his opponents in court.

"That means a lot," she finally replied. Smiling at him, she went over and gave him a brief hug, feeling obligated. He hugged her firmly, with both arms, before she stepped back. He smelled like some kind of fancy soap. "Have a good evening."

"You too, Journey."

He stood and watched as she got in her car and backed out of the driveway. Journey waved at him as she drove off, anxious to get home to her remote and a big bowl of cookie dough ice cream. She didn't even give thought to why her hands were shaking.

Chapter 3

• • • •

A COUPLE OF WEEKS LATER, Journey was mindlessly typing away on her computer at work. The layoffs had in fact happened, but thankfully Journey's department hadn't been hit. She hated it for the people who got the axe, but she was hugely relieved to still be employed herself.

"You wanna go to lunch today?" Christina asked her, hopping onto her desk as she usually did. "Since we still have jobs and all."

"Girl," Journey chuckled and shook her head. "I brought my lunch. Eating out really isn't in the budget like that."

"It's on me. I think I can spring for some wings."

"You don't have to do that."

"I do a lot of stuff I don't have to do. Come up in here every day looking fly, giving these repressed dudes a thrill..."

"Stop it."

"But for real. Take that tired sandwich or whatever you brought with you back home and come out with your girl. I'm sure you could use a breath of fresh air by now."

"It's nine-thirty."

"That's all?? Damn, I feel like I've been up in here all day!"

Journey giggled as a new instant message alert popped up on her screen. She leaned in to read it, and her smile faded slightly when she saw it was from her supervisor.

Christina noticed. "What's wrong?"

"Owen wants me to come see him."

"For what?" Christina twisted around, trying to peer at the message.

"He didn't say."

"Oh. Well, I'm sure it's probably nothing," Christina dismissed with a wave of her hand. "You know how Owen is; he tends to make mountains out of molehills sometimes."

"Right," Journey agreed, though she couldn't help being a little nervous. Owen didn't usually call them to his office; if he had something to say, he'd instant message or email it. For something super urgent, he'd call. Journey couldn't help but wonder what was so important that he had to tell her in person so early in the day.

She tried to ignore the thin thread of dread that coursed through her as Christina headed back to her desk. Quickly scanning her mind to try to think of what she might have done wrong, she locked her computer and headed towards Owen's office, trying not to look as nervous as she felt.

"Come on in, Journey," Owen greeted her after she lightly knocked on his open door. "This won't take too long."

Trying not to take that as a bad sign, Journey stepped into the small office and stood behind the chair in front of the desk.

"You can sit down," Owen offered.

"That's all right. I'd rather stand."

"Okay." He shot her a strange glance, then shuffled through a few papers on his desk. "Well, the reason I called you in here is because I wanted to see where your head is in regards to your future here."

Oh no. "Oh, um..." She tried to shrug casually. "I want to be here for as long as you all will have me." *Or until I can get to where I do hair full-time.*

"That's good to hear because I'm going to recommend you for a promotion to supervisor."

Journey blinked, clearly thrown. "Say what?"

"I'm putting you up for promotion. You've been here for six years and have been an excellent employee. It's time you got rewarded for that."

The grin shot across her face. This was just the good news Journey needed to hear. "Are you serious, Owen? Please tell me you're not just messing with me."

"Of course not. You know I don't have a sense of humor."

"True." Journey placed a hand on her chest as relief washed over her. "Thank you *so* much for this; I can't tell you how right on time it is."

"Well I'm glad you're pleased, but nothing is set in stone yet. It's just a recommendation right now, but I don't see why it wouldn't be approved. You have a great track record and you've been meeting or exceeding standards since you've been here. And there *is* an opening thanks to someone retiring, so I'd say your chances are very good."

"I appreciate it, Owen. Thanks for thinking of me. I guess I'll just keep my fingers crossed, huh?"

"Yeah. I'll let you know what comes of it, one way or the other. In the meantime, though, please keep this to yourself."

"Absolutely," Journey quickly agreed, even though she already knew she was going to be telling Christina. "Is there anything else?"

"No, that was it. Keep up the good work. Thanks, Journey."

Journey tried to contain her giddiness as she headed back to her desk. When she passed by Christina, who looked at her questioningly, Journey just indicated that she'd talk to her later. She went back to work with renewed energy, feeling more positive about things than she had in a while.

• • • •

"SO WHAT DO YOU THINK?"

Journey turned to Carrie, the nice lady who was showing her around Barone School of Cosmetology, or BSC. She hadn't been able to stop smiling since she arrived. "I love it! It's way nicer than the pictures online."

"Oh yeah, we just renovated some areas and updated a lot of our equipment and supplies. We're gonna be updating the site in the next couple of days. But I'm so glad you like it!"

"I really do. Thanks so much for giving me a tour; I know it's the end of the day and all."

"It's no problem at all. Hopefully getting to peek in on a couple of the classes gave you at least a little bit of an idea of how things are. These are our evening students, on the year-long program. We also have day classes and that's a nine-month program, but you have a day job, right?"

"Right."

"Yeah, so this evening program is where you'd be, most likely. If you want to put in an application, just let me know. Our next semester is going to be starting in a few weeks. We'd love to have you join us."

Journey didn't hesitate. "Absolutely. I'm ready."

"Great! Come on to the office and we can get started!"

Journey's excitement continued to grow as she filled out her application, then talked to an administrator about payment options. Hearing how much all of this was going to cost only made her hesitate for a second. She'd be getting a little more cushion if she got the promotion at work. And even if she didn't, she'd find a way to make it happen. She was tired of putting off her dream.

"Gotta jump in," she told herself as she headed back out to her car later. Her fingers happily tapped the steering wheel as she sung extra loud along with the songs on the radio, whether she actually knew the words or not. She couldn't remember the last time she felt so excited.

She headed to Olivia's to pick up Theo, the smile still on her face when she knocked on the door.

"What are you so happy about?"

Journey hadn't expected to see her mother there again. Determined not to let Clarice dampen her good mood, Journey just stepped forward and gave her a big hug. "Hey, Mama!"

"Girl...you pregnant or something?"

"What?? No!"

"Well, you sure glowing like you are."

"Can't I just be in a good mood?"

"Uh-huh," Clarice hummed, turning and sauntering back into the living room. Journey shook her head as she stepped inside, closing the door behind her.

"Is Theo ready?"

"I don't know. He's back there in the back with Mama. Theo!" Clarice yelled as she plopped onto the couch, immediately kicking her thin legs up onto the ottoman. "Your mama is here!"

Almost immediately, hard footsteps could be heard running towards the living room. Theo ran right over to Journey and threw his arms around her waist. "Hey, Mama!"

"Hey baby! You have a good day?"

"Yes, ma'am."

"That's good and everything but I've told you about running in here," Olivia admonished Theo as she emerged from the back of the house, though there was a smile on her face.

"Sorry."

"And I've told *you* about yelling in here, too," Olivia turned to Clarice, her smile faded.

Knowing Oliva would put her out if she talked back, Clarice just contritely replied, "Sorry."

Coming over to hug Journey, Olivia looked at her with a playful suspicion. "What's got you so cheerful?"

Journey grinned harder. "I've had a really great day. But the most exciting thing is that I enrolled in cosmetology school, finally."

"Oh you did? That's wonderful!" Olivia pulled her in for another hug. "I'm so happy for you!"

"What's cosmetology?" Theo asked.

"It's doing hair and nails, sweetie," Journey replied.

"I know you've been waiting for this for a while; I'm glad you're finally going ahead and doing it," Oliva commented, rubbing her granddaughter's back.

"You can afford that?" Clarice asked with a raised brow. "I thought you were struggling."

Journey remained undeterred. "I can manage."

"You can't put Theo in an after-school program but you can put yourself through school?"

"Clarice, mind your business!" Olivia snapped. "If you can't be supportive then just shut up."

"And anyway, that's what financial aid is for," Journey continued. "It's not ideal, but if I wait to save all the money for that, I'll be applying for AARP at the same time."

Chuckling, Olivia waved a hand at her. "Don't even worry about it. However you need to get it done, get it done. I'm just proud of you for knowing what it is you wanna do and going out and doing it."

"Me too, Mama," Theo concurred, hugging Journey again.

"Thank y'all so much," Journey gushed, rubbing Theo's low-cut black hair. She'd just given him a haircut the previous evening. "I'll take all the support I can get."

"I just don't want you to get your hopes up," Clarice spoke up somewhat hesitantly, eying Olivia. "I'm not trying to be negative...I just know how it is trying to juggle a bunch of stuff at once. Eventually, something always falls off. Just saying."

"Theo, get your stuff so we can go," Journey instructed. She wasn't going to let her mother dampen her spirts. Clarice had a way of bringing a dark cloud over bright moments, and Journey wasn't going to let her do that this time.

"And *you* go get your stuff so *you* can go," Olivia told Clarice sternly, after Theo left the room. "I told you to hush if you couldn't be positive and I guess you thought I was playing."

Clarice's jaw dropped. "Mama!"

"Get!"

Journey stifled a laugh as Clarice stomped to the back to get her purse. Olivia just shook her head.

"You didn't have to do that on my account," Journey informed her.

"Yes, I did. She's always bringing stuff down when she doesn't have to. So she can do that at her own house."

"Well, I appreciate you having my back. You get lifetime free hair services, you know."

"I don't believe in letting folks do stuff for me for free that they've spent time training for. But I love you for wanting to."

Shortly after, Journey and Theo left. She surprised him with dinner at IHOP, even though that wasn't really in her budget. It was Theo's favorite restaurant and Journey felt like celebrating her good news, even though Theo didn't know a whole lot about what they were celebrating.

"So you're gonna be doing homework and stuff like me?" he asked her as he munched on a piece of bacon.

"Not the same kind of stuff, but yeah."

"You gonna have to take tests?"

"Yep."

"What happens if you get a bad grade?"

"Bad grades aren't allowed in our house, remember?"

"But I can't put you on punishment like you do me."

Journey chuckled. "True. But not passing my assignments is punishment enough."

"Does Daddy know you're going back to school?"

"Not yet."

"When you gonna tell him?"

"Not sure. Whenever I talk to him next, I guess."

Dino was actually supposed to meet Journey at home to bring her the long-awaited money he promised her, but she didn't want to tell Theo that and get his hopes up for seeing him. Turns out that was a good decision because Journey hadn't heard from him all day. And when she finally got Theo home and ready to take his bath, she tried to call Dino and he didn't answer, nor did he respond to any of her texts.

"Figures," she muttered, throwing the phone to her bed. "He doesn't even have the balls to tell me he doesn't have it this time."

After she put Theo to bed, Journey took a shower and checked her phone again for any messages from Dino, already knowing there wouldn't be any. She shook her head and pulled out the information for BSC, the smile automatically coming back to her face. She couldn't *wait* to get started.

When her phone rang with a video call and she saw it was Roz, Journey excitedly answered. "Hey, girl."

"What you doing?"

"Just looking at this stuff for cosmetology school. I finally enrolled today."

"You did?" Roz gasped, her face brightening. "Go 'head, girl! I'm glad you finally took that leap."

"Yeah, I'm not thrilled about going into more debt over it but if I keep waiting, it might never happen. And I'm not trying to be at Metro forever, even though they *did* tell me I might be getting a promotion soon."

"Yeah, you're just killing it all the way around. I'm so proud of you, girl. And even if you have to struggle some in the beginning to get your career off the ground, it's worth it to do something you love every day."

"You're right about that."

"And you know if there's any way I can help, just say the word."

"Thanks, girl."

"Now, can I tell you something and you not get onto me about it?"

"Lord. What did you do?"

"Had a little...meetup with Dick."

"Who is Dick?"

"It's more a description than a name. I needed some, girl, and I won't be seeing Cooper for a while. Wasn't no way I could've waited that long."

"So you cheated on him again?"

"You don't have to make it sound like that. Cooper and I have a unique kind of relationship. And who knows what he's doing when he's not down here, 'cause he loves to get it in as much as I do."

"So why are y'all together, then?"

"It just works for us right now. Who knows how long it will last. And anyway, you know I'm more on the free side than I am the monogamous side. I'm not *totally* against monogamy, but I *do* like being able to do whatever I want without feeling guilty."

"I see."

"I just think everyone should be free to do what they please without being judged, as long as it doesn't break the law or hurt anybody. We only have one life to live..."

"Roz, relax. I'm not judging you."

"Oh, good, 'cause I was already about to choke on that platitude. Oh yeah, before I forget, Dad asked about you today."

"He did?"

"Yeah, probably wanted to know how your car was running. He asked for your number but I wanted to make sure it was okay with you before I gave it to him."

"Oh yeah, girl, that's fine. Go ahead," Journey replied absently, flipping through the BSC class catalogue in front of her. "That's sweet of him to worry about that."

"If only he would be that sweet towards Mom, too."

"Yeah." Journey didn't want to comment on Clyde and Molly's marriage, especially after what she overheard Clyde say about how Molly's weight gain affected him. She was sure that it wasn't an easy situation for either of them.

The friends continued to talk for a while, with Journey cornrowing her hair into a new style as Roz waxed her legs, before they called it a night. Journey adjusted her satin bonnet and snuggled under the covers, her newfound optimism soothing her into a restful sleep.

Chapter 4

• • • •

"YOU'RE LIKE A HUNDRED dollars short."

Dino shrugged. "Best I can do right now."

"Do you think I can tell the light company that? *'Well y'all, this is the best I can do this month so y'all are just gon' have to be happy with this.'* We'll be sitting over here in the damn dark."

"Don't be dramatic, Journey."

"Don't tell me how to be after you dodge me and then *still* come up short after putting me off for over two weeks and act like it's no big deal."

"Look, I can't give you what I don't have. And I'm really not in the mood to argue with you right now."

"Oh yeah? Well, *I'm* not in the mood to-"

"Hey, Daddy!"

Journey clamped her mouth shut as she turned to see Theo running towards Dino, who seemed relieved at the disruption. He opened his arms to his son, swinging him around in a circle and making Theo laugh uncontrollably.

"I didn't know you was here," Theo commented when Dino set him back down.

"*Were* here," Journey corrected.

"Were here."

"Yeah, I just stopped by to talk to your mama real quick," Dino replied. "I'm about to head out."

"Can I go with you?"

Dino looked at Journey. "If it's okay with your mama."

Theo looked up at Journey pleadingly. She wanted to say no, but knew that would be petty. She didn't want to be one of those women who used their children to punish their exes. Theo didn't have school the next day so there was no legitimate reason for Journey to deny him.

"Of course it's okay," she finally confirmed, smiling down at Theo. "Go get your shoes on."

"Grab some other clothes, too; might as well spend the night," Dino called after Theo as he ran off to his room. He glanced at Journey with what she considered a mocking smirk. "Right?"

She cut her eyes at him. A string of colorful language danced through her mind that she was itching to spew but she didn't want to risk Theo hearing it. It was times like this that she wondered what she ever saw in this man.

"Whatever, Dino."

"I'd think you'd be glad I'm taking him off your hands for the night."

"Theo isn't a burden or a headache I'm trying to get rid of. That's *your* way of thinking, isn't it?'

Dino's smirk faded. "Don't play me like that, Journey. I've *always* been there for my son."

"When it's convenient for you, sure."

"I resent that."

"You can resent it. Doesn't make it any less true."

Dino started to say something else, but stopped and shook his head. "You know what? I'm not going back and forth with you."

"Uh-huh."

Journey proceeded to ignore him as they waited on Theo to come back out. When he finally emerged, overnight bag in tow, Dino didn't even bother checking to make sure he had everything before quickly ushering him out the door.

Sighing, Journey stood in the middle of her small living room, feeling suddenly exhausted. She dug her hands into her hair, mindlessly scratching her scalp, before sighing and going to continue fixing the dinner she had started before Dino showed up.

Once she was in the kitchen, though, she looked at the fixings she had pulled out and lost all desire to cook. Throwing it all back into the fridge, she grabbed a frozen pizza from the freezer and slid it into the oven. Figuring she'd make the most of her evening, she pulled up YouTube on her Firestick and began watching hair tutorials, which was one of her favorite ways to spend her free time.

An hour or so later, she had finished her pizza and was practicing a new braiding technique on her mannequin head when her phone rang. Not recognizing the number, she ignored it, but it began ringing again immediately. She tried to think of any bills she might be so behind on where a collector would call her, but though it left her pockets rather dry for the time being, she was current on everything, for once. She finally decided to answer it, since whoever it was apparently would keep calling until she did.

"Hello?"

"Journey," a familiar voice greeted.

She paused. "Mr. McMillan?"

He grunted. "Didn't we talk about that?"

"Oh, sorry. Mr. C."

"Still a little formal for me, but better."

"I wasn't expecting to hear from you..."

"Roz said you didn't mind her giving me your number."

"Oh yeah." Journey had forgotten all about that.

"Is this a bad time?"

"Oh no...it's fine. Um, what's up?"

"I just wanted to make sure everything was okay with your car."

"Oh. Yeah, everything's fine with it. I got some more oil, like you suggested."

"Good. I'm glad to hear it."

"It's really sweet of you to be so concerned."

"Of course. I know how some car batteries can get problematic after you have to jump them off. I just hate the thought of you being stranded somewhere. Do you have AAA?"

"I probably should, but no."

"Well, I hope you do get it, but until then, keep my number. Make sure you call me if anything ever happens. I'll take care of you."

Something about the way he said that made Journey drop her comb. Glancing down at it but not bothering to pick it up, she moved the mannequin head to the side. "I appreciate that."

"Don't mention it. How is everything else going with you?"

"Hmm?"

"I just realized that as long as we've known each other, we've never really *talk*-talked, you know?"

"True..."

"So let's rectify that. Unless you're busy?"

"Oh, no, not really. Just practicing some hair stuff since Theo is with his dad."

"How old is your son now?"

"He's seven."

"And you're divorced, right?"

"Thankfully."

"So you and your ex-husband don't get along, I take it?"

"I mean, we're far from best friends but we usually get along okay, considering."

"Considering..."

"That I don't have a lot of respect for him. He doesn't do what he's supposed to do."

"Don't tell me he doesn't pay child support."

"Guess I'd better hush, then."

"That's unacceptable, Journey. If he's not paying child support, I can refer you to a lawyer friend of mine. And before you say it, you wouldn't have to worry about paying him. I'd see to it that everything is taken care of."

Journey's jaw dropped. "Wow, really?"

"Absolutely. You didn't make that child by yourself and you shouldn't have to pay for everything by yourself."

Journey was surprised at how appreciative she was to hear that, even though it was common sense. Having someone sympathize with her was warming. "You're right about that."

"So just say the word and I'll make it happen."

"Thanks, Mr. C. I'll definitely keep that in mind."

"My pleasure." He paused. "So you're all alone this evening?"

"Yes."

"You don't want any company?"

Now it was Journey's turn to pause. Her widened eyes darted around the room, as if Clyde would somehow pop out from around some corner. It was a simple question that had scrambled her brain for a second.

"Uhh," she sat up straighter, "I'm about to go to bed, actually. Long day tomorrow, you know."

"Understood. When will you be coming back by the house?"

"Uhh, not sure. Why?"

"Just wondering. Would be nice to see you again."

"Oh." Journey didn't quite know how to respond to that. "I'm sure I'll be over there soon enough, to see Ms. Molly."

"And what about me? I live there, too, you know."

Journey was trying to think of a response to that when Clyde chuckled. "You can relax, Journey. I'm just messing with you."

"Oh!" Journey giggled, feeling relieved. "Why you gotta do me like that, Mr. C?"

"I didn't make you uncomfortable, did I? If I did, I apologize."

"No need. I can take a joke. No big deal."

"Good. Well, you have a good night, Journey. Talk to you soon?"

"Sure. Good night, Mr. C."

Journey hung up the phone, trying to ignore the uneasy feeling that had crept up on her. Shaking it off, she told herself she was tripping and then went to get ready for bed.

• • • •

TURNED OUT JOURNEY would be seeing Clyde again sooner than she thought. A couple of days later, she was right back over at his house, cutting Roz's hair while she was there hanging out with Molly. Clyde wasn't home, and part of Journey was glad about that. She wasn't sure how she felt about his newfound mission to befriend her. As far as she was concerned, the polite detachment they had going on was working just fine the way it was.

"Did you find out about that promotion yet?" Roz asked as Journey got her clippers ready.

"No, not yet. Still waiting on official word. Owen hasn't said anything else about it since he first told me he was recommending me."

"Are there other people up for it, too?" Molly asked, holding a bottle of burnt orange nail polish against her hand. "Do you think this color is too garish for me?"

"Not if you like it. And I doubt I'm the only one in the running, but Owen gave me the impression that I had the best chance at it. I've been there long enough and have an impeccable record."

"So when are they supposed to make the decision?"

"Not sure. I imagine pretty soon. They might just be dragging it out as a formality, or working on the offer they'll present to me. I'd go from hourly to salaried, which would be a big step up."

"Well, I need for them to go ahead and make it official, then," Roz stated, taking a seat in the chair in front of

Journey and removing her huge hoop earrings. "No need in showing you the menu if they're not gonna let you eat."

"Speaking of eating, what are we gonna have tonight?" Molly piped up. "And I do not want any of those salads, as delicious as they are."

"You wanna order a pizza?" Roz suggested.

"Ooh, I'd love pizza! But, I shouldn't," Molly's shoulders slumped. "Clyde would never let me hear the end of it."

"He's not the boss of you, Mom; you can eat what you want. And anyway, pizza doesn't have to be bad. It's all about what kind you get."

"I guess that's true."

"Well, to me, pizza is a waste of time if it doesn't have a lot of meat and extra cheese," Journey quipped, revving up the clippers and gently pushing Roz's head forward. "I never got into the whole cauliflower crust craze."

"Ugh, Cooper tried to get me to start eating that," Roz commented. "I tried it just to shut him up, and was not a fan. You know we actually argued about that?"

"Arguing about pizza crust, huh? Yeah, y'all definitely don't need to live in the same city."

"I *do* wonder what he'd do if he found out about the date I went on the other night."

"Are we calling them dates now?"

"They're dates. Just because the main goal is sex doesn't mean it's not a date."

"Uh-huh."

"And who knows what he's doing when he's away from me."

"Yeah, you've said that before. So again I ask...why are y'all together?"

"I've told you; this just works."

"Well I would imagine that you two would have discussed this kind of thing when you decided to be a couple. Maybe he would agree to keeping it semi-open and you wouldn't have to feel paranoid every time you met up with Dick."

"Dick? Who is that?" Molly asked.

Roz started to turn her head but Journey stopped her. "More of a description than a name, Mom."

"Goodness."

"And I'm not into open relationships. I like to be free but not *that* free."

Journey shook her head. "I swear, I don't get you at all."

"I can't say I do either," Molly agreed, adjusting her blue housedress around her large thighs. "I don't expect you to settle down and get married or anything but I can't say this is the kind of relationship I want for you."

"I know, Mom. You want grandbabies. I'd probably get a dog or something before I stretch myself out giving birth."

"Does Cooper want children?"

"He's never mentioned it to me. But too bad, if he does. He can go knock somebody else up."

"That's a great attitude to have," Clyde clipped as he entered the room. His eyes flitted to Molly and Journey before resting on his daughter. "I'm *so* proud right now."

Sucking her teeth, Roz started to turn her head again before Journey again stopped her. "I'm grown, Dad. And not every woman wants to have kids."

"True. And they're not obligated to. But most women don't give their men permission to go impregnate someone else just because they don't."

"We really don't need to have this conversation, Dad."

Journey was focusing on Roz's head, glad that Roz's haircut wouldn't take all that long. She immediately felt different upon Clyde entering the room. The ease she had felt just moments before was now replaced by an almost crawling anxiousness that almost made her actually squirm. She didn't know why she was starting to get like this around him all of a sudden but she knew she hated it.

Clyde's attention was with Journey, eyeing her clingy black top and curve-hugging jeans as she cut Roz's hair with the skill of any seasoned barber. He noticed she still hadn't looked at him yet, and he only averted his eyes when he noticed Molly glancing at him curiously.

"Hi honey," she greeted him hopefully.

"Hey there." Clyde nodded, then after a beat, added, "You all right?"

"I'm good. Glad you're home."

"Thanks...it's good to be home. Did you have any of the salads today?"

"Oh, um...I had one for lunch." Molly's voice was nervous. "I kind of wanted something else for dinner."

"Something else like what?"

"I don't know..."

"We were thinking about pizza," Roz spoke up, defiance making her voice louder than necessary. "I'm gonna place the order as soon as Journey is done with my head."

"Pizza?" Clyde spat. His eyes narrowed. "And whose idea was that?"

"Mine." Roz's voice was clearly challenging. She lifted her head to glare at her dad, and Journey let it happen. She knew Roz was always ready to come to Molly's defense and she wasn't going to try to stop it, especially since Molly was already looking away guiltily. "It was *my* idea."

"Right." Choosing to let it go for the moment, he turned his eyes back to Journey. "Journey, how are you? You're looking nice."

"Um, thanks," Journey replied, casting him a quick glance before turning her attention back to the design she was cutting into Roz's hair. She noticed just like the other women did that he complimented her but didn't do so with Molly. Even his voice had changed. "And all is well over here."

"Good to know. Everything still all right with your car?"

"Yes, sir."

"Stop that 'sir' nonsense."

"Can't help it; just showing respect."

"I know you respect me. But we've talked about you being so formal."

"Right."

"Well, I'll be in my office. But Roz..."

"Yes?" Roz droned.

"If you're really that unhappy with Cooper, just break it off. Seems like you're just wasting each other's time."

"I'll remember that. And I'll refrain from saying how much time is being wasted every day you let go by without spending any real time with Mom."

"Roz..." Molly pleaded, glancing at Clyde as if she feared he would think she put Roz up to the comment. "Please don't."

"I didn't. I said I'd *refrain* from saying it."

Shaking his head at his daughter, Clyde just left the room without further comment. He didn't feel like getting into it with Roz again.

"Why do you do that?" Molly hissed as soon as Clyde left. "You're just upsetting him."

"And what about the way he upsets *you*?" Roz retorted. "I swear, you always cowing to him is about as upsetting as him treating you like an afterthought."

"I do not *cow* to him. I'm just understanding of why he is like he is. I'm the one who turned him off by gaining all this weight. We used to be a lot closer before I did that."

"Mom...I don't have the energy right now," Roz sighed. '

"All done." Journey finally finished Roz's head and handed her a mirror while she brushed the fallen hairs from her shoulders. She was thrilled to be finished so she could get out of there. "What do you think?"

"That design is *hot*!" Roz praised, turning to see the swirly line that now adorned the left side of her head. "I love it!"

"Good!"

"See, that's the benefit of keeping my hair this short. These designs are just like another accessory. Can change 'em every few weeks."

"It looks great on you, sweetheart," Molly commented from her perch on the bed. "You totally have the face for that. You could be right in any magazine with any other model."

"I could, couldn't I?" Roz winked playfully, giving a sexy pout in the mirror. "No but really, thanks for that. But I'm satisfied just prettying the models up; I don't need to be one, myself."

"I think you should do both. Journey, why are you packing your things so fast? You have another appointment or something?"

Journey didn't want to say that she was in a hurry to get away from their normal familial tension but more so, get away from Clyde. "Not an appointment but some stuff I need to do before the night is over with, that's all. And I've gotta go get Theo."

"You need some help getting this stuff out to your car?" Roz asked her.

"Oh no, I got it. Go ahead and order y'all's pizza."

"I wish you could stay and hang out with us," Molly pouted. "I love our girls' nights."

"Me, too. And we'll have another one really soon, Ms. Molly. Maybe the next time I'm over here doing your hair. One thing about being a single mother is that my time isn't always my own."

"I can't relate but I can sympathize. And you know Theo is more than welcome to come over here with you, if that makes things easier. He's a great little boy."

"I appreciate that. But my time here is a reprieve from being somebody's mama for a while," Journey quipped with a chuckle, though it wasn't really a joke. "But it's good to know I can do that if I need to."

"Of course!"

"Well, I appreciate you hooking me up, girl," Roz said as she ordered her and Molly's pizza via the app on her phone. "Cooper will be here tomorrow night. He actually likes rubbing on my nearly-bald head."

"Glad it works for ya," Journey winked at her, hoisting her bags onto her shoulders. "I'll see y'all later."

"You *sure* you don't want anything to take with you? Some juice or something from the fridge over there?" Molly persisted.

"Oh no, I'm good. Thanks, though."

Journey left the room and moved quickly towards the front door, hoping to get out undeterred. But Clyde was waiting for her.

"Let me get those for you," he offered.

"I got it."

"I insist." He relieved her of the shoulder bag she kept all of her hair tools in. "Whoa, this is kinda heavy. You lug this thing around all the time?"

"I'm used to it."

"Can't be good for your back," he observed as he loaded the bag into Journey's opened trunk. "How often do you get massaged?"

"Umm...that's a luxury I don't get the benefit of, I'm afraid."

"Don't think of it as a luxury. Think of it as self-maintenance. The body needs occasional tune-ups just like our cars do." He slammed her trunk shut and slid his hands into his pockets, slowly strolling closer to her. "I bet you'd feel a million times better if you started getting those. And they're not that expensive, depending on where you go."

"I'll remember that."

"I'd be happy to recommend a few places. Or even send you-"

"I can't let you do that," Journey cut him off, tossing her purse onto her passengers' seat. She smiled tightly at him, trying to think of the best out since it looked like he wanted to have another getting-to-know-you session. "I appreciate it, but I'll send myself. Hopefully after I get this promotion, I'll be able to do more stuff like that."

"Oh, you're up for a promotion? That's wonderful! I have no doubt you'll get it. I'll add it to my prayers tonight."

Journey couldn't help but smile. She needed any extra *umph* she could get. "Thanks, Mr. C. Well, I'd better get going..."

"Sure. Get home safe." He placed a hand on her car door before somewhat awkwardly opening his arms. She paused, her eyes flitting to both arms before going to his slightly expectant face. "How about a hug?"

How about a hug? She'd only hugged him that one time out of obligation; Journey didn't know how she felt about the sudden desire to make it a regular thing. But after a couple of contemplative moments, she decided it was harmless enough and stepped into his arms, being sure to leave a decent amount of space between them.

His arms were strong, and his hands were warm. He smelled like some kind of expensive cologne this time. Journey was slightly surprised at how firm his body felt, then she was surprised that she even noticed that. It made her realize that it had been a while since she'd been in a man's arms. She usually kept so busy that she didn't allow herself to think about it.

Clyde's hand was doing a slow slide up and down her back, and he didn't seem to be in any hurry to step away. So Journey did.

"Good night, Mr. C." she muttered, barely meeting his eyes.

His hands returned to his pockets. "Good night, Journey."

Journey quickly got into her car and drove off, wondering why she was feeling she should be ashamed of herself.

Chapter 5

• • • •

A COUPLE OF DAYS LATER, Journey was still scolding herself, though she didn't know why.

It was just a hug with her best friend's father, but something about it felt...wrong. She made sure to keep their middles from touching, her face turned, and her hands planted firmly in place on his back; no rubs, no pats, no lingering slides. It was totally platonic.

So why in the world did she feel like she needed to take yet another shower?

A thought flittered into her head...had Clyde been flirting with her?

Was that what was behind the sudden urge to hug and talk and get to know her better? There was no question he'd been acting differently towards her lately.

Just as quickly, though, Journey dismissed the thought. Clyde had known her since she was an ashy-legged kid. There was no *way* he looked at her like that.

One thing she didn't (couldn't) put out of her mind, though, was the realization of her intimacy drought. It was true she hadn't been in a serious relationship since Dino, and her random trysts since were far *too* random. She dated occasionally, but no one ever lasted very long, for whatever reason. Since Dino, it was hard to let her guard down enough to really get close to anyone. And she was especially mindful of who she brought around Theo. Between him, work, and doing hair, she didn't have a lot of time left for a man, anyway.

That didn't mean she didn't want one, though.

Sighing, she tried to put such thoughts out of her head. It would only make her want something she couldn't immediately have.

She was folding laundry and still trying to keep her mind from wandering when there was a knock on her door. Glancing at her watch, she got up and went to answer it, figuring it was Dino bringing Theo back.

"Hey Mama!" Theo rushed in, hugging Journey around the waist. His force pushed her back a couple of steps, but she didn't care. She just grinned and hugged him back.

"Hey, baby. Have a good time with your dad?"

"Yes, ma'am. He got me a pet."

"What??"

"Cool your jets, Journey," Dino spoke up, stepping inside and closing the door behind him. "It's a fish. And he's keeping it at my spot so it's nothing for you to worry about."

"Oh. Well in that case, awesome!"

Shaking his head, Dino nudged Theo's shoulder. "Hey man, go put your stuff up in your room. Stay in there until I come get you. I need to talk to your mama for a minute."

"Yes, sir." Theo skipped off to his room.

Journey looked at Dino skeptically. "What's up?"

Glancing towards the hallway Theo just escaped to, Dino lowered his voice slightly when he asked, "Can we go in the kitchen?"

"Why? I haven't cooked anything since you said you were feeding Theo before you brought him home. Or did you not do that?"

"Do you have to question every damn thing? And yes, I fed him. Can we just go in the kitchen, please? I don't want Theo to hear."

Journey started to ask what the big secret was, but she just shrugged and headed to the kitchen. It wasn't a huge apartment but the kitchen was the furthest from Theo's room. And if they were going to start arguing, Journey didn't want Theo to hear that, either.

Arguing was the furthest thing from Dino's mind, though. As soon as they were in the kitchen, he backed Journey against the counter and kissed her. She angrily pushed him away.

"What the hell??" she hissed.

"Come on, don't be like that." He stepped back over to her, looking her up and down with clear intention. "It's been too long."

Journey couldn't disagree. But despite Dino's fortunate timing, he wasn't exactly her first choice.

"I can't believe you're pushing up on me right now, Dino."

"Why not?" His hands eased to her waist. He pressed his sturdy body close to hers, and she let him. She was feeling plugged, like every nerve in her body was tingling. And try as she might, she couldn't make Dino's advances not affect her. Her eyes drifted closed as he ran his lips up and down her neck. "You know I've never stopped wanting you."

All Journey could do was moan when his hand began massaging her breast. His fingertips teased her nipples through her thin shirt as he brought his lips to hers. He kissed her lightly at first, test kisses, before deepening it.

Journey moaned and sighed between kisses, letting herself enjoy what he was doing to her. He was right; it *had* been too long.

Her hands tangled themselves in his long locs as he began to kiss down her neck, her chest, and then her breasts through her shirt. She didn't even know when he had eased her neckline down, but her bare breasts were out and he was devouring them like snow cones in the summertime. The sensible voice in her head told her to stop, that Theo might come out of his room, but the horny voice reminded her that Dino had told him to stay in there until he went and got him. Thank god.

Her hips began to wind involuntarily as Dino continued to lick one breast and fondle the other, driving her insane. If nothing else, he knew where her spots were.

Quickly rising to full height again, Dino reclaimed her lips forcefully. They kissed hungrily, Journey's hands clawing at him while he reached between them to unbutton his pants.

"Pull your pants down," he ordered against her lips. He pulled a condom from his back pocket.

She wasted no time complying. Pretty soon they were joined, sexing against the kitchen counter, trying to contain their sounds of pleasure. Journey grabbed Dino's behind, pulling him deeper. She just allowed herself to get lost in the moment and get her itch scratched, and not think about how much she was going to regret this in about an hour or so.

And sure enough, after they finished and Dino had cleaned himself up, said goodbye to Theo and left, Journey was kicking herself. She cleaned the counter and muttered how stupid it was to keep giving in to Dino, considering they could barely get along any other time.

Finally, she sighed. "Whatever," she threw her hands up. "Nothing I can do about it now."

And, she rationalized to herself as she went to check on Theo, it was damn good.

• • • •

AFTER THEO WAS IN BED, Roz called and asked if she could come over. She sounded upset about something and Journey guessed it either had something to do with Cooper or Clyde.

Turned out to be both. She had in fact had an argument with Cooper, which she fussed about for a couple of minutes, but most of her energy went to venting about Clyde.

"He pisses me off so much, girl," Roz fumed, flopping onto her back on Journey's bed. "The way he treats Mom..."

"Did something happen today?"

"She asked him if they could spend time together this weekend and he brushed her off. Left her sitting in her room crying. She called me and it took everything I had not to go over there and tell him off. I love my dad but he's *so* wrong for that."

"Aww man. Yeah, there's really no defending that. I hate to hear Ms. Molly was in there crying by herself."

"I wanted to kill him."

"So you haven't spoken to him about it at all?"

"I started to. I was headed over there when I called you and asked if I could come here. 'Cause really, what's the point? He's just gonna make excuses or tell me I don't know what I'm talking about."

Journey grabbed a couple of the gummy worms Roz had brought over and stuffed them into her mouth. "I can't imagine being in their position. It's gotta be rough, dealing with what they deal with."

Roz looked over at her. "Meaning?"

"Look...I'm not condoning how Mr. C. acts. I've seen how distant he is towards Ms. Molly and that can't be easy to take, no matter how much she makes excuses for him."

"Right!"

"*But* I also don't know what it's like to see the spouse I've been with for years and years grieve so hard that they stop caring about themselves, without being able to do anything about it," Journey continued emphatically. "And it's easy to sit on the sidelines and condemn but...it has to be different when you're *in* it."

Roz looked at her thoughtfully, then turned her gaze to the ceiling, stretching a gummy worm with her teeth. Finally, she sighed and dropped her hands to the bed beside her.

"I guess it *is* easy to say what I would and wouldn't do from the outside looking in," she finally conceded. "I mean, I hate how he treats her, I do. But...he *did* mention a little while ago how difficult it was for him. I brushed it off at the time, but...maybe he has a point. When I think about it, they *were* a lot closer before my grandparents were killed. That really changed everything."

"I can only imagine."

"And I was out of the house by then so it's not like I had a front-row seat to how things really were between them. Mom barely even let me come over there, so there's no telling how she was with Dad. I just wish they could get past this stage they're in. Between me and you, I can't say *I* love how Mom has blown up, either."

"Of course not. She used to be like a size ten, at most."

"Yeah. And really, I wouldn't be surprised if Dad was getting his *needs* met elsewhere."

"What, you think he's cheating?"

"I don't claim to know what goes on in their bedroom but Mom has never been cagey. She wears her emotions on her sleeve; you know that. If she and Dad were doing anything, she wouldn't act so desperate for any scraps of attention from him. And it's just a little hard to believe that Dad has gone all these years without sex *at all*. And if he's not getting it from Mom..."

"He's getting it from somewhere."

"I'm sayin'."

"What if you found out he did?"

"I'd want to make sure Mom never found out. But personally, I can't judge. I'm not married but it's not like I'm the poster child for monogamy. Hell, maybe that's where I get it from."

"It's not a birthmark."

"Hmph."

"Well, speaking of getting it in..." Journey flopped down next to Roz on the bed. "I got with Dino."

"Yeah? Thank *god*. When?"

"Earlier, after he dropped Theo off. Right against the kitchen counter. And what do you mean, *thank god*?"

"You were way overdue."

"Not *way*..."

"Please. I don't know how the hell you can go months and months without it like you do. I'm losing my mind after two weeks."

"I keep myself busy so I don't think about it."

"Ain't that much 'busy' in the world. How was it?"

"Ugh. Frustratingly awesome. If there's one area Dino and I are in sync, it's sexually."

"And let me guess; you're regretting it."

"Well...I don't need to keep dipping into that pool with Dino. I don't even like him."

"Girl, some of the best sex I've had has been with men I didn't like. You release all kinds of delicious aggression on each other."

"I'd rather do that in kickboxing."

"You don't have time to go to kickboxing. And you don't have to feel guilty about anything. So you got your itch scratched by your ex; big deal. You're both grown and single. You both know it doesn't mean anything. So chill out."

"I guess."

Journey's phone beeped with a text, and she sat up to check it, automatically fluffing the back of her flattened hair. When she saw who the text was from, her jaw dropped.

Hope you're having a good evening.

Now Clyde was texting her? She glanced over her shoulder at Roz, who was still pulling gummy worms apart with her teeth. Glancing back down at her phone, Journey closed the message and put it back on the nightstand. Guilt was running through her like a stream she suddenly became aware of.

But why? She didn't ask him to text her. The text wasn't anything inappropriate. It was actually rather generic. But it was the fact that he'd sent it at all that was making her itch.

She turned towards Roz to mention it, but when she opened her mouth, what came out was, "You know...I still want to help Ms. Molly get some of that weight off, if I can."

"That's so sweet of you, girl. I honestly don't know if she'd stick to it but you'd have a better shot than just about anybody else right now at least getting her to start."

"Well, talk her into it. Better yet, I'll call her myself. She'll get some of her confidence back once she starts seeing some results."

"Probably, yeah. But when would you have time to do that?"

"I'll make time."

"You're so awesome."

Journey didn't feel awesome. The funny feeling was even funnier because she felt like she couldn't discuss Clyde's recent actions with Roz. She told Roz everything. Part of her felt she didn't want to tell Roz about the text and the hug and random phone conversation because it might up the already sky-high tension between Roz and Clyde. But the other part knew that wasn't *quite* it.

So she just stuffed more gummy worms into her mouth and said nothing.

Chapter 6

• • • •

JOURNEY DIDN'T WAIT for Roz to talk to Molly about working out with her. The next morning before work, Journey stopped by and asked her herself.

"You'd seriously want to do that?" Molly asked with a flattered hand on her chest.

"Come on, Ms. Molly; I've offered this before."

"Yeah, but..."

"I just hate seeing you so unhappy," Journey continued, placing a warm hand on Molly's knee through the bedspread. Clyde was, thankfully, in another part of the house, retreating to his office after letting her in. "And you haven't had much luck with trainers. I'm certainly no expert or anything but I can still help you. Imagine how good you'll feel once those pounds start falling off."

"That *would* be wonderful," Molly admitted, sighing. "I *am* sick of being so disgusting."

"See, you've gotta stop that. You're overweight but *not* disgusting. And more importantly, you're a great person, regardless of your size."

Smiling gratefully, Molly placed a hand over Journey's. "You're such a sweetheart. But I'd hate to infringe on your time like that. I know you have a lot going on."

"It doesn't have to be all that time-consuming, though. We can start out just walking around the neighborhood, resistance bands, light weights..."

Molly's cheeks flushed. "Walk around the neighborhood? I'm trying to remember the last time I've even been outside."

"Why?"

"I can admit I'm embarrassed. Don't want a lot of people seeing me like this."

"Forget people. This is about *you*. But if it makes you that uncomfortable, we don't have to do it."

She looked at Journey regretfully. "I'm sorry. I don't wanna be a baby about it but most of our neighbors knew me before I let *this* happen," she informed, waving her hands around her body. "Maybe it's all in my head but I just feel they'll judge me or even take pictures of me through the window to post online."

"Ms. Molly. I know people can be cruel and all, but-"

"I know, I know. They probably don't care about how much I weigh. It's just my own paranoia that I have to get over, and I will. In the meantime, though, would you mind if we just use the treadmill?"

"Oh, you have a treadmill?"

"Yeah. Clyde bought one along with a bunch of other exercise equipment years ago for when trainers came to the house. It was mostly for my benefit but so far, he's the only one that's been using it."

Journey didn't want to think about Clyde working out.

"Well yeah, we can totally do that, if you want."

"Good. At least at first. Thankfully I'm not so obese I can't move around. I admit I *do* spend too much time on this bed, only 'cause I've gotten used to it. That can't be helping any."

"No, but we're gonna fix that. If I didn't have to go to work I'd say we could start this morning, if you wanted. I just want to help you feel better, Ms. Molly."

Molly gave her a grateful grin while Journey tried to keep the guilt from creeping back in. While it was true that she had offered many times before to try to help Molly lose some weight, she'd be lying to herself if she didn't admit that the reason she was pushing it now was to assuage her own guilt. Even though she was fuzzy on exactly what she should feel guilty *about*, since she and Clyde hadn't done anything, Journey felt different around him now. And not different in a good way, though she couldn't describe it as 'bad', either.

But she pushed those thoughts out of her mind. This had to be stress or something; there was no way Clyde saw her as anything other than his daughter's BFF. Just like there was no way she saw him as anything more than her best friend's dad.

"Well..." Molly hedged, "If you're *sure* it won't be an inconvenience for you..."

"It won't."

"Then I happily accept your generous offer."

Smiling, Journey leaned forward and hugged her. "I'm so glad."

"I insist on paying you, though."

"Oh no. That's not necessary."

"What's not necessary?" Clyde asked, entering the room. Journey glanced at him with a tight smile.

Molly looked at him excitedly. "Honey, Journey is being nice enough to make time to work out with me. I was telling her that she should be paid for that."

"I agree. And that's extremely kind of you, Journey. We haven't had much luck with trainers around here."

"Well, I certainly can't call myself a trainer. More like a workout buddy. And I'm happy to do it."

"We're going to pay you for your time."

"I'm not doing this for the money; I just want to help Ms. Molly."

"Nevertheless-"

"Y'all, please, I appreciate it but you don't have to worry about paying me anything," Journey interjected as she stood. The familiar urge to make a quick exit was hitting her again. "Y'all are like family to me. For now, though, I need to get going or I'll be late for work."

"This isn't over," Clyde insisted, eying her. "I'll drop it for now, but I didn't get to be the one of the top lawyers in the city by not knowing how to make things happen."

Journey's face flamed.

"He *is* very persuasive," Molly agreed, grinning. "If you could have seen him on our first date-"

"Molly, I'm sure she doesn't want to hear about that," Clyde interjected, quickly blocking the trip down memory lane. "That was ages ago. A lot has changed since then."

Her smile fading, Molly looked down at her lap. "You're right. Sorry."

Journey hated that she was in the middle of yet another uncomfortable scene. She could only imagine how things were when Clyde and Molly were alone. But she figured they probably didn't communicate much at all if there was no one there to keep up appearances for.

"Yeah, well..." she hedged after a moment. "Maybe you can tell me about it next time, Ms. Molly. I'd love to hear it."

Molly beamed gratefully. Journey winked at her and picked up her purse, only casting a quick glance at Clyde before striding out of the room.

She was almost to her car, seemingly home free, when Clyde caught up with her.

"Journey, wait a second."

"I don't have a second, Mr. C. I have to go." Journey unlocked her door, not caring how testy she sounded.

"I feel like I need to explain some things..."

"You don't have to explain anything to me."

"I'm not a monster, you know."

Journey paused getting in the car, finally looking at him. His eyes seemed hopeful for understanding.

"Maybe I'm not the one you should be trying to convince of that," she snipped. "Ms. Molly is the one that should get your support and encouragement. She's clearly desperate for it. I don't need anything from you."

She got into her car and drove away as quickly as she could, wishing there was a way she could help Molly without having to see Clyde. Even though she had known him for years, being around him was going from making her squirm to making her skin crawl.

• • • •

JOURNEY THOUGHT HER morning was looking up when Owen called her into his office.

"Finally," she muttered, locking her computer. "I've been wondering when they were gonna make the decision. I'm overdue for some good news."

"Come in, Journey," Owen said when she appeared in his doorway. "And close the door."

Trying to suppress her bubbling excitement, Journey did as instructed and took a seat in front of his desk.

"How are you?" he asked her. His eyes were on his computer screen.

"I'm good. Great, actually. How about you?"

"I've had better mornings, honestly. I have to do some things today that I don't particularly enjoy."

"Is it time for the reviews already?"

"No, not that. We've been informed that some more layoffs have to happen."

"Damn, really? How many?"

"A few." He fiddled with his mouse, eyes still averted.

"Damn. That's gotta be tough."

"Very. Especially when it's one of my best workers." He finally looked at her.

Journey's stomach dropped. "*M-Me??*"

"I'm sorry, Journey. I tried..."

"Why *me*? I've had a damn near impeccable record!"

"Yes, you do. But unfortunately they're mainly looking at seniority, and there are a couple of people that have been here longer than you."

"So?? What, my work means nothing? It's all about whose been here the longest??"

"Journey, I hate telling you this, please believe me," Owen assured, his voice pained. "I pleaded your case, showed them your records, sung your praises. But at the end of the day, it was simply out of my hands. They *did* agree that you were an excellent employee and are giving you a generous severance package. More generous than anyone else is getting, in fact."

That didn't make Journey feel any better. In fact, she felt herself begin to panic. She couldn't afford to lose her job; she was just managing to stay afloat as it was. What was she supposed to do now?

"Your last day won't be for another couple of weeks or so," Owen was saying. "I'd suggest maybe applying for positions in some other departments, and I'll recommend the hell out of you if you do."

Journey's hand was clutching her shirt over her chest, her heart racing a mile a minute. Hurt and anger were vying for position in her mind. The rational part of her knew this wasn't Owen's fault, but the irrational side didn't care and was itching to go off. She wanted to curse, throw something, break something...but she knew that wouldn't change anything. Not only would she still be fired, she'd probably be banned, not even getting to work the final two weeks.

Managing to gather herself, she dabbed at the tears at the corners of her eyes and smoothed out her shirt.

"All right, well," she sighed. "Thanks for trying, Owen."

"I'm really sorry, Journey. I feel terrible about this."

"I know." She tried to manage a smile. Owen had been good to her. And she knew that he probably did try to do everything he could. "I'm gonna, um...I need a minute before I go back to my desk, if that's okay."

"Absolutely," Owen quickly agreed. His curly brown hair fell onto his forehead. "Take all the time you need."

Smiling tightly, Journey got up and walked out, feeling like she was walking through water. Had she really just been laid off?

She started towards the bathroom, but thought better of it and went to her car, not wanting to run into anyone. Christina texted her, asking where she was and revealing that she'd gotten the axe too, which only made Journey feel worse.

Releasing a long breath, she leaned her head against the headrest, her fluffy twistout bushing around her face. She just sat there with her eyes closed, mentally running down what she had in her bank accounts and how much she still owed on her bills. The severance was a mild relief, but it would only last so long; if she didn't want to blow through what savings she did have, she knew she'd have to find some way to bring in at least as much as she'd been making, and quick.

After another twenty minutes or so, she finally got out of her car, not caring about fluffing her flattened hair. She trudged towards the building, wondering how in the world she was going to scrape together enough enthusiasm for work, when she was almost bowled over by Christina.

"Whoa, girl, you almost knocked me down!"

"Sorry." Christina looked angrier than Journey had ever seen her. Her face was practically red.

"Where are you going?"

"What do you mean, where am I going? Home!"

"Why?"

"Didn't you get my text? They fired me!"

"Yeah, I got it, and I'm sorry I didn't respond; I was trying to process being laid off, myself."

Hearing that calmed Christina down some, but not much. "I'm sorry, girl. I thought if they'd keep *anybody*, they'd keep you."

"Yeah, well. Apparently all that matters is how long you've been here."

"One of many jacked-up policies they have. Not my problem anymore."

"Why are you leaving now? Didn't Owen tell you that you still have another two weeks? That's what he told me."

"Yeah, he said that. And I told him to go to hell."

"Christina!"

"What? They're not gonna lay me off and then expect me to come back up in here every day for a two-week stroll to the fiery furnace. I'm *out*."

"So you're not gonna apply for something in another department? That's what Owen suggested."

"Why? So I can be hearing about more layoffs in another few months? Pretty soon they'll hardly have anybody left up in here, and the few people they *do* have will be doing the work of everybody they canned, for the same mediocre pay. I'm good on that."

"So what are you gonna do?"

"I've got some money saved so I'll be all right for a minute. But I've been looking for something else for a while now, anyway. Maybe this is what I needed so I can finally focus on doing something I actually want to do. I'd gotten too comfortable doing this shit."

"Well, I'm sure gonna miss seeing you every day. You were part of what kept me sane around here."

"Girl, we're gonna keep in touch," Christina assured, reaching around to fluff Journey's hair. "And anyway, you don't need to be worrying about this shit, either, the way you do hair. Aren't you going to be starting school soon?"

"Damn! I forgot about that. After this, I wonder if I should put that on hold for a while."

"Put it on hold for what? You were gonna go nights and weekends, anyway; you can still do that while you look for something else. And you already said you were getting financial aid."

"Yeah...I don't know. I just feel blindsided. There I was thinking Owen was calling me in to finally promote me and I got fired. This was the *last* thing I was expecting."

"Honestly, I'm not that surprised. These are some cheap bastards." Christina slid some gold-rimmed shades onto her face and adjusted her purse strap. "I'll talk to you later, girl. Keep your head up. And I'll be calling you when I need this color re-done."

With that, Christina lifted her face to the sun and strutted towards her car, the heels of her black boots clicking against the pavement. Journey watched her drive off and wished she could have such an unbothered attitude.

She managed to get through the work day, taking Owen's suggestion and applying for any position she was qualified for in other departments, and a couple that she wasn't. She tried to think positively that everything would work out fine; that this was just a temporary setback.

As she headed to Olivia's to get Theo, she called her ex-husband.

"What's up, baby?"

Journey rolled her eyes. "Just because we got busy one time doesn't mean you can start calling me that. Look, Dino, I'm gonna really need you to step up with the child support. Pay what you're supposed to pay and be more consistent with it."

"I do the best I can, Journey."

"No, you don't, Dino. And it's not enough, anyway, especially now."

"What do you mean, especially now?"

"I got laid off today."

"Aww damn. Well, good."

"What do you mean, *good*??"

"Now you can come work with me. We can build an empire together."

Journey didn't want to laugh, but she couldn't help it.

"What's funny?"

"Dino, be for real."

"I'm dead-ass."

"Look, I need a *real* career. I'm going to be starting cosmetology school soon - at least I hope I am - and I need something bringing in the dollars. Hocking tea and cable service and gummy healing vitamins isn't something I'm trying to be bothered with."

"You mock but plenty folks make a grip off that. My boy and his wife just won a new car. That could be us."

"No, thank you."

"So I'm just good enough for an occasional fuck and that's it?"

"You pushed up on *me*, remember? And it doesn't have to happen again."

"Why don't you just get back with me and stop trippin'? You know that would be best for Theo. And it's not like you're dating anybody else."

"Is this supposed to entice me?"

"And I'm still in love with you. You know that."

Journey couldn't help but smile at that. Not because she felt the same way, but because it was nice to hear. She couldn't even remember the last time she'd heard it.

"That's sweet, Dino," she replied, her voice softening a bit. "And I respect that. But...I don't feel the same way about you. I'm not trying to rekindle anything. I just want you to do what you're supposed to do. That's it."

Dino was quiet for a moment. Then he cleared his throat and said in a gruff voice, "Yeah, aight. If that's how you want it."

"That's how I want it."

• • • •

BY THE TIME JOURNEY got to Olivia's, she was feeling slightly better. Still a little freaked out, but not as much as before. But she knew she wouldn't be able to hide anything from Olivia, who had a knack for knowing when something was wrong. So Journey went ahead and told her.

"Oh no; they laid you off?" Olivia exclaimed.

"Yep. Not too long after I got there this morning."

"I'm so sorry, baby. Are you okay?"

"I'm not great. My head has been all over the place all day, trying to figure out how I'm gonna work this."

"When is your last day gonna be?"

"In two weeks. They're giving me severance, which will hold me for a while. And I have *some* savings, but not a ton. Hopefully I'll get one of the other positions in the company that I applied for, though. I'm trying to think positively."

"That's a wonderful attitude. And in the meantime, you know I'll do whatever I can to help."

"Thanks, Grandmama. You're already a huge help to me. Did you say Theo was 'sleep?"

"Yeah, he's back there. Why?"

"Can I talk to you about something?"

"Of course. Come on in the kitchen."

Once they were settled at Olivia's round wood kitchen table sharing a bowl of grapes, Journey tried to figure out what to say. And how *much* to say.

"I've been...feeling a kind of way about somebody," she finally revealed.

Olivia's eyebrows lifted. "Really? It's been a while since I've heard you say you have a crush."

"I don't know if I'd even call it a crush. It's just...a feeling. Like when I'm around him, it affects me."

"In a bad way?"

"In a confusing way. I don't quite know what to make of it. Can't say this has ever happened before."

"And I'm guessing you don't like that this is happening."

"It's like...it makes me uncomfortable, but I don't totally hate it."

"I think I know what you're talking about. I experienced something like that many years ago with one of my work superiors. He was older and married, but there was a certain way he looked at me that made me uneasy. At first I tried to stay away from him, but over time, I found myself liking it. And wishing he would do more than just *look* at me."

Journey couldn't help but grin. "Grandmama!"

"What? Can you say that you haven't thought that about this man?"

Now Journey was blushing. "Once or twice."

Olivia eyed her. "Is this someone who's off-limits? Or do you just not want to be attracted to him?"

"A little of both, to be honest."

"Well, baby, all I can say is to use good sense. You're a grown woman who knows right from wrong. And if this is someone it's not possible for you to stay away from, and you can't talk to him about it..."

"I *absolutely* can't talk to him about it."

"Then you'll just have to do your best to get past it. Maybe it'll fade over time."

"How did you get over the thing with your superior?"

"Started focusing on his negatives, even if I had to make them up. He wore brown too much, his nails were dirty, his car had leather seats..."

"Wow, really? Leather seats?"

"I was grasping at straws. But it worked. After a while, he became just another man in the hallway."

"Hmm." Journey stuffed a few grapes into her mouth and thought about Olivia's advice. It stayed on her mind even after she got Theo home, fed, and in the bath. Focusing on Clyde's flaws wasn't a bad idea. And she certainly had plenty of material, with how he acted towards Molly. Really, given how she'd seen his coldness firsthand, she was surprised she felt anything towards him other than contempt.

She flipped through the mail and saw her official cosmetology school acceptance package. She grinned, automatically excited, but when she got to the breakdown of how much everything would be, her smile faded. Of course she had seen all of this already when she visited the school, but seeing it the day she got laid off made the numbers seem much bigger. Most of it would be covered by financial aid, but not all of it. So she'd have to figure out how to cover that part.

Feeling a headache coming on, she quickly put the papers down and told herself not to stress. Things would work themselves out, though she wasn't sure how yet. It was just something she needed to keep telling herself so she didn't go crazy.

While Theo got ready for bed, Journey tried to put everything out of her mind and veg out with a movie.

"Nothing is gonna change tonight," she told herself, curling up in the blanket Olivia made for her. "So I'm just gonna forget about it until tomorrow. Tomorrow is another day."

A few minutes into the movie, Theo came in with a sheet of paper in his hand. "I forgot to give you this, Mama."

When Journey saw what it was, she fought to keep her face even. "A field trip, huh?"

"It's gonna be so much fun!" Theo exclaimed. "They said we're gonna be gone all day."

"Yeah, I see," Journey replied, trying to sound at least a little enthusiastic.

"I've gotta turn it in by Friday. Can I go?"

Journey saw that the trip was fifty dollars, not including lunch or snacks. The temporary zen she had managed to force a little while before was now replaced by an overwhelming anxiety. She couldn't afford this. But when she looked at her baby's excited face, she couldn't make herself deny him. Once again, she'd just have to figure something out.

"Sure you can, baby," she made herself say. "I'll sign it so you can take it back before Friday. For now, though, go on to bed; it's too late for you to be up."

"Yes, ma'am." Theo lunged forward and hugged Journey. "I love you, Mama."

Smiling and tearing up, she hugged her son back with both arms. He was always a bright spot for her, regardless of how murky the rest of her life became. The only other thing that could've lifted her spirits right then besides her son was someone telling her she hit the lottery.

After Theo went to bed, Journey tried to call Roz.

"Hey, girl," Roz answered in a whisper.

"Roz...what are you doing?"

"I'm under the covers."

"Under the covers where?"

"At Dick's."

"Oh." Journey shook her head. "Dipping back into the well, huh?"

"Girl, I can't help it. It's just too good. He certainly lives up to his name."

"I thought it was a description more than a name."

"Whatever. It fits."

"Why are you under the covers, though?"

"He's asleep. We finished literally a couple of minutes ago. I'm about to get up outta here after I get the feeling in my legs back."

"Wow."

"Everything okay?"

"Well, to be honest, I-"

"Ooh!"

"What??"

"Uh, I'm gonna have to call you back," Roz panted. She moaned loudly. "He woke up and wants some more."

Rolling her eyes, Journey just said "Bye," and hung up. She was frustrated because she really hoped Roz would've been able to give her some suggestions or perspective on everything she had going on. She just needed someone to bounce thoughts off of.

To her surprise, her mind drifted to Clyde. She had never before gone to him for advice about anything, and she wasn't sure what he'd think about her doing it now, despite him urging her to call if she needed anything. Would he think it was a ruse; just a sly way for her to get closer to him? Maybe he'd think she was responding to the signals he'd been sending of late and try to ramp things up. Who knew how he'd try to 'get to know her' next.

"Nope, not going there," she muttered with a fierce shake of her head.

Desperate, she called Clarice, someone she almost never called, especially for advice. And after she broke down what was wrong and heard her mother's suggestion, she remembered why.

"You need a sugar daddy."

"Ugh...I'm serious, Mama."

"Hell, I'm serious, too. Worked for me. You think I'm with Senior for his body?"

Journey scolded herself for ever bothering to talk to her mother about anything serious.

"Bye, Mama."

Chapter 7

. . . .

JOURNEY COULDN'T BELIEVE she had to go to work on a proverbial two week plank. Every day she plastered on a smile and trudged through the door, she prayed that Owen would call her back into his office and tell her that they'd worked out a way to keep her, or that someone else had quit and there was no need to let her go. But that call never came, and Journey had to resist the urge to relay the explicit epithets that scrolled through her mind continuously all day.

For all of the pep talks that she gave herself, and all the assurances that things would work out, it was becoming harder to believe it. It seemed that ever since Owen issued her two-week notice, things started to slide even further downhill. Aside from having to pawn her old DVD player and a gold necklace Dino had given her when they were dating to get the money for Theo's field trip, and Dino avoiding her after she refused his request to rekindle their relationship, her microwave stopped working and she cracked the screen on her cell phone after accidentally dropping a book on it. Relatively small things in and of themselves, but both things that would cost money to fix. Money Journey just didn't have.

And when she got home from work on this particular day, she got notice that her rent was going up.

Frustrated tears sprung to her eyes before she could stop them. Too much was happening at once.

"What's wrong, Mama?" Theo asked her, noticing the tears.

"Nothing, baby," Journey quickly replied, wiping her eyes and forcing a smile. "I'm all right."

"You're crying."

"It's nothing for you to worry about. Plus, not all tears are sad tears." *Sometimes they're pissed-off, frustrated, wanna-burn-something-down tears.*

"Oh. Can we have pizza tonight?"

"We don't have any pizza. I'm heating up that lasagna."

"But I want pizza."

"Well, too bad, Theo. I said we don't have any pizza."

"Can't we just order some?"

"No, we cannot."

"Why?"

"*Theo!*" Journey screamed, making him jump. "I said no, dammit! And you know better than to question me when I tell you something! I said we're not having pizza and that's what I meant, so stop asking me!"

His lip quivered as he shrank away from her, which normally would have calmed Journey down, but now it just annoyed her more.

"Go to your room," she dismissed, her voice tired. Her hand slid to her forehead as yet another headache began to sprout. "Go take a bath or something. Just...get out of my face."

As Theo hurried away from Journey, she flopped onto the couch, wishing she could just be left alone to sulk. The last thing she felt like being right then was anybody's mother. And unfortunately Theo wasn't old enough to fend for himself.

"*What* am I gonna do about this shit?" she muttered to herself, an arm draped over her eyes. Her mind surprisingly wandered to Clarice's suggestion of a sugar daddy. Even if she knew anyone she could have that kind of arrangement with, the thought of sleeping with some old man just to keep her bills paid disgusted her. Things were bad, but they weren't *that* bad.

Journey allowed herself a few minutes of pouting before making herself get up. After popping a couple of aspirin, she slid the frozen lasagna into the oven, changed clothes, and pulled out her laptop. She hadn't touched her resume in years, but she scoured it for any way she could punch it up without embellishing *too* much. Unfortunately her work history, while respectable, wasn't anything to marvel over. Before Metro Service Group, her jobs were either short-termed or almost too regular to mention. She tried to tell herself that being an assistant manager at a fast food place for a few years was something to be proud of, but she couldn't quite make herself believe it.

After she over-hyped her skills and accomplishments as much as she could without straight-up lying, she began posting her resume to various job sites, scrolling through the available openings. Nothing jumped out at her, which only deepened her frown. She didn't want to be *too* particular, since it was only going to be until she got her cosmetology license, but she wanted to avoid another mind-numbing job if she could.

Knowing she wasn't in any position to be overly picky, she began applying for just about everything she was qualified for. Various office jobs, some call centers, even a couple of managerial positions. She needed something to keep the money coming in, not to mention needing benefits for her and Theo.

By the time the lasagna was done, Journey was mentally wiped out. She and her son ate a quiet meal before he slumped off to bed, still smarting from her earlier admonishing. Journey usually hated going to bed without cleaning the kitchen but this time she just tossed the dirty dishes into the sink, not having the energy to bother with them. When she accidentally dropped a plate and it shattered at her feet on the floor, she just stared at it as if it was a bad joke she was waiting on the punchline for. Then she just kicked the broken pieces aside and slunked to her room, deciding to clean up the mess in the morning. All she wanted to do was go to bed and pray that the next day would be better than this one.

• • • •

"*Why* did I volunteer for this?"

Journey was preparing to go to Molly's for their first official workout session, and it took everything in her not to make up an excuse to cancel. The last thing she felt was positive or encouraging, despite trying to remind herself that things could be a lot worse. But she didn't want to disappoint Molly, so after getting Theo off to school, she gathered her things and headed out.

"Good morning!" Molly greeted her enthusiastically. She was actually off her bed and moving around her room, something Journey didn't see very often. "I'm up and ready to work!"

"I see," Journey replied, forcing a smile and silently telling herself to chill out. She couldn't deny how nice it was to see Molly so happy. "We've got about an hour or so before I need to leave for work."

"Oh, that's more than enough time. I'll probably be ready to quit after ten minutes."

"Aww, don't say that. I bet once we get going, you'll love it."

"Love working out? Me? If you say so."

Journey chuckled. She felt slightly less tense as she and Molly headed to the home gym. After she got Molly going with a slow walk on the treadmill, she engaged her in light small talk to keep her mind off of her own issues. It turned out that it helped keep Molly's mind off of how much time she had left, and the ten minute warm-up went by like that.

"Wow, that wasn't so bad," Molly marveled as she carefully stepped off the treadmill, panting slightly.

"See? So far, so good." Journey smiled as she handed her a towel. "Time to stretch."

After a few minutes of light stretching, Journey led Molly through a series of exercises using resistance bands. They continued to chat about various things, with Molly doing most of the talking.

"Back in college, I worked out all the time," she shared, wincing slightly as she yanked the resistance band towards her. "I was totally one of those girls that were about appearances. My sorority sisters and I used to actually compete with each other over who wore the best stuff and who could get the cutest guy. God, we were shallow idiots back then."

"I didn't know you were in a sorority."

"Yeah. I haven't seen most of them in years, though, since I've let myself get like this. I can just imagine what they'd say about me now."

"If they're your real friends, they won't care about how much you weigh. Especially considering the reason you gained it."

"It won't matter. They might be supportive to my face, but as soon as I'm out of earshot they'd trash me worse than acid-washed jeans."

"Wow. I'm sorry to hear that."

"It's fine. I realized years ago that we were never really friends; just part of the same group. Honestly, what real friends I *did* have, I've pushed away after what happened to my parents. Food was all I cared about. And of course, that spilled over into my marriage."

Journey stiffened slightly as she grabbed a medicine ball and gently tossed it to Molly, readying her hands for it to be tossed back. "I can't imagine how hard that must have been."

"It was unimaginable. I ignored Clyde, *and* Roz, because I was so caught up in my own grief. I preferred to spend the evening with a huge bowl of pasta and a pan of brownies than my own husband. You probably remember; you were around then."

Journey was, but she only knew what was going on through Roz, since Molly hadn't wanted to see anybody for many months during that time. When Journey finally got the okay to come back to their house, she was floored to see how much weight Molly gained. She recalled being tongue-tied, almost not recognizing her.

"Kinda, yeah. You were pretty closed off."

"I was *totally* closed off. My parents' deaths hit me so hard and I didn't know how to handle it. I was *so* distraught; food was the only thing that made me feel better, even if it was just temporary. But now I see what damage I did to myself, and I want to get better."

"And that's awesome, Ms. Molly. We were all worried about you, even my Grandmama. She's had you in her prayers for years. I'm just glad I'm able to help you in some small way."

"There's nothing small about what you're doing for me. God, how much does this thing weigh?? I don't think I'm ready for a twenty-pound ball."

"It's ten, Ms. Molly."

"Ten, really? It feels like more than that."

"It's not, I promise." Journey winked at her.

A little while later, the workout was over. Molly was pouring with sweat and her face was flushed, but she was smiling.

"That wasn't nearly as bad as I expected," she admitted, patting her face with the towel. She looked down at her sweat-soaked t-shirt. "I haven't worked up this much of a sweat in a while. I can't say I tried very hard with any of those other trainers."

"How are you feeling?"

"I feel pretty good, actually. I know I'm gonna be sore later, but I'm sure I can handle it."

"Maybe Mr. C. can give you a massage."

"Clyde? Yeah, right. That would require him touching me. He'd hire someone for that rather than do it himself. Not that I can blame him."

"You're still his wife, regardless."

"Hmm." Molly brushed her sweaty blonde hair from her face. "But I really appreciate you doing this for me, Journey. I'm sure that part of what made it so bearable was having you here to deter me from wimping out. Our conversation helped distract me from focusing the discomfort. And you didn't try to kill me right out the gate. I'm actually not dreading the next time."

"I'm glad to help. Here you go," Journey said, handing her a bottle of water. "This is helping me, too, since I've been slacking on my own workouts."

"Please, you look amazing. And you have a lot going on; it's understandable."

"Well, we can help each other stay in line. But for now, though, I need to get ready for work. Are you okay?"

"Yeah, yeah, I'm fine. Go ahead; you know where the guest bathroom is."

Journey grabbed her things and headed for the bathroom to wash up and change. She was glad that her first workout with Molly had gone well, though she hoped the topic of conversation wouldn't veer to Clyde and their marriage issues every time.

By the time she emerged from the bathroom, Molly was in the kitchen eating breakfast. Journey's breath hitched when she saw Clyde standing near her.

"Hey, Mr. C," she croaked. She cleared her throat. "I didn't know you were here."

"My meeting got cancelled so I had some time to kill," Clyde explained. "How are you, Journey?"

"I'm good."

"Molly's in good spirits, surprisingly. I know it's been a while since she's done any kind of workout."

Journey wasn't sure if he was trying to be snide or just stating facts. "Well, it's the first day. I didn't wanna go too hard."

"Something is better than nothing. How much do we owe you?"

"Oh...nothing. I told y'all you don't have to pay me."

"Journey, come on," Molly piped up. "You're going out of your way, coming over here before work...let us compensate you."

"I don't mind, really."

"Still, I don't feel right with you doing all of this for nothing."

"It's not for nothing. And anyway, it's not like I'm a professional trainer."

"Journey, I'm going to have to insist," Clyde said, pulling out his wallet. He extracted two hundred dollar bills and held them out to her. "There's no way we can let you be so generous and leave empty-handed. And I'm sure there's something you can use this for. Take it, please. I'll feel insulted if you don't."

"He's pulling out the big guns, Journey," Molly informed with a smile. "And he's not gonna stop until you give in."

Clyde was eyeing her in a way that made Journey want to run back to the shower. She looked away, making herself focus on their fancy smart refrigerator.

"Okay," she finally conceded, not having any more energy for the back-and-forth. And she knew she wasn't in a position to be turning down money, anyway, with things going the way they were for her. Money had nothing to do with her offer to help Molly, but she knew it would be stupid of her to keep refusing it. "You've twisted my arm."

"Good," Clyde smiled victoriously as Journey took the money.

"Now I really do need to get to work. I'll call you, Ms. Molly."

"Okay." Molly nodded, swallowing her oatmeal and smiling. "Thanks so much, again."

"I'll walk you out," Clyde offered.

Knowing it would be futile to try refusing him, Journey just nodded and went to get her things. Thankfully, though, Clyde didn't try to engage her in any conversation; he just put her bags in the car for her, thanked her again for her help, and stepped back as she backed out of the driveway. Journey released a breath as she headed down the street, resisting the urge to peek in her rearview to see if Clyde was still watching her.

Roz wasted no time calling. "How'd it go? Is my mother still alive?"

"Funny. It went great, actually. I didn't try to make her do too much too soon. Just some treadmill, resistance bands, and tossing the medicine ball around."

"Yeah, but I know she'll be screaming for Icy Hot later. She hasn't done much more than sit on that bed in forever. Thank you for helping her; maybe this is just what she needed to get back to her old self."

"Y'all are putting *way* too much pressure on me," Journey said, only half-joking. "I'm certainly nobody's savior."

"So you say."

"They insisted on paying me. I finally took it just to end it. I figured Mr. C. wasn't going to let up until I did."

"Yeah, he can be frustratingly persistent. And they *need* to pay you. I don't know why you were turning it down in the first place. It's not like you're rolling in the dough."

"Thanks, Roz."

"Am I lying?"

"You didn't have to say it like that. Though you're not wrong."

"It's like another side hustle. Nothing wrong with that."

"I guess that's a good way to look at it. And I can't front like I don't need the money." Journey stopped at a red light and glanced at her passenger seat. "Dammit!"

"What's wrong?"

"I forgot my purse at your folks' house. Shit!" Journey glanced at the time on her dashboard as she looked for a place to turn around. "Now I'm gonna be late."

"Girl, just call Owen and let him know what happened. It's not like you're ever late any other time. And what are they gon' do, fire you again? You're half out the door, anyway."

"Thanks for the reminder. Let me go so I can call Ms. Molly and let her know I need to come back."

"Just call Dad, if he's still there. He can meet you outside and save you some time."

Journey knew that made more sense, even though she didn't want to call Clyde. "All right. I'll talk to you later."

Figuring she could still make it to work on time if she hurried up, Journey opted not to call Owen. She just called Molly and let her know she had forgotten her purse and was heading back to get it. Clyde was waiting outside with it when Journey arrived, and he must have sensed her hurry because he just nodded and waved after giving it to her. Journey breathed a sigh of relief as she sped off down the street, but that relief was short-lived thanks to an ill-timed flat tire.

"Are you freaking *kidding* me??" she yelled, hitting her steering wheel with both hands. She pulled to the side of the road and turned on her caution lights, getting out of the car and slamming the door in a huff. Her back driver's side tire was completely flat.

"Well, this is just lovely," she muttered, her hands on her hips. Knowing there was no way she was going to be on time for work now, she called Owen to let him know what was going on, then opened her trunk. She was trying to remember everything she knew about changing a tire when she heard a car pull up behind her. Immediately tensing up, she whirled around with her strongest don't-try-to-mess-with-me expression, and was only partially relieved to see it was Clyde.

"Mr. C," she breathed. She started to ask if he'd been watching her or if this was a coincidence, but stopped herself.

Clyde got out of his tan Mercedes. "Got a flat?"

"Unfortunately."

"Do you have a spare?"

"Yes. It's not the best but I have one."

"I'll take care of it." Clyde closed his car door, then paused, looking at her. "Unless you just want to change it yourself."

"That'd be much appreciated, if you did. I was going to pull up a tutorial on my phone. I haven't changed a tire in a while and am admittedly a little fuzzy on the process."

"Understood. I've got it."

"But don't you have to go to work? I wouldn't want you to get your clothes all dirty on my account."

"The house is right down the street; I can go back and change, if necessary."

Clyde proceeded to change Journey's tire, finishing way more quickly than Journey would have. Journey didn't want to just stand and watch, but her eyes kept straying back to him. The sleeves of his white work shirt were rolled up to his elbows, revealing some surprisingly nice forearms. There was something intriguing about someone who always seemed so clean-cut changing a tire with no concern about dirtying up what Journey was sure were expensive clothes.

When he finished, Clyde loaded the flattened tire and Journey's tools back into her trunk.

"Thank you so much, Mr. C," Journey gushed. "I really appreciate your help."

"My pleasure. You really should replace this spare. It's not in the greatest condition."

"Yeah, I know. It's one of those things I never think about when I have some extra cash."

"I'd offer to get you one, but I have a feeling you'd turn it down." Clyde retrieved some wet wipes from his glove compartment and cleaned his hands.

"I can get it myself."

"You're very stubborn, aren't you?"

"I like to think of it as independent."

"Right." Clyde glanced at his watch, pulled out his cell phone and held up a finger to Journey, turning his back as he made a call, speaking in a low voice. When he finished, he turned back to Journey. "You have to head to work now?"

"Yes. I'm already half an hour late."

"I have what I'm sure you'll think is a radical suggestion."

Journey looked at him warily. "What's that?"

"Come get something to eat with me."

"Huh? I thought you had to go to work, yourself."

"I moved some things around in the hopes you'd say yes."

She took a tiny step back without thinking. "Why?"

"It's just something I'd really like to do. I could make up a more prolific excuse but that's really all there is to it."

"Oh..."

"Don't you have some vacation time or something?"

Journey had loads of vacation time because she rarely took any time off, trying to be a model employee. Unless she or Theo was sick, she always went to work; she thought that having great attendance would only help her promotion track. But clearly, none of that effort had mattered.

"I do, actually," she finally admitted.

"So how about playing some hooky today? We can go wherever you want."

It was on her lips to say no, but she stopped herself. What was she rushing to work for? She was pretty much just running out the clock at this point. When she had gone to Owen the previous day to check on the status of her possibly getting hired in another department, he admitted that the chances were slim because so many others were also clamoring for them, so she didn't even have *that* to hang onto.

"Sure," she found herself saying. "Why not?"

Clyde smiled, and Journey couldn't resist a smile, herself. He seemed genuinely happy that she had accepted.

"Let me just call my supervisor to let him know I won't be in," she said.

"No problem."

Journey called Owen and told him she was taking the day off, which surprised him. She didn't try to make up an excuse; she just said she had decided to take the day, and that was that. Owen didn't put up a fuss, though it wouldn't have mattered if he had. The more Journey thought about all she had given that company only for them to kick her to the curb after dangling a promotion in her face, the less she cared about going back in at all.

They decided to go to Thumbs Up Diner, with Journey declining his suggestion of leaving her car at his house and riding with him. This was already feeling too much like a date, and she asked herself for the tenth time why she had agreed to this. She wanted to ask him why he didn't eat with Molly, but she couldn't quite work up the nerve.

After they were seated and had placed their orders, Journey crossed her arms tightly across her stomach as Clyde ran some napkins over the already-clean table.

"Thank you for agreeing to come," he finally said.

"Well, I hadn't eaten anything, so..." Journey shrugged.

They proceeded to make small talk that gradually grew into actual conversation. Journey found herself loosening up slightly.

Clyde rested his chin on his interlaced fingers and looked at Journey intently.

"Something is going on with you."

"Hmm? Why do you ask?"

"I wasn't asking. I can tell it is."

"Did Roz tell you?"

"You know my daughter as well as I do, if not better. Do you really think she'd tell me your business for the hell of it?"

"Okay, true. But it's nothing...just life stuff."

"Journey." Clyde slid his hand across the table, stopping just short of touching hers. "You can take off the armor around me. I'm well aware that you can take care of yourself and handle things; you have nothing to prove. If something is going on, it doesn't make you any less strong to acknowledge it."

Journey blinked. His words were an unexpected comfort, and she almost immediately felt some of the ever-present tension leave her body. "I just don't like to go around whining, I guess. Figured everybody has something to deal with; nobody cares about my stuff."

"*I* care," Clyde quickly assured her. He looked right into her eyes. "I do care about you. And even if it's just to listen or bounce ideas off of, I'm right here."

It seemed like everything around them quieted as Journey became transfixed in Clyde's gaze. His brown eyes were so intense yet still inviting, and she found herself sinking into them like her body would into a warm bath.

She was actually starting to feel rather warm all over, and she abruptly shook her head, breaking the trance between them.

"Um," she cleared her throat, "I...it's just...well, I got laid off recently. They told me they were thinking about promoting me but instead I got a two-week notice. Completely out of the blue."

"That's terrible. I've certainly been there. You feel frustrated, blindsided, maybe even a little betrayed..."

"*Very* betrayed."

"That's one of the drawbacks of corporate America. They can just cut you off at any time like it's nothing, and they will. You can drop dead in their office and they'll just clean you out and have someone else in there the next day."

"That's...graphic."

"But true."

"Yeah. It's not like it was my dream job or anything but it was decent pay and benefits. And I thought I'd been there long enough and established myself to the point of earning some kind of loyalty. But I guess there's no such thing."

"Unfortunately not. At least in most places. So do you have something else lined up?"

"No," Journey sighed, trying to fend off the tension that automatically came with thinking about her job situation. "I've been looking, but no bites yet. I'm starting cosmetology school soon and I'm trying to decide if that's what I should be focusing on right now. I've been going back and forth about that for days."

"Why put it off?"

"I need something that's gonna bring money in. These bills aren't going to stop because my job did. Not to mention my son growing like a weed and needing stuff every other day..."

"I have a solution."

Journey looked at him, curious. "Please don't offer to give me money, Mr. C. I mean, as much as I need it-"

"That's not it," Clyde interrupted. "I'm not talking about just *giving* you money. It's more like an...exchange."

"An exchange?"

The waitress showed up with their meals, and after she left, Clyde leaned forward. "Journey, I'm not good at beating around the bush so I'm just going to be blunt. I'm attracted to you."

She dropped her fork. Surely, she didn't just hear what she thought she did.

"Excuse me?"

"Surely this isn't a total surprise."

"Umm..." If Journey was honest, it *wasn't* a surprise. The shock was hearing him declare it straight out like that. "I guess not, but-"

"And I'd like nothing more than to spend more time with you," Clyde continued, smoothly spreading butter over his waffle as if this awkward conversation wasn't happening. "But I know hanging out with me for nothing wouldn't be beneficial to you. So I'm more than willing to pay you for your time."

"Pay me for my time?" Journey frowned. "What, like I'm some kind of damn hooker?"

"Not at all. I'd never insult you like that." He looked at her, unfazed by her ire. "I'm just talking about spending some time alone with you, uninterrupted by anyone else. It doesn't have to be about anything other than that."

"Right," Journey threw her napkin on top of her uneaten food and grabbed her purse. "I really can't believe you're coming at me like this. You have a wife! And your daughter is my best friend!"

"And you're a grown woman," Clyde countered. "This doesn't have to have anything to do with either of them."

"This is ridiculous!" Journey stood up in a huff. "I should've known this was a mistake. I'm leaving."

"If you change your mind, you have my number." Clyde poured syrup over his waffle and took a bite. "The offer stands."

"Ugh!" Journey stalked out of the diner, more offended than she'd been in a while. She was glad that she had the good sense to drive her own car.

Clyde's words replayed through her mind the whole way home. He seriously told her he was attracted to her like it was the most natural thing in the world. *And* had offered to pay her to spend time with him. Regardless of how mildly attracted Journey might have been to Clyde, there was no way she could do anything like that. She was sure that 'spend time' meant sex, regardless of how casual he tried to make it sound.

She tried to put the whole conversation out of her mind, but it kept creeping back in. Journey laid across her bed, staring up at the ceiling. How had this become her life?

Her stomach started growling and she remembered the steak and eggs she had left sitting on the table at Thumbs Up, and it only made her more frustrated. She should have gobbled up that free meal before storming out. It's not like she had the luxury of eating out that much.

Pushing herself up, she shuffled to the kitchen and opened the refrigerator, groaning at the meager contents. Getting groceries was just another thing she needed to do.

Slamming it shut, she was going to just make some microwave popcorn when she remembered her microwave was broken. She ultimately ended up heating up a can of soup and going back to her laptop to check more job listings. It was a little baffling to her that she hadn't gotten *any* responses yet, outside of the *thank you for applying* form emails. Journey knew it had only been a few days, but time and patience weren't things she had a ton of.

"Things will work out," she tried to tell herself, though it was weak. She was becoming less and less convinced of her own words.

And when she went to get some more aspirin for the sudden headache she was getting and the shelf in her medicine cabinet collapsed, Journey just hung her head. Everything was literally falling apart.

Clyde's words ran through her mind again, though this time Journey was wondering just how much he had in mind when he offered to pay her for her company. And if it would be a one-time thing or an ongoing arrangement, like she was on call whenever he got some time between meetings and court dates. And how would he even pay her? She couldn't imagine he'd write checks for this...

"What am I doing?" she shrieked, shaking her head. She couldn't believe she had allowed herself to start considering such a crazy idea. She wasn't *that* desperate.

Chapter 8

. . . .

JOURNEY COULDN'T BELIEVE that she was still pondering Clyde's offer a couple of days later.

Part of her felt weirded out by his proposal. This was, after all, a man she'd known since childhood, though she didn't think of him as a father figure. Journey was now in her thirties. But it was hard to look at someone who had always been just her friend's dad as anything remotely sexual, even though she *could* admit to herself that she found him attractive.

The fact of the matter was that Journey needed money. She had a child, bills coming in, and debt that she was already trying to pay down. And she was getting zilch on her job search. If she agreed to Clyde's offer but set the terms herself, what was so bad about it? She couldn't imagine him trying to force her to do anything she didn't want to do.

As much as the thought warmed her to the idea, she couldn't forget that there were other people that would be affected by this if they found out. How would Roz react if she even knew this was on the table? *And* that Journey was considering it? She'd said before that she would never judge Journey, but surely this was outside the realm of what she was talking about. Journey didn't want to lose Roz as a friend over this.

And of course there was Molly. Journey genuinely loved her, and she saw firsthand how hurt she got about Clyde's standoffishness. There's no telling what it would do to her if she found out that he was attracted to his daughter's friend more than he was to her. She might even start questioning Journey's real motivation for offering to help her work out, thinking she was just feeling guilty for the torrid affair they'd surely been carrying on right under her nose.

It was just too much, Journey decided. While she could absolutely use the money, it just wasn't worth it, in the long run.

If only Dino would do what he was supposed to do. Journey had barely heard from him since she rebuked his offer to build a multi-level marketing empire together. Sometimes it amazed her just how childish he could be.

So when he finally called, she figured he was done pouting and was ready to finally step up.

"What up?" he greeted her.

"You tell me."

"Sorry I haven't returned your messages."

"Is there a reason why you haven't?"

"I've just been busy, that's all."

"Uh-huh."

"Look, I'm gonna come by with some money later."

Music to Journey's ears. "Good, 'cause I need it. How much are you bringing?"

"I'm not sure yet. Hopefully I can wrap up this deal I'm working on and give you a little extra but at the very least it'll be a hundred or so."

Journey had to bite her tongue. A hundred dollars wasn't much at all. Not to mention, as behind as he was, there was no such thing as him giving her 'extra.'

But in an effort to keep the peace, she kept those thoughts to herself. "Just let me know when you're on your way."

"Okay." He paused for a second. "Where's Theo?"

"Still at Grandmama's. I'm gonna go get him in a while."

"Maybe I'll take him to get something to eat later on. Have some father-son time."

"I'm sure he'll be glad to hear that. He hasn't heard from you in a while."

"That's my bad. Just let him know I'll see him later."

"All right."

"So...have you thought any more about what we talked about?"

"If you're referring to the stuff about me joining your pyramid schemes, no."

"I keep telling you that's not what it is."

"Whatever you want to call it, Dino. I'm not interested."

"That's not really what I'm talking about, anyway. I meant about you and me."

"I'm still not interested in that, either."

"Wow. So it's like that."

"You act like this is out of the blue. I told you already that I didn't think we should get back together. We don't work as a couple."

"We've both matured since we got divorced. It'll be different this time."

"Would it? I *still* can't really depend on you, Dino, and that's not something I'm looking for in a man. And I don't want to get Theo's hopes up for nothing."

"If we both *really* commit-"

"Dino! Just let that go, all right? It's not gonna happen."

"Fine, then," Dino spat. "Be like that. Your loss."

Journey snickered but managed to stop herself. "Whatever you say."

Dino hung up.

• • • •

LATER, AFTER JOURNEY had picked up Theo from Olivia's and gotten him back home, she was scrolling through more job listings when Roz called.

"What are you doing?" Roz asked her.

"Job hunting."

"Still nothing, huh?"

"Nope. And I'm running out of positive platitudes to tell myself, especially since more things are going wrong than right. You know the damn AC went out in my car yesterday?"

"Oh no..."

"Yeah. That's fun to deal with this time of year. And there's no telling how much it'll be to fix so for the time being, I just have to deal with it. I swear I just feel like I cannot catch a break lately."

"Journey, girl, I'm so sorry...I hate you're going through it like this. You need me to give you a few dollars?"

"Roz, I can't take your money."

"Why can't you?"

"I'm managing. Once I find a decent-enough job, hopefully things will start getting better."

"You need to quit being so proud. I'm your best friend; you know I have your back."

"I know you do. And I love you for it."

"I hope you know I'm gonna send you something anyway, and you can't stop me. It won't be enough to solve all your problems but it's something. So just take it and shut up."

Journey couldn't help but laugh. She loved her some Roz. "Okay, okay, fine. I appreciate it."

"And you better not try to send it back, either."

"I won't try to send it back."

"I know you like to handle everything on your own but let folks who love you be here for you. And as far as the job search, I'm sure something will come along. It's only been a few days."

"I'm starting my last week at Metro. I had hoped to have something else lined up by now. I don't have time to dawdle. Before I know it, that severance they're giving me will be gone and then I really don't know *what* I'm gonna do."

"What about the hair you do on the side? That won't hold you over?"

"That's supplemental income, at best; not enough to live off of yet. Some weeks I have multiple people hitting me up and others, its crickets. It's better than nothing and it definitely helps but I need something consistent until I can get through cosmetology school."

"What kind of places are you looking at?"

"Just about anything in an office or call center. I don't love that but it's what I know. But with the way things are going, I might have to swallow my pride and go back to working retail or fast food. God forbid."

"Ugh, I know that would suck. I hated working in fast food and swore I'd never go back to that again, I don't care if I had to sell off parts of my body."

Roz's statement made Journey remember Clyde's offer. "Wow, you hated it that much?"

"I really did. Nothing wrong with it; it's an honest living. But if ever the makeup game started slacking and I needed to go back to a regular job, I'd do just about any legal thing I could to avoid going back to *that*."

"Really?" Journey sat forward in her seat curiously. "So...you wouldn't be opposed to, say... getting a sugar daddy or something like that?"

"Hell no, I wouldn't be opposed to it! If there was someone I could stand doing that with that was willing to keep my bank account full, I'd be down."

"Sometimes it's not even about sex, though; it's just about companionship. Like in *Pretty Woman*."

"Even better, then."

"You don't find it degrading at all?"

"I think degradation is relative, to a degree. I wouldn't do anything I wouldn't want to do. It could even be looked at as a sponsorship of sorts. Why are you asking?"

"Mama suggested I consider it; said that's how she initially got with Senior."

"I *knew* it! I never wanted to say anything but I had a feeling it was something like that!"

"Yeah, I figured there had to be some kind of incentive for her to stay with him for so long, too, 'cause they hardly act like people in love. It's been years so I guess they're just used to each other by now."

"Is he still breaking her off?"

"Girl, you know Mama and I don't confide in each other like that."

"I wouldn't be surprised if he was. No offense, but it's not like he's much of a looker. And isn't he damn near seventy?"

"Somewhere in the neighborhood, I guess. And you don't have to worry about offending me; Senior and I have never been close. We hardly even acknowledge each other whenever I *do* see him. The one thing I *do* appreciate about him is that he never tried to act like my father after my real dad died."

"He knows his place. I like that in a man."

"Hmph."

"But seriously, if you have a chance at that kind of arrangement and you can stomach it, do what you have to do. You have a child to take care of. It doesn't have to be forever; just be up front with Mr. Sugar Daddy about what you will and won't do. Like I've said, I'd never judge you. And really, it's nobody's business but yours."

"True."

"I'd even understand if you didn't tell me. Hell, to be real, you don't know *every* little thing about me, either."

"Really?"

"Girl, no. You know more than anybody else, but there's some stuff I'm gonna take to the grave."

"Ashamed?"

"Partially. I'd love to be all bad bitch about it and say I don't care what anyone thinks, but that'd be a lie. Your opinion, and Mom's, matters to me."

"And your opinion matters to me. But I can understand where you're coming from. I guess we've all done some things we don't want to broadcast, regardless if it's to your closest friend or not."

"Exactly."

The conversation with Roz stayed on Journey's mind long after it ended. Even though she was sure that Roz didn't have her dad in mind when she suggested Journey get a sugar daddy if she could, *technically*, it shouldn't matter. And Roz didn't ever have to find out about it.

There was still the issue of Molly, though. Journey knew her conscience would start eating at her after a while. Part of her felt guilty for considering it at all. It might've been easier if Clyde was married to some random woman, but he wasn't. It was someone Journey was going to have to see on a regular basis, and she didn't know if she could be in Molly's face pretending like she wasn't *carrying on* with Clyde behind her back.

She resolved, yet again, that she just couldn't do it. What she didn't want to ask herself, though, was why she kept entertaining the thought after already coming to that conclusion more than once.

• • • •

"WHEN IS DADDY GONNA get here?"

Journey checked the time on her phone again. Dino still hadn't called or come by to get Theo, and it was almost eight o'clock. She knew he most likely wasn't coming, but she was trying to keep hope alive for Theo's sake.

"Probably just running late, baby, that's all."

"Can you call him?"

"Sure." Journey knew Dino probably wouldn't answer, and she was right. The call went right to voicemail. She looked at her son regretfully. "He didn't answer."

Theo looked crestfallen. Journey could just wring Dino's neck for this. Was he really so petty to stand up his son just because he was mad at her? In hindsight, Journey wished she hadn't even told Theo anything about Dino coming until he actually showed up.

Journey pulled her son into a hug, running her hand along the top of his head. "Don't be sad, baby. You know he'd be here if he could."

"You think he got in an accident or something?"

"I sure hope not. Look, go finish getting your stuff together for tomorrow and I'll try to call him again."

When Theo left the room, Journey called Dino and sent him a text, both of which were ultimately ignored, though she saw that he had read her text. She hoped nothing serious was wrong, but she had a feeling it was nothing more than Dino being in his feelings about her turning him down. He didn't usually let anything going on between them affect his relationship with Theo, but apparently this was one of the rare times he did.

She wasn't going to waste any more time trying to get Dino to do the right thing. If he wanted to act like a baby at the expense of his son, that was on him.

When she finally made her way back to Theo's room with a prepared excuse (lie) explaining Dino's no-show, she was relieved to find him sprawled across his bed, having dozed off. Journey gently removed his sneakers, noticing that they were quite worn on the bottom. Thankfully he didn't care about name brands yet because he was either growing out of or wearing down a lot of his clothes and shoes.

Journey just sat on the corner of Theo's bed for a while, watching him sleep. He was a good boy who didn't give her a lot of trouble. She wished she could do more for him; even little things like going to IHOP or getting him a new game every once in a while, or taking him on a fun day trip somewhere. But he didn't ask for much because he knew Journey couldn't afford many luxuries, which she hated. They weren't doing that bad, but there wasn't a lot of room for extras. Journey had gotten so used to that that she didn't even realize it anymore.

The more she sat there watching Theo sleep, the more fed up with her situation she became. She was beyond tired of this. It was time to put her own needs first, for once.

Quietly leaving Theo's room, she went to get her phone, passing by the stack of bills on the coffee table. Giving herself no time to second-guess her decision, she sent a simple text:

I'll do it.

Chapter 9

· · · ·

IT WAS TIME FOR ANOTHER training session with Molly, and Journey was nervous. She didn't know how she was going to manage acting like everything was everything knowing what she had agreed to do with her husband.

She tried to put that out of her mind, though, and stick to her resolve that this was something she needed to do for herself. She wasn't in love with Clyde. All she wanted from him was his money.

It was easier said than done remembering that when Molly started confiding what she hoped to get from the workouts.

"I really hope I get to where Clyde wants to sleep with me again."

Oh god, Journey thought.

"I'm sorry; does that make you uncomfortable?" Molly quickly asked, pausing her dumbbell curls. "There's just not many people I can talk to about this kind of stuff."

"No, of course; you can talk to me about anything," Journey made herself say. "I can listen, if nothing else."

"I really appreciate that. My own sister won't even listen to me."

Journey looked at her, surprised. "I didn't even know you had a sister."

"We're not close. I haven't even seen her in years. She thinks I'm weak for letting myself go like this, and that I'm just using our parents' deaths as an excuse to be lazy."

"She really said that?"

"That and more. But I'm not worried about her; she's always been mean."

"Still, though. I can't imagine my own sister saying that to me. You'd think something so tragic would bring you closer."

"Hmph. Thankfully I had Clyde when all of that happened, but then of course, I started pushing him away. Now I want us to get closer and he doesn't seem interested. I see him every day but still miss him so much."

"Have you two considered counseling?"

"He actually suggested that a few years ago but at the time, I didn't want to go. Now, I admit I'm a little afraid to bring it up again. I mostly just want to concentrate on getting this weight off. Hopefully once he sees how serious I am about it this time, he'll start letting me back in again. That's why I'm so glad that I have you to help me with this and keep me on track."

Journey wished Molly would stop being so nice. It was only making her feel worse.

"I'm sure that Mr. C. will come around," she finally said. "The fact that he's even still here at all means a lot, especially nowadays when people get divorced for way less."

"True," Molly agreed with a pant before finally dropping the dumbbell to the floor. "I *do* appreciate the fact that he's still here. There have been so many times I wondered if he was gonna be gone when I woke up."

"I'm sure he wouldn't even consider such a thing."

"It wouldn't surprise me if he has. Clyde can hold a grudge and be majorly vindictive when he wants to be."

"Really?" Journey swallowed.

"Thankfully he saves most of that for his opponents in court. The worst he'll do to me is just act like I'm not here."

Journey had to ask herself again why she wanted to be involved with such a man. She already knew Clyde was no boy scout, but the things she continued to learn about him didn't do anything to improve his image.

All I want is the money, she reminded herself.

"Have you been walking every day, Ms. Molly?" Journey tried to change the subject. "Just a few minutes a day on the treadmill or the bike makes a difference."

"I've been doing a few minutes. Sometimes just five, other times I can crank out a little over ten."

"That's great! Don't try to overdo it but I want to make sure you're at least getting some regular movement in."

"I am. Instead of waking up and turning on the TV, I roll out of bed and put on my sweats. It actually feels good to be sore from working out instead of just from being big and sitting in the same spot all day."

"I'm glad to hear that you're motivating yourself."

"I'm trying to. Between this and the nutritionist Clyde hired, I'm already starting to feel a difference."

"That's what I wanna hear."

They finished the workout and Journey washed up and got ready for work. Clyde thankfully wasn't home, so she was able to make an uninterrupted exit.

But as she drove to work, she couldn't make herself stop replaying Molly's words. Try as she might, Journey just couldn't shake the guilt over what she had agreed to do. She pulled over into the closest parking lot and called Clyde.

"Clyde McMillan."

"I can't do this."

"Journey?"

"Yes, it's Journey. Or are there other women you've propositioned?"

"Hang on a minute." There was some rustling, and the sound of a door closing. Then Clyde came back to the line. "Tell me what's wrong."

"This whole *arrangement* is wrong! I just left your wife and she was talking about how much she wanted to get closer to you and how she misses you so much and all of that, and it made me feel like the scum of the earth."

"Journey..."

"I can't keep going over there claiming to be her friend, knowing what I'm intending to do with her husband. Especially since I'm sure it would devastate her if she found out and probably send her spiraling back to where we're trying to pull her out of."

"Journey-"

"I can't do it. I just cannot do it. I'll get a job at McDonald's or something. They'll hire damn near anybody."

"Journey, I need you to calm down."

"How can I calm down? Hell, how can *you* be so calm about this? Have you done this before?"

"No, I haven't. Never even considered it. Look, Journey, my attraction to you has nothing to do with my wife. I'm not leaving Molly; I'm *never* leaving her."

Journey cocked a skeptical brow. "Really?"

"Yes, really. Is that what you were worried about?"

"Well, anybody can see you don't seem to like her very much."

"Nothing could be further from the truth. I love Molly and always have. And I'm always going to be here for her."

"Okay, I've avoided asking you this question but since we're on this 'indecent proposal' tip, I'm gonna stop being shy. When is the last time you've shared any kind of affection with her?"

Clyde was quiet for a moment, and Journey wondered if he was going to tell her it was none of her business. But when he finally spoke, he admitted, "It's been a while."

"What about conversation? When's the last time you actually talked to her, and not just about eating salads? Do you even spend time together when it's just the two of you?"

"Honestly, not much, no."

"Wow. Just...wow."

"Like I've told you before, I'm not a monster. I don't love the way my marriage is. And it'll take more time to explain than a phone call, but every time I look at Molly, it's like a kick in the gut, remembering how she used to be. And it's not all about her physical appearance, as she thinks it is. I wasn't able to help her at one of the lowest points in her life. It's been hard to cope with that. And now that I've made peace with the distance between us, she wants to get closer again."

"Don't you want that, too?"

"Part of me does. The other part is still angry. And it's not easy to just let it go, as much as I know I should. I don't even intend to be so cold towards her; it always just comes out that way when I see her. And when she starts looking devastated and I start to feel guilty, I get a flashback of one of the times she would scream at me to get out of the room because she didn't want to be bothered, or just didn't want to look at me. There were times she didn't even want me in the same house."

Journey felt her stance soften a little. "It got *that* bad?"

"This isn't even the half of it."

"Why would she lash out at *you* like that, though? She wasn't the same way towards Roz, was she?"

"It was a Black man that killed her parents. And seeing me...at times she even asked if I was the one that did it. Actually *accused* me of doing it. The same kind of people I work to put behind bars every day. You have no idea how that felt."

"Oh damn." Journey's chest hurt with empathy. "I had no idea."

"I'm not trying to throw a negative light on her or make myself seem like the victim; this is just how it was. And it was tough dealing with that."

"I can't even imagine. I'm *so* sorry for assuming..."

"No need; I get it. I usually keep the intricate details to myself because I don't want to appear as if I'm blaming her. She's been through enough. And if I have to look like the bad guy, so be it. Hell, sometimes I feel like I am."

Journey actually had tears in her eyes. She knew the issues between Clyde and Molly were deep, but had no idea it was like *that*. She felt awful for jumping to conclusions without knowing all the facts.

"And I take it Roz doesn't know about this?"

"No. And I'd appreciate it if you didn't tell her. She's always been Team Molly and I wouldn't put it past her to think I was exaggerating or fabricating, trying to exonerate myself."

Journey wanted to defend Roz, but she couldn't deny that was probably exactly what her friend would do.

"I'll keep it to myself," Journey promised. "I won't mention it again."

"It's actually kind of healing to get some of this off my chest. I used to try to get Molly to go to counseling but she always refused me. And by the time she changed her mind, I was refusing *her*, almost as a way of punishing her. It's been a tough past few years."

"I'm...I'm really sorry. No one should have to go through what either of you went through."

"True. But that's life, I suppose. Look, I have to head to a deposition; if you're having second thoughts, I completely understand. I'd like to meet you tomorrow morning, and we can discuss everything – regarding me and you – in more detail then. I'll send you the address. If you decide not to show up, no hard feelings. And we never have to speak of any of this again. All right?"

Sniffling, Journey nodded. "All right."

"Have a good day, Journey. And thanks for listening."

Journey wiped her eyes as she ended the call. After composing herself, she pulled out of the parking lot and headed to work, wondering what she was going to wear the next morning.

• • • •

JOURNEY'S SKIN WAS tingling with anticipation.

She had no idea what exactly was about to happen, but a small part of her was actually looking forward to it. Ever since she spoke with Clyde the day before, their conversation played repeatedly in her head. The anguish in his voice was clear when he talked about what he went through with Molly, especially the part about her accusing him of murdering her parents. And Journey suspected he probably *still* hadn't told her everything.

This new information made her feel closer to Clyde, and Journey's earlier guilt had given way to empathy...and a strange curiosity. If nothing else, she wanted to hear exactly what it was Clyde wanted from her.

So she dropped Theo off at Olivia's (after lying about having an interview) and headed to the address Clyde texted her. She was surprised to pull up to an apartment building almost twenty miles away from his house.

"Well, this just gets more and more interesting," she muttered to herself, killing the engine. She checked her lipstick, fluffed her hair, and adjusted her off-the-shoulder sweater before opening the door. Her hands rubbed together anxiously as she headed towards the building, glancing around her as if someone she knew would pop up at any second.

After Clyde buzzed her in, Journey rode up the mirrored elevator, her nerves getting more frantic the closer she got to his floor. As nervous as she was, she didn't want to turn around and go home. She was prepared for anything. She just hoped Clyde had some kind of alcohol.

Clyde opened the door mere seconds after she knocked on it, and Journey felt herself tighten up at the sight of him.

He was dressed casually in a stark white t-shirt and dark jeans, a tumbler of brown liquid in his hand, and Journey openly stared him up and down.

"Are you going to come in?"

He was looking slightly amused by her reaction to him, and Journey felt her face flush. She silently told herself to get it together as she stepped into the apartment, briefly closing her eyes when she got a whiff of his cologne.

"How are you?" he asked her, closing the door. "I'm glad you decided to come."

An icy hot feeling rushed over her at his statement. She tried to remember just how many condoms she had with her.

"Yeah, I-um, me too. And I'm fine."

"Agreed." Now his eyes were roaming over *her*. "Would you like a drink?"

"Yes, please," she replied quickly. "Whatever that is you have is fine."

"You like Martell, huh? Didn't take you for the type." He winked at her as he headed over to the bar. "Please, have a seat. Get comfortable."

Fat chance of that, she thought as she moved over to the plush cream couch, rubbing her damp palms on her jeans. Her eyes mindlessly took in the crown moldings, shiny hardwood floors, and African art before wandering back over to Clyde.

Has he always had those biceps?

Journey tried to remember how old Clyde was. It wasn't something she ever thought about and she realized she had no idea, and wasn't going to try to work up the nerve to ask. She only knew Roz mentioning at some point over the years that he and Molly had conceived her right before they graduated from undergrad, so he couldn't have been more than twenty, maybe twenty-two years older than Journey, since she and Roz were the same age. The thought somehow put her a teeny bit more at ease.

Clyde poured Journey's drink and refreshed his own, then headed over to join her on the couch, his eyes on hers. Journey fought not to look away, but did at the last second, feeling like she had lost some kind of challenge.

"Here you go."

She wordlessly took the offered drink and wasted no time taking a long sip.

After downing some of his own drink, Clyde set it on a coaster on the coffee table in front of him and clasped his hands together, looking at her.

"I can tell you're a little nervous so let me put you at ease. Nothing has to happen that you don't want to happen. I'd like to think that goes without saying, but I still wanted it stated for the official record. I'll never try to persuade you to do anything you don't want to do; you have my word on that."

"I believe you. But you know what might help some?"

"What's that?"

"If you stopped talking like a lawyer and just spoke like a regular guy."

Chuckling, Clyde dropped his head briefly. "It's so ingrained in me that I don't realize I'm doing that most of the time. I'll try to...*chill out*, as they say."

Journey smiled. "Good."

"Okay, so...I really do just enjoy being around you, Journey, so even if this ends up being all we do, I'm fine with it. But I won't lie...I *would* like to be intimate with you."

Her breath hitched in her throat as her smile melted. She felt her nipples harden and she wondered if he could tell through her sweater. Licking her lips, she verified, "In what way?"

He reached over and took her hand, brushing it across his lips. "I can tell you exactly."

She bit her bottom lip as he leaned closer to her so he could whisper in her ear. Her eyes widened slightly.

"Are you serious?"

"Very."

"That's what you're into, huh?"

"I am. You think you'd be down with that?"

It wasn't really Journey's thing, but she could handle that better than what she *thought* he wanted.

"Yeah. I'd be down with that."

"Then come with me."

He stood, her hand still in his, and waited for her to follow suit. Journey kept the glass of cognac in her other hand as she let him lead her to the master bedroom. He passed the huge four-poster bed and guided her to the chaise lounge, then once she was seated, went into the adjoining bathroom.

Journey waited as she listened to him run some water. She stretched her legs in front of her, feeling slightly looser than when she arrived.

Clyde emerged from the bathroom with a basin of warm, soapy water. Kneeling in front of her, he gently removed her ankle boots and socks, rolled up the hem of her pants a little, then proceeded to wash her feet.

"Beautiful," he whispered, running the soft cloth along the bridge of her foot.

Journey just sipped her cognac, thankful she'd given herself that pedicure a few days earlier.

After washing her feet, Clyde pulled a small bottle of edible massage oil from his pocket and poured some into his palms, rubbing them together to warm it. Journey eyed his gold wedding band before turning her eyes away with another tension-relieving sip of cognac.

Her eyes slid closed when he began massaging her foot. A slow warmth spread over her body, and she knew it wasn't just the cognac. Clyde surely knew what he was doing; he gently pulled her toes and kneaded her soles, hitting pressure points that were sending shock waves all through her body.

"How does that feel?" he asked her, his voice low.

All she could do was moan and lean back.

He took his time, spending a good half hour on each foot. Journey felt like liquid; she'd never had a foot massage so good.

But Clyde wasn't done. He lowered his head and ran his tongue over her toes, stroking the yellow polish and continuing up to her ankle. Journey gasped, her eyes opening as her toes disappeared into Clyde's mouth and she felt a new kind of warmth. She hadn't thought this would affect her so much; men had sucked her toes before and she felt nothing. But now, she was definitely feeling something, and it was delicious. The languid relaxation that she was feeling just moments before was now overtaken by a budding arousal that was throwing her for a huge loop.

She continued to sip her cognac as Clyde sucked her toes, trying to hide just how much it was getting to her. Moans kept escaping before she could catch them, and her chest was heaving harder by the second.

"Mmmm..." Clyde moaned, clearly enjoying it as much as she was. His hand caressed her foot as he savored her toes, then slid his tongue in a line down the bottom of her foot. When he tongue-kissed her heel, Journey was done trying to be cute.

"Oh *shit*!"

"You like that? Or you want me to stop?"

All she could do was whimper. "No...don't stop."

His whispers, his moans, his hands, the sight of his flexing biceps, and his thick tongue were sending Journey over the edge. The orgasm took over her body with full force, and she screamed out, unable to help it. The now-empty glass fell to the floor as her hands gripped the top of the chaise over her head, her body rolling with the wave of the orgasm. Clyde continued to feast on her, wanting to get every ounce of reaction she had. It was only when her body fell limp that he finally gently lowered her foot.

She was thankful that he didn't say anything; he just let her come down off her high. When she did, she was hesitant to open her eyes, slightly embarrassed at how loud she'd gotten. He must have sensed that she would need a minute, because when she finally dared to ease her eyes open, Clyde had left the room.

Releasing a long breath, Journey looked around the room, then at the empty tumbler by her shiny, bare feet.

Did that really just happen?

She finally made herself put her socks and shoes back on. Her legs were a little shaky as she stood, not even bothering to retrieve the glass before gingerly heading back towards the living room, her body still on a low buzz. Clyde was at the large picture window, one hand in his pocket while he sipped from his glass with the other.

Wow, that shirt is really stretching across his back like-

He turned when he heard her enter the room. She immediately looked away.

"You okay?" he asked.

She just nodded.

Clyde didn't try to engage her in conversation. He could tell she was a little embarrassed and he didn't want to make her any more uncomfortable.

Turning back towards the window, he instructed, "Send me your account information, if you don't mind. I'd prefer to just deposit straight into your account than give cash. Payment would be easier and more efficient that way. Is that all right?"

Journey briefly wondered about the possibility of Molly possibly seeing those transactions, but she erased the thought. She'd bet Molly had little to do with the handling of their household finances, as she'd never had a job as long as Journey had known her. And Journey was sure that Clyde was savvy enough not to pay her from any account that Molly might have access to, anyway.

"Yeah. Yeah, that's fine," Journey agreed. "I'll send it to you."

"I'll deposit the money as soon as you do. And I'll pay you for yesterday, also."

"Okay." Journey wanted to get out of there, but didn't know how to say so. Her feet were still tingling.

"You can just leave, if you want. I won't take it personally."

His back was still to her, and she breathed a small sigh of relief as she grabbed her purse from the couch and quickly walked out.

Once in her car, Journey took a minute to collect herself. Part of her still didn't believe she had really just gone through with that. The fact that she had shown up at all, but also that all he'd wanted to do was suck her toes...and that she had enjoyed it as immensely as she did.

She quickly sent him her account information as requested before starting her car and driving off. Her middle clenched whenever she thought back to what Clyde did to her. If this was all it was going to be, she could absolutely handle it.

And when she got home and saw the five hundred dollars he had deposited into her account, she couldn't help the smile that automatically spread across her face. They hadn't discussed amounts (it wasn't like she had a pricing list for this kind of thing) so Journey didn't have any idea how much he would be sending her, and this was more than expected.

She felt like she had been handed a blessing on a silver platter.

Chapter 10

• • • •

IT WAS JOURNEY'S LAST day at Metro Service Group.

She didn't have time to be sad because she was still reeling from what Clyde had done to her two days earlier. He called and asked to meet her after work, and it didn't take much to convince her. Again, he made love to her feet with his mouth and hands, to the point where Journey was actually begging him not to stop. She still blushed when she thought about it.

"I haven't been able to find anything yet," her coworker Hannah commented. "I applied for one of the positions in the other departments but didn't get it."

"Honey, you and everybody else they canned applied for those positions," Margaret, another coworker, informed with a flip of her hand. "Thankfully, I was getting ready to retire, anyway. But I feel for y'all young folks. Everybody scrappin' for the same stuff for nothing. These folks will bring in their baby-faced nephews before they hire any of y'all."

"What about you, Journey? Have you found anything yet?"

"Hmm?" Journey had slipped into fantasizing mode again. "I'm sorry, Hannah. What did you say?"

"I asked if you were able to find another job yet."

"Oh...yeah, I found something else, thankfully. A friend's parent referred me."

"Ugh, you're so lucky!" Hannah groaned. "I've gone on a couple of interviews but that's it. I might have to go back to working at the grocery store until I find something better."

"It's better than nothin,'" Margaret reminded.

"I guess, but it just feels like a step back."

Journey was tuning them out again. Her mind was on that apartment twenty miles away. It was driving her crazy trying to figure out just what was so different about Clyde's actions from anyone else's. What exactly he did to make her yearn for more. She was actually anticipating the next time, if nothing more than out of a sick curiosity as to why he was so different.

It had only been two times; maybe the novelty of being with him heightened the sensations. *Surely* it was a fluke.

Thankfully, she was saved from the paralyzing task of initiating another encounter, because he texted her and asked if she was available later. Actually blushing, she put off responding for another twenty minutes or so, not wanting to seem too eager by agreeing as quickly as she wanted to. But from that point on, she was eying the clock and itching to get out of there.

Clyde had told her he wouldn't have a ton of time, so her feet were moving even faster out of the office when the clock struck five o'clock. She didn't take the time to say goodbye to any of the coworkers she'd been working with for years, or to thank Owen for at least trying to help her move up in the company. There were no tears, like there were for some of her colleagues. Thanks to Clyde, she didn't have to dread this day like they clearly had.

She almost panicked when she got a call from Roz. They hadn't talked much in the past few days, which usually meant Roz was super busy with work or had met a new side piece. Journey hadn't been eager to reach out to her friend because she didn't trust herself to act as she normally did, knowing what she was doing with her father.

Hesitating, she answered the call. "Hey, Roz."

"What's up, girl?" Roz sounded chipper.

"Oh, nothing much. Just leaving work."

"Wasn't today your last day?"

"Yeah."

"How are you holding up? I can imagine you'd be a little shook since you haven't been able to find another job yet. Or have you? I know we haven't talked in a few days; I've been out of town on that movie shoot."

"Oh, uhh..." Journey didn't want to flat-out lie, but she didn't know how to answer so as not to invite a lot of follow-up questions. "I found something temporary. It's not even worth mentioning."

"Temp jobs are better than nothing. And sometimes they *do* lead to something permanent, if you wow them enough."

"True. But I don't see that happening here; it was understood that this couldn't turn into a full-time thing."

"Bummer. Did they say how long you *will* be there, at least?"

"Ahh...could be a few weeks. It's kinda up in the air right now."

"Gotcha. Well, hey, I'm still glad for you. I know you were stressing over that. And something better still could come in any day. And in the meantime, I've been hyping you up to my makeup clients."

"Thanks, girl."

"Oh, I've been meaning to thank you, too."

"Thank me for what?"

"For your help with Mom. She's over the moon about the progress you've helped her make."

Journey's fingers dug into the steering wheel, that familiar guilt starting to creep across her. "You don't have to keep thanking me. And I'm glad she's happy."

"Happy ain't the word, girl. She's practically glowing. When I was over there the other day, she was actually up and moving around, and I haven't seen her do that in years unless she absolutely had to. And truth be told, I can see a difference myself, too."

"Well, I can't take all the credit for that. The nutritionist is probably making more of a dent in things. You know how folks say that changing their diet made all the difference, even when they barely worked out at all."

"Stop selling yourself short. The nutritionist is great and no doubt has helped, but you're the one she trusts. They're not the ones that talk to her and hype her up and inconvenience themselves to come work with her. That's all *you*."

Hearing Roz say that Molly trusted Journey made her wince. Once upon a time she would've been proud of that but now she felt anything but deserving.

She cleared her throat. "It's not an inconvenience."

"Call it what you want, but getting up extra early to go over there before work is a sacrifice. Speaking of which, are you still gonna be able to do that with this new temp job, or is your schedule totally changing?"

"I can still do it. The temp thing is a little more flexible." Journey just prayed that Roz didn't ask her exactly where she was working.

"Well, that's good," Roz finally replied. "I know it would disappoint Mom if you weren't able to work with her anymore."

She'd be more disappointed if she knew what I was doing with her husband.

"Well...she doesn't have to worry about that. I'll keep at it as long as I can."

"Good. Well, I need to go so I can get ready for a client. I'll try to call you later."

"All right."

Journey ended the call, releasing a long breath. That could've gone worse.

A little while later, Journey was at Clyde's apartment. Their greetings were still rather awkward; there were no hugs or kisses. Just hollow pleasantries and automatic glasses of Martell.

"Last day of work today, right?" Clyde asked her as she stood in the living room sipping from her glass. She still wasn't to the point where she could just come in and make herself comfortable.

"You remembered that?"

"Of course." He looked at her, sliding a hand into his pocket. Journey noticed how he looked in his blue shirt and gray slacks, then she tried *not* to notice. It was evident that Clyde had been getting *plenty* of use out of his home gym.

Why have I never noticed just how fine he is?

Feeling weird even thinking such a thing, she shook her head to try and jar the thought.

"Well that's...that's really sweet of you."

"How are you feeling?"

"About the job? I'm not crazy about being unemployed but I can't say I'll miss working there, in particular. It was always just a means to an end."

"Hopefully my assistance will help you stay afloat until you can find something else."

Journey hoped her dark skin hid her blushing. "It is. It feels strange to thank you for...what we do."

"You don't have to thank me again."

They stood there for a few silent moments before Clyde took her hand and led her to the bedroom, taking the lead again. Journey had to wonder when she would ever *really* loosen up around him, or if this would continue long enough for her to even get to that point.

Clyde got the basin of sudsy water and gently cleaned her feet, then slowly massaged them, as he always did. This time he used strawberry oil. Journey thought that she would get used to this after a couple of times and it wouldn't affect her so much, but it still made her squirm as much as it had the first time. His hands were magic.

What *did* change this time, though, was that Clyde didn't stop the massage at her ankle. His hands slid up to her calf, prompting her to gasp softly and sit up straighter. She wanted to ask him what he was doing – and why – but his hands felt too good to say or do anything to make them stop.

She stiffened slightly when the massage continued under her flowy knee-length dress and his hands greeted her thigh for the first time. Her chest was heaving heavily as she dared to look at him, wondering if he was really going to be bold enough to go where he was heading. She kept her mouth shut, only releasing shaky breaths, silently daring him to do what he was teasing.

But his fingers only went as high as her upper thigh. He massaged her thickness, getting dangerously close to her v-spot. His fingertips grazed the sensitive skin of her inner thigh and Journey shivered so violently that he looked up at her, silently making sure she was all right, though his fingers never stopped.

This was a whole new sensation. Journey wasn't able to contain her moans, and arousal started fueling a slow body roll. Her leg fell open slightly as if giving access to his fingers that kept getting achingly close to her wetness, and part of her wanted to tell him to touch her; to stop all this torturous teasing. He didn't even lift her dress; his hands and forearms remained hidden underneath it, adding another element of mystery since Journey couldn't see exactly what he was doing.

The orgasm was building, and Journey realized she didn't want to be the only one feeling it this time. Before she could talk herself out of it, she grabbed his left hand and slid his index finger into her mouth, tasting the strawberry oil. His momentary surprise quickly gave way to a spine-stiffening pleasure, and he groaned from somewhere deep in his throat, which only made Journey wetter.

When Journey started grazing her foot along Clyde's body, he closed his eyes and shuddered, which gave her a strange sense of power. It fascinated her that something so small could have such an affect. And anytime her foot got close to his groin, he came closer to losing it.

"Ahhhh..." His head fell back, his composure slipping. His breathing got deeper and deeper, his hips undulating slightly, and Journey's arousal intensified the more she watched him. When she finally pressed her foot to his groin, he lost it. Journey had never before heard him curse, but he did plenty of it then.

"Shit! *Fuck*, Journey!"

Before Journey could gloat too much, he grabbed her foot and began devouring her toes, sending an automatic shock wave through her body. She hit the chaise with her fist, trying her best to hang onto her composure, but it was no use. She fell back, screaming in pleasure, amazed once again that someone sucking her toes could make her go crazy like this.

As usual, Clyde got up and left the room as she gathered herself. She went to the bathroom and patted some cool water on her face, avoiding looking at herself in the mirror. Part of her still couldn't believe that she was participating in this, and more amazingly, that she was enjoying it so much.

Clyde was on the couch when she finally went back to the living room. He motioned for her to join him.

"I have something for you," he told her, handing her a black velvet box.

She eyed it curiously. "What's this?"

"Open it and see."

"I-I can't. I shouldn't."

"It's not like it's an engagement ring, Journey. Don't read more into it than necessary. Open it."

Cautiously taking the box, she opened the lid. Her eyebrows shot up in mild surprise.

"So it's not an engagement ring but a...toe ring?"

"Yeah. And an ankle bracelet. Thought they would look alluring on you. And they compliment that nose ring."

"Oh wow..."

"Wear them. Pawn them. I don't care. Just wanted you to have them."

"I appreciate it, Mr. C., but-"

"When are you going to start calling me Clyde?"

Journey blushed. "Guess I'm not there yet."

"What do I have to do to you to get you there?"

Her face was on fire now. His question revved up her simmering arousal, but she wasn't bold enough to do anything about it.

"I don't know," she finally mumbled.

"Are you all set for cosmetology school?"

The change in subject momentarily jarred her, and she wasn't sure if she resented it or appreciated it. "Um, as ready as I can be, I guess."

"What does that mean?"

"There's just some stuff I need to get, working what financial aid doesn't cover into my budget-"

"Send me the information. I'll take care of it."

Journey's eyes bugged slightly. "I didn't tell you that to get you to pay for it."

"I know."

"You're already giving me...you're doing enough."

"If I can lift that burden off of you, I'm more than willing to do it."

"Why?"

"Why not? Money is not an issue for me. No use being blessed with all that I have if I can't share it with the people I care about."

"I-I didn't know you were so generous."

"Because you didn't *really* know me. But hopefully that's changing."

Journey hated that she was blushing again. She felt like some inexperienced high schooler. "I guess part of me just still doesn't feel right about all this."

He placed a hand on her knee. "This is as far as it's ever going to go, Journey. You never have to worry about me trying to have sex with you."

"You don't want to have sex with me?"

Journey hadn't meant to ask that, and she immediately looked away, embarrassed. Clyde patiently waited for her to ease her eyes back to his before responding.

"In any other circumstance, I'd love to have sex with you." His voice was low and smooth. "And I won't act like I haven't thought about it. There's a part of me that *aches* at what I won't get to do to this body of yours."

Journey felt like she was going to burst into flames. Now *she* was aching at the thought of what he wanted to do to her. "Oh..."

"But we both know why that can't happen."

"Right. Of course." Journey hated to admit it, but she almost wanted Clyde to want her more, even if she had to turn him down.

Lord, I'm losing it. I need to get out of here.

"All right, well...I'm gonna go," she finally announced.

"Let me know that you've arrived safely. And don't forget to send me your school information."

"All right."

She grabbed her purse and left. When she got to her car, she couldn't hold back the smile that shot across her face. She never planned on asking Clyde for any more than he was already doing for her financially, but his offering to pay for her cosmetology school tuition and fees was a huge burden off of her. She hadn't felt this weightless in a while, and she wasn't going to try to hate the feeling.

By the time she got to Olivia's to pick up Theo, Clyde had put the latest deposit into her account. Journey grinned, thinking of the bills she could pay off with it. She'd already replaced her dead microwave and cracked phone thanks to him. Things didn't seem as dreary as they had just weeks before. Her relief was starting to push whatever guilt she'd been feeling further and further out the door.

She took some time to compose herself before going into Olivia's house. Even though Journey had confided in her about the inappropriate feelings she was having, there was no *way* she could tell her about the arrangement she had with Clyde.

"Hey, Mama!" Theo greeted her with a wide smile.

"Answering the door again, huh?"

"Mama O is in the bathroom peeing."

"Nice. Remind me to teach you what 'discretion' means."

"Huh?"

"Hey, baby; I didn't even hear you knock," Olivia commented as she entered the room, rubbing lotion on her hands.

"I didn't. My little man here opened it before I had a chance to," Journey replied, kissing the top of Theo's head.

"I saw her car pull up," Theo shrugged. "And she's not a stranger."

"Boy..." Olivia shook her head.

"Did you eat yet? I was gonna take you to IHOP," Journey told her son.

Theo gasped excitedly. "Really??

"Yep. Go get your stuff together."

Theo ran out of the room and Olivia looked at Journey with surprise. "You're in a good mood for someone who just had her last day on the job."

Journey shrugged, her unbothered expression fixed. "I figure everything happens for a reason."

"That's a great attitude. What are you going to do now, though? Have you found something else? Any way I can help you, you know I will."

"I appreciate that, Grandmama, but I think we'll be all right. I found something temporary that will tide me over for a while. And I *am* getting severance pay from Metro."

"What about long-term, though? Are you going to be able to do the temporary job while you're going to school?"

"I should, yeah. It's pretty flexible."

"Have they told you how long they're gonna need you for?"

Journey tried to keep her face even. "I don't know, but I'm kinda feeling like I'm on an interview right now. What's up with all the questions?"

"Just trying to make sure you're all right."

"I'm fine, Grandmama. You don't have to worry so much."

"I just know how it can be, when you're trying to do everything on your own. Or is Dino finally doing what he's supposed to do?"

"Dino isn't doing anything."

"See? Now I'm even more worried."

"Please don't be. I'm working everything out."

"Still, though. Oh, I made some lemon pound cake, if you want some."

"Oh, yum!" Journey followed Olivia into the kitchen, hoping this snack break would make Olivia chill with all the questions. No such luck, though.

"So how many resumes have you sent out?"

Resisting the urge to roll her eyes, Journey accepted the large slice Olivia handed her on a saucer. "A bunch. Not sure how many."

"More call centers?"

"Not if I can help it."

"What kind of places are you applying to, then?"

"Grandmama!" Journey finally exclaimed, her patience gone. "Can you please stop??"

Olivia frowned slightly. "What's wrong with you?"

"You are killing me with all these questions! I appreciate your concern but I'm really not in the mood to get grilled about this. I told you I was fine; can we please just leave it at that?"

"I'm not trying to grill you about anything. Just wanted to see what you were doing about your situation."

"I'm a grown woman; I can handle my situation just fine. Matter of fact, I'm just gonna go." She stood from the table.

"What about your cake?"

"I'm good on the cake."

"Journey, calm down..."

"I'm plenty calm. Come on, Theo!" she called towards the back of the house.

Olivia followed her into the living room. "I wasn't trying to upset you, baby. I'm just concerned."

"Right."

Theo skipped into the living room and Journey quickly ushered him towards the door without another word. She hadn't been this anxious to get away from Olivia since the time she took four cookies when she was only allowed three.

"Journey."

Journey paused at the door and looked at her grandmother.

"Don't ever think you can't talk to me about whatever is going on with you."

Olivia had a knowing gleam in her eye that Journey didn't like. She quickly opened the door and practically pushed Theo out of it, slamming it shut behind them.

• • • •

AFTER SHE AND THEO got home from their dinner date, Journey looked into what she needed to do to get Theo into the after-school program, and was relieved to see he was still able to join despite it already being a couple of months into the school year. She'd rather pay for that than endure more interrogation from Olivia every time she went over there, and risk her finding out more than Journey wanted her to.

As much as she tried to avoid it, her mind kept wandering back to Clyde's apartment. The things he did to her...she couldn't forget it or write it off as nothing. And knowing that there were more things he wanted to do to her but couldn't left her with an embarrassing amount of yearning.

As crazy as it was to admit to herself, he had her open a little bit.

She pulled out the box with the toe ring and ankle bracelet he gave her. Shiny and silver, she could admit he had great taste. And it was sweet of him to get them for her, though she suspected they were more for his pleasure than hers. He was overly enamored with her feet.

She was lightly fingering the jewelry when her phone rang. Seeing that it was Roz, she hastily pushed the box to the floor, then shook her head.

"It's not like she can see this," she muttered to herself, retrieving the box with one hand while she picked up the phone with the other. "Hello?"

"What's up, girl? You at home yet?"

"Yeah. Why?"

"I wanted to come over there. My client cancelled on me and I'm not in the mood to go home by myself."

"Where's Dick?"

"Girl...don't get me started on that. He might be with his wife or something."

"What??"

"What?"

"You never told me your side dude was married!"

"They're separated. But apparently she wants him back. Or something. I don't care."

"Why...so..."

"I'm not in love with the dude. He just scratches my itch until Cooper comes back into town. You see I don't even use his real name."

"Do you even *know* his real name?"

"That's real funny. Of course I know it. I just keep it light by not acknowledging it."

"Wow."

"That's not judgment I hear in your voice, is it?"

"No," Journey quickly assured. "I'm certainly in *no* position to judge."

"What do you mean by that?"

Squeezing her eyes shut, Journey kicked herself for the slip. "Just that I've done stuff people might wanna condemn me for, too. I mean, who hasn't?"

She was trying to sound lighthearted, and she hoped Roz fell for it.

"True," Roz finally agreed. "So can I come over?"

"Of course, girl, come on," Journey replied, though she really wanted to say no. She didn't know how she was going to handle being in Roz's face and not letting on that something was up. She was just going to have to put Clyde totally out of her mind for a while.

But as she looked back at Clyde's gift, she wondered just how long she would be able to keep all this up.

Chapter 11

• • • •

JOURNEY WAS A COUPLE of months into cosmetology school and absolutely loving it.

She finally felt like she was doing what she was meant to do. She'd never looked forward to her days as much as she did now. Learning about the chemistry of hair and doing fingerwaves, roller sets and flat twists was fascinating to her. And since she was now able to go during the day instead of just nights and weekends, she'd be able to finish and dive into her career full-time that much faster. She'd never been so happy.

Of course, this was mostly thanks to Clyde. He was the one that made all of this so easy for her. All she had to worry about was going to school and not how she was going to pay for it or have all of her supplies. Or that paying for it would add to her debt, which had now been paid down considerably.

Clyde was still very much a part of her life and routine. They still saw each other a couple of times a week, and Journey's guilt about it had melted to almost none. She figured since she and Clyde weren't having sex, she didn't really have anything to beat herself up about. That didn't mean she wanted anyone to find out about it, though, which was why she spent decreasingly less time with Roz and Olivia. Whenever they pointed out her scarcity, she just said she was putting in extra time at the school salon or practicing techniques.

Unfortunately, though, she couldn't make herself pull this with Molly. She still went by in the mornings to work out with her, and that was when her melted guilt would bubble slightly. It took herculean effort to not feel like a heel whenever Molly would comment about her high hopes for her marriage.

"Clyde has been really impressed with the progress I'm making," she informed one morning, grinning proudly.

"I'm impressed, too. What have you lost, about twenty pounds now?"

"Closer to thirty now, actually. I've become practically *obsessed* with getting this weight off. I've even started working out at night, too."

"Really?"

"Nothing too strenuous; I don't want to overdo it and hurt myself. Usually it's just getting on the exercise bike or using the resistance bands while I'm watching TV. My knees let me know when I need to stop."

"I'm so happy for you, Ms. Molly. You are *killing* it."

"All thanks to you."

"You're the one that's doing the work."

"But you got me going. And you *keep* me going. You know Clyde actually hugged me yesterday?"

Journey tried not to look startled. "Yeah?"

"*Totally* shocked me. He said he was proud of me for being consistent with everything, then he just reached out and hugged me. Our first one in years. I actually cried. Isn't that great??"

"It sure is," Journey agreed, pasting a smile on her face. There was a funny feeling coursing through her, and she didn't want to believe it was jealousy. She had no right to feel such a thing, and she knew it. But hearing that Clyde appeared to be warming up to Molly didn't make her as happy as it should have.

She wanted to change the subject, but Molly forged ahead.

"I'm feeling more positive about my marriage than I have in years. Hopefully next time he'll give me more than a hug, if you know what I mean."

Journey playfully nudged Molly in the arm. "Are you being naughty, Ms. Molly?"

"I'd *love* to be!"

"Oooh!"

"I know I'm nowhere near thin or anything yet, but losing this weight has me feeling sexier than I've felt in years, though I admit I still don't have the confidence to actually act on it." Molly tucked some sweaty blonde hair behind her ear and resumed pulling the cable on the rowing machine. "It would kill me if I made a move on Clyde and he rejected me. But at least we're back to sleeping in the same bed."

"Oh...y'all were sleeping separately?"

"Yeah, most of the time. I'd like to say it was just because I'm so big, but honestly it was – and I'm so ashamed to admit this – because of some of the terrible things I said to him when I was grieving. It's a wonder he still stayed in the same house, as bad I was."

"You said something *that* bad? I can't imagine it."

"Journey, I accused him of being my parents' killer simply because he's Black. I'll never forget the look on his face when I said that. I'm sure he'll never totally forgive me for it."

Hearing her confirm what Clyde had told her only made Journey's respect for him increase. Part of her thought – hoped – that he'd been exaggerating to further justify his attitude towards Molly. But apparently not.

"Does Roz know about this? Have you told her what you said?"

"Oh god, no! I could never tell her I said something like that to her father. I know they butt heads a lot, but she'd *surely* have his back on this. How could she not? And I don't want her opinion of me to get any lower than it is."

"Well...hopefully he recognized that you were grieving and probably in shock and not in your right state of mind. He has to know that you wouldn't say such a thing otherwise."

"I've apologized a million times, and still don't really feel like it's enough. I treated him *so* badly, Journey, and that horrible accusation just pushed everything over the edge. He eventually said he understood, but things just haven't been the same since. But maybe now we're finally turning a corner."

"For your sake, I hope so." Journey made herself say it, even if she didn't totally feel it.

• • • •

JOURNEY WAS TREATING Theo to dinner at Outback. Thanks to Clyde, she was able to splurge a little more, and Theo was thrilled about it.

"Can we do this every week, Mama?" He munched on his French fry.

She smiled at him. "I don't know about every week, but more often than we used to."

"Am I gonna be able to have a birthday party?"

"I don't see why not. Nothing huge, though. You know what you want to do?"

"Sky Zone."

"The place with all the trampolines? We should be able to do that, you and a few friends."

"Cool! Can Dad come?"

Journey took her time chewing her steak. "Sure."

"Good. I'll go ask him."

"What do you mean, you'll go ask him?"

"He's right there."

Journey's head whipped around to where Theo was pointing. Dino was sitting in a booth, hugged up with a woman sporting long blue braids.

Clearing her throat, Journey shook her head. "No, looks like he's on a date. You can call him later, if you want to. Your birthday isn't for a couple months, anyway."

"But he's sitting *right there*," Theo insisted, pointing again.

"I'm aware of that, Theo. I said you can call him later."

"Who is that woman?"

"I don't know."

"Dad!" Theo called out, waving his arms. Dino looked over at them and Journey could see him curse under his breath.

She scowled at her son. "What did I tell you, boy??"

"But-"

"You sittin' up here hollering in this restaurant like you don't have any home training. You keep being hardheaded and you won't be going to Sky Zone or anywhere else. When I say something, I mean it!"

Dino reluctantly wandered over to their table, followed closely by his blue-braided companion.

"What's up, y'all?" Dino greeted, avoiding Journey's eyes.

"Hey Dad!" Theo slid out of his seat and hugged Dino around the waist. He was rather short for his age, apparently taking after Dino's average height. "I didn't know you were gonna be here."

"Yeah, me and Shelly are just getting something to eat before the movie."

"You're going to the movies? Can I go?"

"Sure!" Shelly chimed in, a little too perky for Journey's taste. "It can be like a family night."

"Pump the brakes a minute," Journey spoke up before Dino could. She looked right at Shelly. "No offense, but I have no idea who you are. So all this *family* stuff is a little premature."

"Well, it can't be *that* premature, considering Dino has been my man for a while now," Shelly revealed. "You've heard of me, at least."

"No..." Journey's eyes were now on Dino. "No, I haven't."

"Well, I...I haven't gotten a chance to call lately," Dino managed to say. "I've been a little busy."

"Yeah? Business is picking up?"

"Some, yeah..."

"We've been in Miami," Shelly grinned, holding onto Dino's arm. "Dino said he wanted to celebrate me joining his business. Said we're gonna build a whole empire together."

"*Did* he?" Journey couldn't believe this man's nerve. Dino still wouldn't look at her. "Well, that is beautiful. But unfortunately, Theo can't join y'all tonight. Maybe another time."

"Yeah, hopefully. He's around the same age as my daughter. Dino is so cute with her. You should see the new bed he bought her."

Journey wanted to grab the chair next to them and knock Dino over the head with it. He was buying *beds* for his new girlfriend's child but couldn't give Journey any money for Theo?

"I would *love* to see it," Journey replied emphatically. "That would be a good thing to take note of. You know, for future reference. I'm sure you'll be getting something like that for Theo soon, huh Dino?"

His brown skin flaming, Dino nodded, his eyes on the floor. "Of course. You know I'm gonna take care of my boy."

"Sure."

"Dino, let's go finish eating so we can get to the movie on time," Shelly urged, gently grabbing his arm with both hands. "You know how I hate missing the previews. And you promised me the big box of M&Ms."

"Oh, well y'all better get going, then," Journey urged. "I've never liked missing the previews, either."

"Bye, Theo. And it was nice to finally meet you, Journey!"

"Oh, the pleasure was all mine, *believe* me."

As Journey figured, the evening didn't end before Dino called her trying to explain.

"I have a perfectly good reason for that shit you heard earlier."

"No, you don't. There's not an excuse you can give that would justify you spending money on your girl but having nothing for your son."

"It's not like that, Journey."

"What's it like, then? Because you haven't brought anything over here in weeks, and you've been dodging my calls trying to ask you about it. And did you have this girlfriend when you were pushing up on me with the same *let's build an empire* shit you fed her?"

"We were messing around, but we weren't official. I wanted *you*. But you weren't trying to hear me, so I went on and got with her."

"I bet she'd *love* to know she's just your fallback."

"Don't be talking like you gon' rat me out. This isn't even about her, J."

"You're right. It's about you doing more shit for her and her child than you do for your own. So unless you're about to tell me that you've hit the lottery since the last time I talked to you and there's a check for Theo in the mail, there's really nothing you can say to defend yourself."

"Look. I came into some money, and she asked for my help. I didn't *plan* on giving it to her..."

"But you did. And took her to Miami, to boot. What's your excuse for that?"

"Groupon deal."

Journey released a sarcastic chuckle. "You know what, Dino? I don't have time for this. You clearly still don't get it, which is just too sad for words. How 'bout I just go ahead and file child support and be done with it?"

Pause. "We agreed not to go there!"

"We agreed not to go there as long as you were paying it on your own regularly. Have you been doing that? I'll go ahead and answer for you. *Hell* no."

"You're acting like I don't do *anything*. I help out with some stuff. I guess you're forgetting about the time I-"

"I'm not going back and forth with you about this. We're never gonna agree. Go spend *all* your time with Shelly, for all I care. I'll do what I need to do on this end."

"And what does *that* mean?"

"Bye, Dino."

Journey hung up on him, then ignored it when he tried to call right back. He wasn't the only one that could be petty.

"We'll see what happens the next time you want to come get Theo," she muttered to herself. "You wanna make things difficult for me? I can do the same damn thing."

• • • •

"YOU WANT ME TO WATCH Theo? Why?"

"Uhh, because he's your grandson. I wouldn't think there'd need to be a reason."

"You usually ask Mama, or that bald-headed friend of yours. You never even call me, let alone ask me to babysit."

"Well, it's a new day."

"Nah, I'm not going for that," Clarice retorted. "Something's up and you just don't want to tell me."

The truth was, Clyde wanted to see Journey. He had called and asked if she had time to come by, and she was eager to go, but had no one to watch Theo. She was still avoiding Olivia because she didn't want to risk her finding out what was going on, and she didn't want to lie to Roz about her plans. She and Dino weren't speaking, so that left Clarice.

"Nothing is *up*, Mama," she finally insisted. "You don't spend enough time with your grandchild. Are you busy or something?"

"No, I ain't busy."

"Well, can you watch Theo or not?"

"Yeah, okay," Clarice conceded. "I'll watch him. But one day, whatever you hiding is gon' come out, I hope you know. It always does."

"I'm not hiding anything. I just have something to do."

"Uh-huh. Bring him on over. Make sure you feed him first."

Relieved, Journey took a quick shower, rounded Theo up and sped him over to Clarice's with his new tablet and some Chick-fil-a. She didn't want to acknowledge to herself that she was this anxious to see Clyde, or why. This was just supposed to be a thing for him to play out his foot fetish fantasies and for Journey to keep her bank account from going dry until she found another job.

Never mind that her job search had stalled to practically a halt. She just concentrated on cosmetology school, not finding more work. The thought really hadn't occurred to her until then. Had she really gotten *that* comfortable with this arrangement with Clyde?

"Journey, I'm glad you could come by," Clyde greeted when she arrived at his apartment. "Come on in."

Journey noticed he didn't greet her with cognac as he usually did. He was still dressed in his suit from work, jacket and all.

"No problem," Journey replied as she entered, adjusting her purse strap on her shoulder. She eyed him as he closed the door. "Is something wrong?"

"No, but we *do* need to talk. Have a seat."

Suddenly nervous, Journey took a seat on the couch and eyed Clyde as he joined her. He sat close enough so his knee touched hers. She glanced at this before looking at his face.

"What's going on?"

"Journey, I wanted to thank you again for all of your help with Molly. She's made more progress with you than she did with all of the other trainers I've hired for her combined. And she's in much better spirits, also."

A little thrown, Journey lightly lifted a shoulder. "I'm glad I could help. Is that what you called me over here to tell me?"

"No, that's not the main thing. The main thing is that I feel like it's time for us to end our arrangement."

"Wh-what? Why?"

"I just feel like it's time. I've loved every minute of our time together, but I don't want to be guilty of not knowing when to quit."

Journey recalled Molly gushing about Clyde hugging her, and she wondered if his desire to stop their trysts had anything to do with him wanting to resume intimacy with his wife. That was supposed to be a good thing, if that was the case, but Journey actually felt a little slighted. It felt like she was being tossed aside and she wasn't thrilled about it.

"I'll still help you out financially, if you need me to," Clyde continued, noting her silence. "I'd be more than glad to do that."

Surprisingly, the money wasn't Journey's main concern.

"Journey?" Clyde said after a few moments of her just looking at the floor silently. He took her hand. "Say something."

She *wanted* to say that she didn't want them to stop what they were doing. That she was actually enjoying it, and wasn't ready to give it up. But she didn't have the nerve.

"I'm just kinda surprised, is all," she finally managed to say. "This is kind of coming out of nowhere."

"This doesn't mean that I don't want to enjoy you tonight," he informed her, his voice dropping. Journey's smirk was automatic as she boldly looked into his eyes. "I've been thinking about what I want to do to you all day."

Journey was immediately wet. The effect he had on her still blew her mind.

"Is that right?" She bit her lip.

He nodded, lustfully eying her up and down. Removing his glasses, he leaned in close and Journey wondered if he was going to kiss her. That was something they hadn't done.

But instead, he nuzzled her neck, inhaling her sweet scent. Journey's eyes slid closed as she automatically leaned into him, loving it. His hand caressed the other side of her face before slowly sliding down her neck and shoulder, the backs of his fingers barely grazing her breasts. Her intake of breath at the action was sharp, and she wanted him to do more.

She got her wish. In the next few minutes she was on her back, and Clyde was sliding her lace panties to her feet.

Is he really about to...

He was. Clyde's head was between her legs, and Journey immediately gasped and gripped the back of the couch. Her hips actually lifted, and Clyde's hands gripped them to keep her in place.

"Ah-ah-ah-ahhhhh..."

Journey couldn't form any words. What Clyde was doing to her was scrambling all of her mentals.

"I'm aware of what I told you before, regarding how far things would go between us," he muttered between licks and kisses. "But I *had* to taste you at least once. I've dreamt about it, Journey...fantasized at inopportune moments, jerked off to thoughts of you so much it drove me crazy. Please don't be upset with me."

If Journey was upset about anything, it was that he held this particular pleasure from her for so long. And she felt strangely flattered that he fantasized about her so much. "I'm not..."

"Do you want me to stop? Just say the word."

"Keep going," she whispered. "Please."

And so he did. The more Clyde feasted on her, the more surreal the whole experience became for Journey. Was this really happening? Why was she *letting* this happen? And how in the world did he get *this good* at it??

He whispered how amazing she tasted as he continued helping himself, and driving Journey to new levels of pleasure she thought were unrealistic and only existed in novels. He pushed her legs as far back as he could get them, wanting full access, and introduced her to titillating areas she didn't even know she had.

She grabbed the back of his head, her fingertips digging into his tapered salt-and-pepper hair. Every part of her was quivering. Pleasure waves rolled through her with such force that it was almost painful, but she loved it. She loved what he was doing to her. She loved that his desire to please her was so intense.

And when the convulsions hit and she knew the orgasm was coming, she hoped his neighbors weren't home because she couldn't do anything but scream at the top of her lungs.

"Clyde! *Oh my god, CLYDE!!*"

"Mmm, yes..." Clyde continued nibbling on her, slowly tapering off to faint kisses on her inner thighs. "Finally got you to say my name."

Journey just laid there, panting, shaking, and marveling at what had just happened.

Chapter 12

• • • •

"IT WAS FOR THE BEST," Journey stated as emphatically as she could manage. "Best to end our arrangement before anyone found out about it. Quit while we're ahead. Go out on top. End with a bang..."

Journey continued to talk to herself in her bathroom mirror, citing every trite banality she could think of to convince herself that she was okay with Clyde calling off their arrangement. The sensible part of her knew it was for the best. But the carnal woman in her could not forget about his oral skills, or make herself not want more of it.

It had been three days, and she still clenched up whenever she thought about it. Clyde had really saved the best for last; the foot action he had been giving her was amazing enough. But it was *nothing* compared to what his tongue could do between her legs. Ever since that day, she'd tried to recreate that feeling, pulling out toys and vibrators that she hadn't used in months from their hiding place in her closet. But it was a waste of time. None of it even came close.

Clyde had turned her out.

She ran her hands down her face and groaned in frustration. This wasn't what was supposed to happen. All it was supposed to be was her allowing Clyde to play out his suppressed fantasies while blessing her bank account as a thank you. And *she* was supposed to be the one to end it. Him completely blowing her mind and giving her undoubtedly the best sexual experience she'd ever had was *not* in the plan.

She didn't know how, but she was going to have to get over this. It was cool while it lasted, but it was over. And Clyde was still offering to support her financially, which was her main reason for agreeing to all of this in the first place. Not to mention, if Roz or Molly found out, she'd be mortified.

Speaking of Molly, she called Journey and asked her to come over with her hair tools. She sounded a little excited on the phone, and Journey had to muster up some enthusiasm to match. She really didn't want to go but couldn't bring herself to decline.

"Sure, I can come over," Journey made herself say. "What time?"

"What time is good for you? Do you have class or something?"

"No, not today. I'll have to bring Theo with me, though, if I can't get my mama to watch him for a while."

"Bring him! He's more than welcome. He can hang out in the movie room and watch whatever movie he wants. There's a popcorn machine in there, too."

"Oh, he'd love that. You might not be able to get him to leave."

Molly giggled. "So just come whenever you're ready, though I'd like to be done by seven, if possible. Roz should be getting here in about an hour."

Journey froze. She *absolutely* wanted to back out now. "Oh…Roz is coming, too? Well, that's cool."

"Yeah, she's squeezing me in. Things have really picked up for her lately, so I'm glad she's able to make it. So, will I see you later?"

"Of course, yeah," Journey forced out, literally kicking herself. "I'll get over there as soon as I can."

"Thanks *so* much, Journey."

"Great," Journey muttered as she hung up the phone. Two of the *last* people she needed to be around were both going to be in her face.

Grudgingly, she rounded Theo up and headed over to Molly's. She started to text Clyde and see if he was going to be there, but she didn't want to come across as thirsty. She'd never checked to see where he was before; she didn't need to start now.

Thankfully, Clyde wasn't home. Journey tried to put him out of her mind as she got her things ready to do Molly's hair.

"I am *so* glad you could come over," Molly called out from her walk-in closet. "I was gonna try to just do my own hair for once but figured I'd get someone who knew what they were doing, since this is kind of a special occasion."

"Oh? What's the occasion?"

"Clyde and I are going on a date!"

Journey dropped her curling iron. Thankfully, no one was around to see that or the stricken look on her face. "Wow...that's great! Um, whose idea was it for y'all to go out?"

"His, actually. Can you believe it?" Molly emerged from the closet, all smiles. Journey almost couldn't believe how much weight she had lost so far. She hadn't seen Molly move around without maximum effort in years, but now she was practically floating. But Journey was sure that was more thanks to Clyde than it was about her ongoing transformation.

"Wow," Journey croaked again. "I'm really happy for you, Ms. Molly. I know you've wanted this for a while."

"*Years!* I almost thought I was gonna *faint* when he asked me!"

"Welp, my handsome godson is all set up with *Avengers: Endgame* and a tub of hot buttered," Roz announced as she strolled into the room. "And whose gonna faint?"

Molly giggled. "I was, when your dad asked me out for tonight."

"Hell, I wanted to faint too, when I heard about it." Roz smiled at Journey and went over for a hug. "Feels like I haven't seen you in forever, girl."

"I know, right?" Journey chuckled as casually as she could.

"How's school going?"

"Girl, I'm loving it. I think I'll actually hate when it's over."

"Really? I surely could never say that about school." Roz chuckled as she loudly clapped her hands. "Aight, Mom, let's pretty you up so you can wow Dad tonight."

Molly beamed excitedly while Journey turned her face away, pretending to inspect the cord on her curling iron.

The ladies made their usual chatter as Journey and Roz worked on Molly, though no one seemed to notice that Journey was more withdrawn than usual. Or so she thought.

"Okay, so what's up with you?" Roz asked her when they were outside later.

Journey glanced at her as she tossed her bags into her backseat. "I don't know what you mean."

"Don't do that. You know what I mean. You barely said anything in there."

"Oh. Just...didn't have much to say, that's all. Got some stuff on my mind."

"And you don't wanna tell me about it?"

Journey looked both ways down the street. "Not yet."

"You've been looking up and down the street ever since we came outside. Somebody following you or something?"

"Girl, stop. No." Journey didn't want to admit that she was watching for Clyde's car. She forced herself to look at her friend's suspicious face. "I didn't even realize I was doing it that much."

"Be straight up. You don't like how I was just talking about hooking up with Dick again, do you?"

"What? Since when have I cared about that?"

"Since I told you he was married."

"I told you I wasn't judging you. You're a grown woman. I just hope you're being careful, that's all, and haven't hooked up with someone that has a psychotic wife."

"Please. She's so busy with her office stuff that she probably doesn't even notice when he's gone. But even if she did, I could take her."

"I'm gonna just assume you're joking and head home." Journey opened the driver's door. She figured Clyde would be coming home soon if he was planning on taking Molly out, and Journey wanted to be gone when he did. "I need to get going."

"Aren't you forgetting something?"

"No, I think I have everything."

"But-"

"I'll talk to you later, girl."

Roz just stood and watched as Journey backed out of the driveway, then abruptly screeched back in. She just stared at her friend with a cocked brow as Journey hopped out of the car and rushed towards the house.

"You could've told me I didn't have my child," Journey muttered, ignoring Roz's amused expression. "And this is *not* to be mentioned again!"

Once she and Theo were home, Journey tried to put the previous couple of hours out of her mind. She didn't know why she was feeling some kind of way about Clyde taking Molly out. She shouldn't have cared at all. If anything, she should be happy for Molly. But to her mortification, Journey was actually a little jealous. She didn't like the thought of Clyde doing to Molly what he'd done to her.

She was still going back and forth about all of this when Theo came and stood in the doorway of her bedroom.

"Mama?"

She glanced up, distracted. "Yeah?"

"Can I go over to Dad's?"

"No." The answer was quick.

Theo frowned. "Why?"

"Are you questioning me??"

"I want to go see Dad."

"I said no. You'll see him when he comes over here."

"When is that gonna be?"

"I don't know."

"Can you call him?"

"Theo!" Journey slapped her hand against the bed. "Go to your room and leave me alone. I'm tired."

Theo turned and stomped down the hall. With a sigh, Journey flopped onto her side, already back in her musings about Clyde and Molly. Her mind wandered back to what he did to her on their last encounter, and her body woke up. She could almost feel his hands on her and see his head between her legs.

Simply, she wanted more. How could she not?

Grabbing her phone, she repeatedly typed messages to Clyde, then erased them. She didn't know what to say. How would she look, crawling back to him asking for another round? He might think she felt something for him deeper than she did.

She wasn't in love with him; she just liked how he made her feel. Loved it, even. That's all it was.

When there was a knock on the front door, she glanced at her watch as she slid off her bed. She peeked into Theo's room as she passed, seeing that he was lying across his bed, pouting.

"Who is it?" Journey called out as she approached the front door.

"Open the door, Journey."

"Roz?" Journey quickly checked the peephole before opening the door. "What are you doing over here? I thought you were meeting Dick tonight."

"He can wait. I need to handle this first." Roz stomped into the apartment without invitation.

"Handle what?"

"You. For what you've been trying to hide lately."

Nervousness shot through Journey. There was no way she could know about her and Clyde...was there?

"Okay..." Journey stalled as she closed the door. "I don't know what you're talking about."

"Save it, girl. I've been knowing you too long. You can't hide this kind of shit from me."

"Roz..."

"I saw how anxious you were all night," Roz interrupted, crossing her arms over her small chest. "Quiet, distracted, in a hurry to leave, the way you kept looking up and down the street like you were on the run, damn near forgetting your own child. Just admit it; you didn't want to see Dad."

Journey swallowed hard, feeling her body go cold.

"Something's going on with you two," Roz stepped closer to Journey, practically getting in her face. "And I know what it is."

Chapter 13

• • • •

JOURNEY WILLED HERSELF to stay calm.

There's no way she could know about me and Clyde. He certainly wouldn't tell her. Or did she follow him to his apartment? Or me? Does she even know *about his apartment?*

Crossing her arms over her breasts, she forced a slight frown. "And just what is it you *think* you know, Roz?"

"You resent him."

"What?"

"You resent Dad. More specifically, you resent me for *having* Dad while your father died and you never developed any kind of relationship with Senior."

Breathing an internal sigh of relief that Roz didn't know the real deal, Journey dropped her arms. "Nothing could be further from the truth. I do not *resent* anybody."

"I beg to differ," Roz retorted, following Journey further into the living room. "You've never been that comfortable around Dad. And I've noticed that he's seemed to want to get closer to you lately."

You don't know the half of it.

"Maybe you two should spend some time together; get to know each other better," Roz continued, dropping onto the couch. "Y'all never really did much over the years besides exchange pleasantries."

"And I'm fine with that."

"Come on, Journey. I bet it would make you feel better. I know I'm not usually the loudest member of my dad's fan club but he *is* a good father. You're my best friend; no reason he can't be a father figure to you, too. I don't mind sharing him."

Rubbing her eyes, Journey wished she could will Roz to stop talking. There was no way she could *ever* look at Clyde as a father figure now. When she thought of him, it was visions of her toes in his mouth and his tongue between her legs.

"Umm...that's a nice idea and everything, Roz, but I'm cool with things between Cl-, umm, Mr. C. and I the way they are."

"Really?"

"Yes, really."

"Then tell me why you've been so distant towards *me* lately," Roz challenged, looking directly into her eyes. "And don't try to say you haven't."

"I've just been busy with school and...my temp job and stuff," Journey replied weakly. She fiddled with the hole in her distressed jeans. "It's nothing for you to take personally."

"Well, I'm taking it personally. You don't even take my calls half the time; you just shoot me some weak text saying you'll hit me back, and then you 'forget'. It's like you're a damn guy."

"Roz..."

"We don't hang out or anything. You say it has nothing to do with my cheating on Cooper with a married dude. So what is it? There has to be *something* going on."

"I've just been getting acclimated to my new schedule. That's all."

"It's been months, Journey. It doesn't take that damn long to get acclimated."

"Roz, can you just rest assured that I'm not upset with you about anything and leave it at that?"

"Nah, girl." Roz shook her head. "Something is going on with you. If you just don't want to tell me what it is, fine. I don't have to know a hundred percent of your business. But whatever it is has you acting different, whether you want to admit it or not. And I miss my girl."

Feeling guilty, Journey finally looked at her friend. She hadn't considered how her sneaking around with Clyde would affect her friendship with Roz, even if she didn't know about it. Journey also hadn't considered that she'd make Roz even more suspicious by distancing herself like she'd been doing.

"I'm sorry," she said sincerely. "You know you're still my girl. I guess I've just been so caught up in my own stuff lately that I've let some things fall off, including our friendship. But please know you mean as much to me as you always have. I'd *never* want to lose you as a friend."

"Yeah?"

"Of course!"

"Prove it, then. Let's go out this weekend."

"Now *you* sound like a damn guy."

They both laughed. Journey realized in that moment how much she missed Roz, too. She told herself again that it *was* a good thing that Clyde had ended their arrangement. She and Roz could get back to how things used to be between them.

"Okay, fine," Journey finally agreed, nudging Roz's arm playfully. "You've talked me into it."

"Good! And who knows; you might meet somebody. Finally find someone to put some arch in that back on the regular."

Journey just chuckled and shook her head. She tried not to think how whoever that guy ended up being would have a hell of an act to follow.

• • • •

"JOURNEY GARNETT, I want you at this house *today*," Olivia demanded.

She knew this was coming eventually. Journey had been avoiding Olivia as hard as she'd been avoiding Roz.

"I have some stuff to do today, Grandmama," she tried to say. "I don't know if I'll have time."

"Make time. I really don't care *what* you have to do, just make sure you have your butt over here before the day is over with."

"Yes, ma'am," Journey grudgingly replied before hanging up the phone without a goodbye. She half expected Olivia to call her right back and get onto her for that, but thankfully she didn't.

Journey dreaded this. Ever since Olivia had grilled her about her job prospects after her layoff from Metro, Journey had stopped taking Theo over there. She figured spending the money on the after-school program was worth not having to endure endless questions about how she was going to support herself. Honestly, Journey was paranoid about Olivia finding out her secret. She was already suspicious enough, and Journey had never been good at lying to her.

But just like with Roz, Journey realized she'd probably only been making things worse by becoming so scarce so suddenly. If she'd just made herself continue on as usual and worked extra hard at keeping her game face on, Olivia might have never suspected a thing.

Journey could kick herself for not thinking of that sooner, but it was too late now. So after class, she picked Theo up and headed over to Olivia's. When her phone rang, she hoped to high heaven that it was Olivia canceling her order for Journey to show up. But she got an all new kind of anxiousness when she saw it was Clyde calling.

Peeking in the rearview at Theo, she was glad to see he'd already dozed off. She pulled into a nearby gas station parking lot, took her phone off Bluetooth and answered.

"Hello?"

"Journey," Clyde greeted her smoothly. "How are you?"

"I'm good. A little surprised to hear from you."

"Why is that?"

"Because you...you know. Of what you said the last time I saw you."

"That didn't mean that I never wanted to talk to you again, Journey. I'd like to think that we're at least friends now, right?"

"None of my friends do what you do."

Clyde chuckled. "Touché. But still. I just don't want us to go back to how things were before."

"I don't think that's possible."

"I'm glad to hear that. Though I'd love to hear why you don't think so."

"Because, I..." Journey checked to make sure Theo was still asleep and slightly lowered her voice. "Because I won't be able to forget what you used to do to me."

"Is that right?"

Journey bit her lip at the drop in his voice. She hated that he sounded so seductive.

"Yes," she managed to reply simply, running a hand along her thigh.

"I certainly won't be forgetting it, either. And I won't embarrass myself by admitting how many times you steal my thoughts over the course of a day...or what I did in the shower this morning while thinking about you."

Journey was certified horny. And she blamed her next statement on that.

"I don't have to be *just* in your thoughts."

When there was a pause, Journey began to feel mortification take over her arousal. She started to try to act like she was joking when he finally replied, "Really?"

"Yeah."

"Where else would you like to be?"

"Come on, don't tease me..."

"Believe me, I'm not. I'm just pleasantly surprised. And hating that I have to compose myself since I'm sitting in my office right now with the door open."

"So..." Journey softly ran a finger between her legs. "Where would *you* like to be right now?"

"With you," Clyde answered without hesitation.

Journey grinned. "Seriously?"

"Very. Would that be possible? Or would you think I was a total hypocrite for requesting that after what I said the last time?"

"The thought never crossed my mind. And yes, it *would* be possible, I think."

"I have some client meetings that should end around six. If you'd like to meet me at my place, let me know. I'd only have until about nine o'clock, though."

Journey wanted to ask if he had another date with Molly that night, but she didn't. In that moment, she didn't care about Molly. All she was thinking about was where she was going to take Theo while she went to meet Clyde, because her body was already aching with want.

"I'll let you know," she muttered, glancing again in the rearview. Theo was still knocked out. "I should be able to make it work."

"I hope you can. I'll be awaiting your message. I can't wait to taste you again."

A moan escaped her lips, but Journey was too horny to be embarrassed. If she could've snapped her fingers and been with Clyde right then, she would've. "I can't wait, either."

They ended the call, and Journey had to take several moments to gather herself. If her son wasn't in the car, she absolutely would have pulled out her lipstick-shaped stimulator and taken the edge off. Clyde had gotten her more worked up in that single conversation than Dino had in all the times they had phone sex back in the day.

When she finally calmed herself down enough, she continued on to Olivia's. She could only pray that this berating wouldn't last long because she wanted to go home and get showered and oiled up for Clyde, and there was still the matter of who she was going to get to watch Theo. But she grinned when she got a perfectly-timed text from Roz:

Hey, girl. A client of mine is having some kids thing tonight; something for charity. Can I borrow your kid to make myself look good? I won't have him out too late. Or he can just spend the night at my place if I do.

Journey wanted to scream, she was so happy. Roz's timing was just as good as finding a hundred dollar bill on the ground right then.

She quickly texted a reply:

NO problem. He's all yours. I'll let you know when I get to the house.

Feeling much better now that her plan to see Clyde was definitely on, she texted him to let him know she'd be there later before gently waking Theo up so she could get on with this showdown with Olivia. The sooner she got it over with, the sooner she could go home and get ready for the orgasms she'd been daydreaming about.

Thankfully, Olivia wasted no time getting to the point of her summons. She sent Theo to lay down in her room and joined Journey on the couch.

"You've barely brought yourself or my great-grandbaby over here in forever. And I want to know why."

Journey shrugged. "No reason in particular. I just decided that it would be good for Theo to spend more time around other kids, that's all. He enjoys the after-school program."

"I thought you didn't want to spend the money on an after-school program when I'm right here. And you know I love spending that time with him."

"It's nothing personal, Grandmama," Journey lied.

"You actually had Clarice babysitting him. You never ask your mama to do that."

"I realized she doesn't spend much time with him at all. They don't have much of a relationship."

"Uh-huh. And that's all it is, huh?"

"That's all it is."

"Something in my spirit tells me there's more going on that you're just not telling me."

"Nothing is *going on*; I'm just handling my business. My schedule is different than it used to be. That's all."

"You doing something illegal?"

"What?? No!" *Immoral, maybe, but not illegal.*

"There has to be a reason you've gotten so secretive lately."

"Grandmama...I wish you would just trust me. Part of the reason I haven't come over here as much is because I don't want to be interrogated. I'm a grown woman and with all due respect, I don't have to tell you everything."

Olivia blinked, slightly taken aback. She and Journey had always been close; Journey confided in her almost as much as she did in Roz. Journey tried to tell herself not to feel guilty. She wasn't obligated to share every detail of her life with her grandmother.

"I see," Olivia replied softly, folding her hands in her lap.

"Look, it's nothing you should take personally," Journey finally said with a sigh. "I'm just going to school, making money, and...kinda seeing someone. That's it."

Olivia's eyes brightened from disappointment to excitement. "You're seeing someone?"

"Yes. I mean, kinda. It's very casual right now and I don't know where it's going, if anywhere. So I haven't made a big deal about it and I don't want to make a big deal about it now. Just know that I'm fine and there's nothing for you to worry about, okay?"

"All right," Olivia conceded, somewhat hesitantly. "I still have that feeling in my spirit, though, and I'm gonna worry about you regardless. I just pray that you're not ending up like your mother."

Journey's eyes snapped to her. "What do you mean?"

"Clarice started acting like this when she first started sneaking around with Senior. He was married when she met him, you see. It wasn't until his wife died that Clarice finally started letting things be out in the open, not that she had been fooling anybody, anyway."

Fighting to keep her face even, Journey just nodded. She hadn't known the part about Senior being married when he and Clarice met. "Oh..."

"And she always insisted that I was being paranoid when I asked her about it, too. That is, before she flat-out told me to mind my own business. We had a good argument behind that. Then *she* stopped coming by here; until she needed something, of course."

"Right."

"So I hope you understand why I'm so concerned." Olivia took one of her hands. "I'm not trying to be nosy because I don't have anything else to worry about. You're my grandbaby and I see something happening that makes me worry."

Not trusting herself to speak, Journey just nodded again, then looked down at their hands.

"But like you said, you're a grown woman," Olivia continued. "I just have to trust that we raised you the right way and leave things to you. Just know I'm here if you need me."

Clearing her throat, Journey gave a tight smile. "Thanks, Grandmama."

"I *will* tell you what I told your mama, though; you can hide stuff from me, but God sees everything. That's all I'm gonna say." Olivia stood. "You want some cake?"

"Sure." Journey stood and followed Olivia to the kitchen, trying to feel as unbothered by that last warning as she made herself look.

• • • •

FINALLY, IT WAS TIME to meet Clyde.

Journey had made it through her visit at Olivia's without telling on herself. Roz had come to pick up Theo already. Journey was all showered and oiled, smelling like a walking mango. She prettied herself up without making it look like she was trying too hard. Lip gloss, afro puff, hoop earrings, jersey dress, sandals that showed off her fresh pedicure and the toe ring Clyde had given her. Satisfied with the result, she grabbed her keys and hurried out of her apartment.

Clyde was waiting on her, having gotten there not too long before she did. He let her in and handed her a glass of Martell, which Journey appreciated because her shyness had returned. She almost felt like she did the very first time they met up, and she silently told herself to quit acting like an inexperienced virgin and snap out of it.

"I'm glad to see you," Clyde informed her.

She smiled and made her voice strong when she replied, "I'm glad to see you, too."

"You have a good day?"

"Yeah. Better now that I'm here."

She blushed at the statement, and Clyde looked mildly surprised. He took her hand and led her to the couch, sitting close to her.

"I've been looking forward to this ever since we talked earlier," he admitted. "It was hard to keep my mind on work after that." His eyes swept over her. "Literally."

Journey wanted to just start taking her clothes off. She wanted what she went there for. Her body was on fire already.

"You're not by yourself on that."

"Not that I want to look a gift horse in the mouth, but..."

"What, you thought I wouldn't want to see you again?"

"Basically."

"I'm not mad at you, Clyde. If anything, I was a little disappointed."

"Disappointed? By me?"

"By you telling me you thought we should end things. I...I was enjoying what we do. Especially what you did to me that last time. Every time I think about it..."

"What?" Clyde leaned closer to her. "Every time you think about it, what?"

She made herself look into his eyes. "It does something to me," she whispered. "And it makes me want it again."

"I want nothing more than to do it to you again. I never wanted to stop."

"Then why did you say we should?"

"That was for *your* benefit. Figured you would only want to put up with me for so long."

"Why are you saying 'put up with you' like that?"

"Journey, come on. I'm fully aware of what this is. While I care about you immensely, we're basically just using each other. In one of the most pleasurable ways possible, but still. I'm certainly not deluded enough to think you have any feelings for me. And since, for whatever reason, you still have yet to *really* loosen up around me, I figured I'd just let you off the hook."

"What if I said I didn't need to be let off the hook?" She inched closer to him, her chest heaving slightly. "That I didn't *want* to be let off the hook?"

His eyes darkened. "I'd say I don't really want that, either."

"Well, then..." She sat both their glasses on the coffee table and slid down the straps of her dress and bra. She boldly grabbed his hand and placed it on her breast, seeing the reaction in his pants and loving it. "We don't really need to do any more talking, do we?"

He licked his lips. "We damn sure don't."

Journey moaned as he palmed both of her breasts, then manipulated her rock-hard nipples until she was whimpering in pleasure. He dove for her neck and she threw her head back, giving him all the access he wanted, wrapping her arms tightly around him as he pushed her onto her back with his body. They both gasped and groaned and hissed loudly, each more expressive than during any of their previous encounters, caution thrown to the wind. Journey lifted her hips against him impatiently, loving how hard he was. In that moment, she wanted him inside of her.

"Journey, sweetheart..." Clyde grunted, his body on top of hers. He ground his pulsing hardness against her. "I want to be inside you *so* badly..."

"Me, too...shit, I want that too..."

"I want to but I just can't go there."

"I know," Journey whimpered, disappointed but understanding. That would be taking things to a *whole* other level. "I know."

"You are *so damn sexy*." Clyde sucked on her neck. "And you smell amazing."

"Clyde..."

"I'm going to be dreaming about these," he whispered, squeezing her D-cup breast before tongue-kissing the nipple and making Journey practically convulse. Her nails dug into his back through his shirt. "Please don't think I can ever get enough of you, sweetheart. I want you as much as I have for a while."

"Good. 'Cause I want you, too."

"You have no idea how much I love hearing you say that."

Journey eyed him lustfully before gently nudging his shoulders, signaling for him to sit up. She could see the question in his eyes but it cleared when she straddled his lap.

His hands immediately went to her lush backside, gripping as her hips began grinding on him. Her arms rested on his shoulders.

"You said you've wanted me for a while...when did that start?" she asked, her eyes roaming over his face. It was almost surreal being this close to him. She didn't want to totally stop their fooling around but it was suddenly important for her to finally get this question answered. "When did you start looking at me differently?"

"About a year or so ago." Clyde's voice still held the slight gruffness from his arousal. He was moving in sync with her, his dick straining against his trousers. "It was unexpected and out of the blue. One day you were over at the house, and I noticed your enticing fragrance; tropical fruit, similar to what you're killing me with right now. I'm sure it wasn't the first time you wore such a fragrance but for whatever reason, I took note of it that day. Then I began noticing how enticing *you* were."

"Yeah?"

"Yes." His hands ran up and down her back.

Journey pressed closer to him, eying his lips. This new information was emboldening her yet she still didn't have the nerve to take the kiss a large part of her wanted. Her hips began a slow circle. "So what made you finally do something about it?"

"Wanted to finally put myself out of my misery." Clyde eyed her lips in return, but instead leaned forward to run his tongue along her chest, to Journey's slight disappointment. "I'd been thinking about you increasingly and figured the only way to get past it was to make it known. If you rejected me, I'd deal with it, but at least I could start trying to get you out of my system."

"Hmm." Journey's hips began to move faster. "What if you decide you want me out of your system later?"

"I don't see that happening," Clyde immediately refuted, lifting his hips to match her steadily increasing speed. He groaned, fisting her dress in his hand as if he wanted to tear it from her body. "Like I said, I know what this is. But you are my fantasy and this has brought me more joy than you would believe; I want this for as long as you want it."

Hearing that made Journey want to scream in relief. Giving up her arrangement with Clyde wasn't something she wanted to do for a while. A long while.

Before long, they were grinding and panting wildly, their lips inches apart from each other. Journey wanted to beg him to kiss her, to fuck her into temporary immobility, and she could tell from the longing look in his eyes that he wanted the same. But even after everything they'd just discussed, she couldn't. He'd already said he couldn't go all the way with her, despite how much he wanted to. No matter how polite, Journey couldn't bear to hear a rejection. She told herself she'd just have to be satisfied with this.

"I wanna come," she whimpered, her cheek pressed against his as she held onto him tighter and bucked against him like a madwoman. Her arousal was sending her into a frenzy. "I'm about to come, Clyde, please..."

"Yes, sweetheart. Come for me. I need to see it...come for me, Journey."

He dug his fingers into the thick skin of her bottom as she rode herself to a loud, panting orgasm on his lap, clinging to him as she rode the pleasure wave. She pulled back and looked at him in wonderment, amazed still that he was able to make her go crazy like he was.

"That was so sexy," he informed her in a whisper, planting soft kisses all over the side of her face.

Journey just whimpered in surrender, unable to speak. Especially when one of his kisses landed dangerously close to her lips.

"Can I see it again?"

He kissed his way down to her chest and gently flicked her nipple with his tongue before taking it into his warm mouth. Journey was already addicted to how he savored her breasts, and automatically arched closer to him.

"Yes..."

He quickly stood, picking her up with him and whipping her around, returning her to her back on the couch. He slid down and resumed suckling her breast, and Journey almost lost it. She grabbed his head, her body rolling and winding all on its own as her arousal reset. When he reached under her dress and slid her panties off, she willingly let him.

"Can this be inside you?"

His fingers slid into her before she could respond, and Journey gasped.

"Shit!"

He continued to pleasure-torture her with his fingers, while returning his tongue to her breasts, sensing how much she loved it. Journey thought she was going to pass out, it felt so amazing. She didn't care about Roz, Molly, Olivia, or even Theo in that moment. She just wanted to make sure she never lost access to this kind of ecstasy.

After a while, Clyde took her to the bed, where he spent the rest of their time together giving her the oral pleasure she'd been dreaming about for days. When Journey finally left, she was already looking forward to the next time.

Chapter 14

• • • •

AS MUCH AS JOURNEY hadn't exactly been looking forward to going out on the town with Roz, if for no other reason than she was worried about the topic straying to Clyde again, she was actually enjoying herself.

They went to Game Time, which was basically a play night for adults. There were various video games, old-school games from back in the day like Hungry Hungry Hippo and Connect Four, and just about every card game in creation. Journey and Roz were in the middle of a surprisingly intense game of Candyland with a couple of other people when Journey realized just how much she was enjoying herself. It had been a long time since she'd had even close to this much fun. When she thought about it, she couldn't even remember the last time she and Roz went out together at all.

"Come on, Journey. We've been challenged to a game of spades over there," Roz informed her, pointing to a couple of guys at a nearby table looking at them.

"How can we get challenged by some guys we've never met?" Journey asked with a smile and an arched brow.

"Okay, so I met the Chris Paul-lookin' dude when I went to get a drink, and he said that women cannot get down at spades as good as men can."

"And you fell for that? He was probably just trying to get your attention, Roz."

"Well, it worked. Now we have to go over there and beat their asses 'cause I've been issued a straight-up challenge and I am not backing down from that. I'm a Black woman, dammit!"

"I'm not sure what that has to do with anything. And need I remind you that you're biracial?"

"My daddy is Black, so *I'm* Black. And these dudes need to be taught a lesson."

"So go ahead. You don't need me. I'm gonna go see if I can avoid embarrassing myself on Tetris."

"Girl, come on! You know how we used to whup on folks back in the day. I don't want to play with anybody else."

"Okay, fine," Journey conceded with an exaggerated sigh, but she was smiling.

Sometimes she forgot about all of the history she and Roz had, and all the things they'd done together. She'd forgotten about all the times she and Roz used to semi-hustle guys when they were in college, because men always assumed they were inferior players. They would come to the table like they already had the game won, and Journey and Roz always enjoyed putting them in their places.

They were quite the pair. Their physical similarities ended at their height, which was just about equal. Where Journey was dark and curvy with a head full of thick natural hair that hung to her shoulders, Roz was fair-skinned and petite with an almost-bald haircut. But they couldn't be closer and loved each other like sisters.

"Hey, girl, where'd you just go?" Roz asked when she noticed Journey's widened smile.

"Hmm? Oh, just some random reminiscing. Come on, let's go handle some business."

"That's what I'm sayin'!"

They ended up playing several games with the men, only losing one. Journey was feeling so positive and relaxed that she began to wonder if maybe she should go ahead and tell Roz everything about her and Clyde. That maybe Roz might appreciate her being forthcoming, even if she got upset (or weirded out) over it. Journey wanted to believe that her and Roz's friendship was strong enough to withstand something like this; they'd been best friends practically their whole lives, after all.

Journey went mentally back and forth about it, thinking that now might be the best time to come out with the revelation, since Roz was so relaxed and feeling good. And when they both went to the bathroom, Journey tried to work up the nerve.

"Girl...we can tell each other anything, right?"

"What kind of question is that? Of course," Roz scoffed, touching up her lipstick in the mirror. Her sepia brown eyes perused her appearance before she leaned in, peering at her head. "It's about time to tighten up my design, here. My hair is trying to grow back out."

"I got you. But no, I asked that because, well...sometimes I wonder just what we can tell each other and what we can't."

"You can tell me anything."

"Really? I know people *say* that but not everybody can really handle being told *anything*..."

"Journey, what's up? Are you trying to tell me that you really *do* have an issue with me and Dick or what?"

"No, it's got nothing to do with that...ugh. I just...I did something kind of embarrassing and I don't know how to say it."

"Just say it. It can't be worse than anything I've done."

"Ohh, I don't know about that..."

"Journey, just come out with it, if you want to tell me. I've told you, no judgment over here. But if you don't feel comfortable, just keep it to yourself. No need in stressing if you don't have to."

"I don't know...I'd just love to get it off my chest finally."

"You sleeping with Cooper?"

"What? No!"

"Then I don't really need to know. If you sincerely want to share, I'm all ears. If you're not ready—and you're clearly not—then just tell me when you are. No biggie." Roz dropped her lipstick back into her purse and patted Journey's shoulder. "Come on, let's get back out there. I told Cornelius I'd play him in Duck Hunt."

"Who?"

"The Chris Paul-lookin' dude."

"Oh."

"And for the record, his friend was doing a *lot* of checking you out," Roz teased as they left the bathroom. "He damn near lost his mind when you bent over to pick up that card you dropped."

"Girl, stop."

"I'm so serious. I know you're out of practice and haven't had any non-Dino dick since Boyz II Men was a quartet, but it might be about that time to start opening up the candy shop to other customers, if you know what I'm sayin.'"

"The plastic plants know what you're saying."

"Anyway. You know I'm not lying."

"I don't even know *how* long it's been since I've slept with anybody other than Dino," Journey admitted. She tried to not to think about whether or not she'd have gone all the way with Clyde if he would have been willing, even though she knew the answer. "It's been a minute, though I don't know about that Boyz II Men quartet time stamp."

"*I* do. And you need to allow yourself time to get your groove on again, and not just on fallback dick with your ex-husband. 'Cause I know you want some."

"What is this, peer pressure?"

"The best kind. And this dude is tall and cute. Might just be the foray you need."

"I don't even know the man's name."

"His name is Porter. Problem solved."

"Oh, well pass me the condoms, then."

"I know that's a joke, but I can."

"Roz...shut up."

"You know you love me."

They went back out to the main floor, and Roz immediately pointed out Cornelius and Porter. When she and Cornelius went to satisfy their Duck Hunt urge, Journey awkwardly stood next to Porter, wondering what the heck she was supposed to say.

"You and Roz seem like y'all have been tight for a long time," Porter finally ventured.

"Oh yeah. Since we were kids." Journey looked up at him. He had to be at least six-five. "You and Cornelius tight?"

"Yeah, we're pretty tight. Frat brothers."

"Nice."

"You want to get in on this game of Monopoly?"

"Uhh...sure, yeah. Since Roz and Cornelius clearly aren't thinking about us."

"No complaints this way," Porter said, smiling down at her. "I'm not thinking about *them*, really."

"Oh," Journey smiled, blushing. Even though Roz had given her the heads-up that Porter seemed interested, his flirtation still caught her off guard. She found herself not really knowing how to respond, which made her feel stupid. It wasn't like she'd never been hit on before.

"You're cute when you're nervous, you know that?"

Journey's cheeks flamed harder. "What makes you think I'm nervous?"

"I'm looking at you."

"I just haven't been out in a while, that's all."

"You work a lot, huh?"

"Yeah, actually."

"I get that. Truth be told, I don't get out much, either. Usually I'm working or spending time with my son."

Journey looked up at him, intrigued. "You have a son? So do I. How old is yours?"

"Ten."

"Mine just turned eight."

"See, I knew we had something in common," Porter winked at her. "Maybe we can meet at the arcade or something one day and our boys can get to know each other."

"Ehh, yeah, maybe. Come on, let's get on that Monopoly."

They continued to get to know each other as they played various games, some as partners and some as opponents.

Journey warmed to Porter considerably, feeling more at ease and trading stories about their sons and the frustrations of co-parenting. She even found herself attracted to him, liking his puppy dog eyes and crooked smile.

When he asked for her number, though, she clammed up again. He was cool, but she didn't know if she was interested in taking things past that night. Then she had to wonder why that was. They were both single, they clearly got along well, they had things in common, she found him attractive...there was no reason why she couldn't get to know him better.

Knowing Roz would never let her hear the end of it if she shot Porter down for no good reason, Journey agreed to give him her number. When he walked her outside, hugged her, and said he'd definitely be calling her, Journey almost admitted that she'd switched the last two digits of her number. But she didn't.

Oh well. I don't really have time to date anybody, anyway, she rationalized to herself. *And I can always just tell Roz he never called.*

• • • •

JOURNEY WONDERED HOW much longer she was going to have to train Molly. She still went to work out with her a few times a week, and it was clearly working. Journey wished she could find a way to stop.

Especially after Molly told her she was planning on seducing Clyde.

"I think I've finally worked up the nerve to do it," Molly confided, flipping her blonde ponytail over her shoulder. Journey hadn't realized how much her hair had grown in the past few months. "And he's been a lot more affectionate towards me lately so I'm daring to think maybe he wants it, too."

"Oh really?" Journey asked, wondering if she sounded as snarky to Molly as she did to herself.

"Yeah. He's hugging me a lot more, checking on me, actually having conversations that he seems interested in...we even kissed once."

"Well, look at you," Journey quipped with a forced smile as an unexpected bolt of jealousy shot through her. She and Clyde hadn't kissed, and until that moment, she hadn't really cared that they hadn't, save for that one yearning encounter. But now she was wondering *why* they hadn't. "You've just been doing all kinds of stuff, huh?"

"Trying to," Molly giggled. "I think now that he sees I'm serious about getting this weight off, he knows I'm also ready to work on our marriage. And maybe he's starting to find me attractive again, since I'm not the humongous whale I used to be."

"Come on, you were never a whale."

"I was as big as a house, Journey, especially compared to how I used to look. But I'm getting back there. I'm just kicking myself for not doing it sooner."

"Well, you're doing it now; that's what's important." Journey put down her dumbbells and placed her hands on her hips, catching her breath. She'd just finished a round of squats and her butt was on fire. "You about done on the bike?"

"Three more minutes," Molly verified. She wiped her flushed, reddened face with a towel. "You look like you've slimmed down some, too, Journey. Though you looked amazing already."

"I appreciate that. Yeah, I guess I *have* dropped a few pounds, huh?" Journey glanced down at her body, twisting her leg to peruse her thick thighs. "I rarely weigh myself so I didn't really notice. Though my jeans *are* a little easier to put on lately, now that I think about it."

"Guess our workouts are helping us both. Even Clyde noticed the change in you."

Journey's head snapped up. "What? What do you mean?"

"He just mentioned that you've lost some weight, too, that's all," Molly clarified with a shrug. "I'm surprised he noticed, since the two of you don't seem to cross paths that much anymore. He's been a lot busier at work lately, sometimes not getting home until late. I can't even reach him at his office or on his cell when I call. He gets like that when he's in the middle of a big case, though."

Journey just nodded, picking her weights back up. She resumed her squats, wondering if any of Molly's calls had ever come when Journey was with Clyde at his apartment.

Then she felt a certain pride spread over her body at the realization that Clyde had noticed a change in her appearance. Her workouts were more for accompanying Molly than improving herself, but now that she knew Clyde had taken notice, she felt herself going deeper on those squats.

She looked over at Molly huffing away on the bike. Even with all of her progress, Molly still had a ways to go. She was still overweight, and would have to contend with a good amount of loose skin when she did get down to the size she wanted. Journey didn't have that issue, and the fact gave her a strange sense of superiority that she didn't expect, but she also didn't hate.

Journey knew Molly was working hard, and was sincerely proud of her. She wanted Molly's marriage to Clyde to improve. But the things Clyde was able to do with his hands and his tongue...Journey wanted that to be reserved for her. It was something she thought about constantly, rendering her unable to fully concentrate on anything else.

If she had her way, Journey would experience Clyde's skills way more often than she did. He was still depositing money into her account every week, but she cared less about the money and more about the pleasure he brought her. And that outdid any amount of money he could give her.

When Journey got into her car after her and Molly's workout, she texted Clyde and let him know she wanted to see him soon. Her body was going through withdrawals and she needed a fix.

• • • •

DINO WAS ONE OF THE last people Journey wanted to see, but he was waiting on her when she got back to her apartment later that day. She sighed and rolled her eyes as she strode by him towards her door.

"What do you want, Dino?"

"Why didn't you tell me you were gonna file for child support?" he demanded, right on her heels. He blocked the door when she tried to close it in his face, and entered the apartment behind her. "That was some real low-down shit, J."

"How is it low-down to file for something I'm supposed to get, anyway? I've been more than patient with you, Dino, and you can't say I haven't."

"Well, what, you just decided to stop? You know I'm working on some stuff; trying to build my business. If you would've just given me a little more time-"

"You've been singing that same song for years and I haven't seen a damn thing. So you can keep that."

"So you don't let me come get my son *and* file child support on me? You on some petty bullshit now that I have a girl, huh? I didn't think you'd be this jealous just 'cause I've moved on and you haven't."

Journey laughed in his face. "What-the-hell-ever, Dino. If I'm mad about *anything* regarding your girlfriend, it's that you spend more money on her child than ours. I have to beg you for a hundred bucks and get the runaround, but you can buy beds and go on vacations with *them*. If you can stand here and say you don't see anything wrong with that, then *you* have the problem, not me."

"I explained all that, Journey!"

"Yet I still haven't gotten anything from you. So I took matters into my own hands, like I should've done years ago."

Dino shook his head, scowling at her. "I don't even believe you right now."

"You better believe it, 'cause I'm done playing with you. We *both* conceived Theo yet I'm the only one that consistently supports him financially. I'm over here busting my ass trying to figure out how to get what he needs while you pick and choose what you're gonna help with. That's *over*."

"Journey-"

"Get out, Dino."

"We're not done-"

"Get *out*!"

"*Fine*!" Dino stormed towards the door. "But don't think this is over!"

"Oh, it's over, baby. There ain't nothing else to talk about."

Dino slammed the door behind him and Journey threw her hands up, resisting the urge to scream. She couldn't believe his nerve!

She was about to head to her bedroom when the door suddenly opened and Dino stalked back in, eyes on her. Before Journey could kick herself for not locking the door behind him, he grabbed her and pressed his lips to hers, crushing her body to his. Journey immediately pushed him away, but he grabbed her again, undeterred. He slid his tongue into her mouth, and Journey's resistance only lasted a few moments before she finally began kissing him back.

They tore at each other's clothes. Dino tried to push Journey to the couch, but she pulled him to her bedroom instead, their wild and sloppy kisses never stopping. Journey reached into her nightstand and threw some condoms at Dino, who wordlessly covered himself before bending her over and entering her roughly from behind. Journey gritted her teeth at the painful pleasure, grabbing the comforter in her fists. Dino pounded into her, slapping her fleshy behind repeatedly and grabbing handfuls of her thick hair. His long locs fell across his face as he continued to work his ex-wife, releasing all of his frustration.

Journey knew this was stupid, having sex with Dino. They didn't even like each other. But this was what they did; have big fights and angry sex. And Journey was enjoying getting the full ride instead of the teasing (though immensely pleasurable) trips she got with Clyde. They'd never gone all the way, even though there was an increasingly-growing part of Journey that wished they could. Everything he'd done to her thus far had been amazing, and she couldn't help but wonder if his dick felt as amazing as everything else he did.

The truth was, the more Journey experienced Clyde, the more she *wanted* to experience.

She tried to push Clyde out of her mind and just enjoy what Dino was doing to her. When he flipped her onto her back and dove on top of her, she eagerly received him, letting him have his way. He leaned down to kiss her and she slapped his face, but he was unfazed, grabbing her chin and holding it in place while he crushed his mouth to hers. Her fingernails clawed his back, leaving evidence of their stupidity.

When Dino finally tired himself out, he rolled off of Journey and laid on his back, panting and looking up at the ceiling. Journey wordlessly and quickly slid off the bed, leaving the room. She went to the living room and pulled her phone from her purse, telling herself she was checking for general messages but knowing that she also was curious to see if Clyde had responded to her text. When she heard Dino enter the room, she nervously dropped the phone. She was bending over to get it when Dino pressed his bare groin against her.

Sucking her teeth, Journey pushed him away and stood upright. She put her phone on the end table. "We're through with that, Dino."

"Who says?" He reached for her.

She slapped his hands away. "Cut it out."

"Did you get yours?"

"What?"

"You heard me." He traced her nipple with his fingertip, and she let him. "You didn't come, did you?"

She rolled her eyes, even though she couldn't help but enjoy what he was doing to her. "No."

"Then we're *not* done."

He grabbed the blanket Journey curled up in to watch TV and hastily spread it on the couch before sitting on it, pulling her to him. She looked between his legs and shook her head.

"And you just *happen* to already have another condom on, huh?"

"Quit fussin' and ride it."

"I'm not proud of this, Dino. You're in a relationship."

Dino's expression sobered. "Yeah. And I'm not exactly proud of myself right now, either; shit got intense and I just acted without thinking. It's only 'cause it's you, J.; I haven't stepped out on her with anybody else. But that's for *me* to deal with. Right now I at least want you to come so just bring your sexy ass here and let me get you there."

Journey didn't bother protesting again. She lowered herself onto him, moving her hips the way Dino always liked.

Part of her hated how good it felt, especially when he began sucking on her breasts like she liked it.

It didn't take long for the pace to quicken and the heat to reignite. Journey was bouncing and grinding on him while Dino was whispering about how much better she was than Shelly when Journey's phone rang. She ignored it, being close to getting her much-needed orgasm.

"Oh yeah...yeahyeahyeah*yeah*..." she muttered, gripping Dino's head with both hands. He tightened his grip on her, urging her on. "*Fuck!*"

Dino grunted as he continued to lick on her damp chest. He tried to pull her face to his for a kiss but she pushed him away, scooting off of his lap. She didn't even look at him as she grabbed her clothes and started to head back to her bedroom.

"Lock the door behind you when you leave this time," she instructed over her shoulder.

"So who's Clyde?"

Journey stopped in her tracks. She fixed an indifferent expression onto her face before turning back towards him.

"Excuse me?"

"The call you just got a little while ago. Who is that?"

"Why are you worried about it?"

"Because the name sounds familiar, that's all. I was just curious."

"Well, it's none of your business. Just get dressed and leave."

He shook his head as he stood and picked up his clothes. Journey stood there with her arms folded, wanting to make sure he actually left this time.

Dino was putting his shoes on when he stopped and snapped his fingers.

"Isn't Roz's dad named Clyde?"

Journey frowned, frustrated that he'd remembered. "Damn, why are you still on that??"

"I ain't *on* anything; I just remembered where I heard the name before, that's all. That's him, right?"

"Yes, dammit, Roz's dad's name is Clyde."

"What's he calling you for?"

"Like he's the only one named that on the face of the planet. And anyway, it's none of your damn business who calls me, Dino. I don't know why you think you have the right to question me."

"I just didn't think y'all were that tight."

"Whatever."

Dino looked at her, his eyes narrowed. "You're hiding something."

"What?"

"You're hiding something, Journey. We've been down since high school; you know I know you."

"I'm not hiding anything, other than my dwindling patience. Whatever I *do* have going on is none of your concern. So pick up your keys..."

"Uh-huh. Yeah, okay." Dino finished putting on his shoes and headed towards the door. "Whatever it is *will* come out eventually, though. Just like you always used to tell me."

"*Bye*, Dino."

He just looked at her knowingly as he walked out the door. Journey rushed over and locked it behind him, then stood against it, biting her lip nervously. She tried to tell herself to chill out; just because Dino knew Clyde was calling her didn't mean he would figure out what was going on. There was no way. And knowing Dino like she did, Journey figured he'd forget all about this by the next day, anyway.

Shaking the whole thing off, she went to return Clyde's call.

Chapter 15

• • • •

JOURNEY WAS ABOUT HALFWAY through cosmetology school, and she finally felt like she was seeing the light at the end of the tunnel.

Her classmates loved how she did their hair during Student Style Days, and a couple of them had asked her to do their hair outside of school. They were also sending other people her way, as was Christina, her former coworker at Metro Service Group. Christina had a sizeable social media following, and once she began shouting out Journey and her skills, Journey started getting a lot more requests.

"I told you I was gonna hype you up, girl," Christina commented. Journey had just finished re-doing her platinum blonde color and Christina was still admiring it in the handheld mirror. "You've got some serious skills."

"I certainly appreciate it." Journey grinned as she took the money Christina handed her. "It's what I love to do. I can't wait until I can do it full-time."

"How much longer do you have to go in school?"

"A few months. And I love school, but I'm ready to be done with it so I can finally start my career."

"You've started it. Just because you're still learning doesn't mean it hasn't started. I'm seeing the styles you post on Instagram; there are people that have been doing hair for years that can't do what you do."

"Awww," Journey blushed, grinning harder. She loved hearing such things about her hair skills. It just made her want to get her hands into every person's hair that she could.

"I love you for having my back so much. Here, let me get the pics."

Christina gladly posed for several pictures, letting Journey get different angles of the color and cut she'd just done on her hair. She then took several selfies of her own, tagging Journey on Instagram and encouraging her local followers to go to her for all of their hair needs.

"Girl, you have my notifications going *off*," Journey marveled, watching her views and follows increase by the second. "I didn't know you had that kind of pull on IG."

"Yeah, I'm kind of a big deal," Christina joked, nudging her friend playfully. "You didn't know?"

"Well, if I didn't before, I surely do now."

"Good."

"So where are you working now?"

"Oh, I got on at my aunt's law firm."

Hearing that made Journey immediately think of Clyde.

"Doing what?" she asked, pushing the thought away.

"I'm an assistant to one of the partners, which I can't say I love, but the pay is great. *Way* better than at Metro. And thankfully they don't expect me to be at their beck and call twenty-four-seven."

"I heard through the grapevine that there are more positions opening up at Metro."

"And they can keep 'em. I'm not interested in going backwards. They called you?"

"No; I kinda thought they would but I guess I'm still not worthy enough."

"To hell with them, anyway. You're doing your cosmetology thing; no need in going back to that hell hole, even if they *did* ask you to. As far as I'm concerned, Metro can kick rocks."

• • • •

BETWEEN SCHOOL, WORKING in the student salon, and the increasing number of clients she had on the side, Journey didn't have much free time. But she was able to allow herself some luxuries she couldn't afford before Clyde started blessing her bank account. She went shoe shopping, ate out more, upgraded her television. Clyde gifted her a spa day, not taking no for an answer when she tried to protest, and after the luxurious massage, facial, manicure, and the most decadent pedicure she'd ever experienced, Journey was hooked. She began going to the spa on her own, even if it was just for regular massages and not more expensive whole spa days. It was amazing how much more relaxed she felt, mentally as well as physically. Just like Clyde said would happen.

She also still made time to go to Molly's and work out with her early in the mornings, after getting Theo off to school. It had reduced to just a couple of times a week, but Molly seemed to be noticeably smaller every time Journey went over there.

"I'm taking these supplements now," Molly informed her, showing her a handful of bottles. "This one is a fat burner, this one is for the liver, this is some kind of diuretic..."

"Wow, you take all these every day?"

"Every day. I think they're helping a lot. I have even more energy throughout the day than I did before. Yesterday I even took a walk outside...in *short sleeves*."

"Whaaaat?" Journey grinned, knowing what a big deal that was for Molly. "And you weren't self-conscious at all?"

"I was at first but then I realized that I was freaking myself out for nothing. It's not like my neighbors sit outside all day watching everything. The few people I *did* see just waved and commented how nice it was to see me out and about. I was just being stupid."

"Well, I'm happy for you."

"Thanks, Journey. I can't tell you how much it means to me that you still come over to work out with me. I know I wouldn't have made this much progress without you."

"Don't give me so much credit. But I'm happy to do it."

"I actually have some extra motivation, since my wedding anniversary is coming up."

Journey looked at her, brows raised in surprise. "Oh it is? What are y'all gonna do?"

"I don't know. Clyde hasn't mentioned it, and I'm trying to tell myself it's because he has a big surprise planned and not because he forgot. Our anniversary hasn't always been an occasion to be looked forward to."

"Oh?" Journey's ear perked up. "Why do you say that?"

"Because ...well, this is a little embarrassing to admit but we mainly got married because I got pregnant with Roz and begged Clyde to make an honest woman out of me. I wanted us to be a family and not just co-parents. It took a while for him to agree, but he eventually did. He's never said it flat-out but I know it wasn't what he really wanted."

So Clyde didn't even want to marry her? This just gets more and more interesting...

"Over the years, though, it became less about obligation and more about love, and we were happy together," Molly continued. "Maybe not over-the-moon, blissfully happy...well, *I* was. Clyde has always been my dream man but I know he can't say the same about me, even when I was a tight-bodied college junior. We were just having a good time with each other; we weren't even a couple. If I hadn't gotten pregnant, I doubt we'd still be together now, I hate to say."

Did you get pregnant on purpose?? Journey had the thought, but knew there was no way she could voice it. It would come across as judgmental and she was certainly in no position to do that.

"Well, regardless, you *are* still together," Journey made herself reply. "I'm sure he hasn't forgotten your anniversary. It's probably on his calendar like everything else."

"Hmph. You'd think that something like this wouldn't have to *be* on his calendar," Molly pouted, plopping onto a workout bench. "Regardless of how we started out, we've been married long enough for him to remember on his own, right?"

Journey didn't want to talk about this but felt compelled to respond, "Hey, don't listen to me...with that sharp attorney mind of his, I'm sure something this important is at the front of it. I just see lawyers on TV who have their secretaries remind them of everything, that's all; that's the only reason I said that."

Molly waved a hand dismissively. "It's fine. That's not the main thing that's bothering me, anyway."

Journey hesitated to ask, but she made herself do so, anyway. "What's wrong?"

"I can't talk to Roz about this kind of stuff 'cause I know she won't wanna hear it. But I ordered a nightie online and surprised Clyde with it the other night. He said it was a nice color, then went to his office. Said he had an opening statement to work on."

"Ouch."

"Yeah. It was pretty humiliating. I really thought he was becoming more sexually attracted to me. But he'd rather work than make love."

"Try not to read too much into that. I'm sure you know how demanding his job is."

"I do, but...I might not be an expert on men – Clyde is really the only man I've been with, to be honest - but I bet most of them would at least put off work for a while when their wives are standing in front of him half-dressed and horny."

Journey's cheeks flushed. "Ms. Molly!"

"Well, I'm sorry, but I'm pretty sexually frustrated right now," Molly confessed. "And like I said, I don't have anybody else to talk to about this. Do you think Clyde might be..."

"Might be what?"

"Do you think he might be cheating? He's certainly not sleeping with me and he's always had a *huge* sexual appetite. Between you and me, he even liked to do things to my feet. But that always weirded me out and I didn't let him."

You don't know what you're missing.

"The feet can be very erotic. Maybe you should try it."

"You think?"

"Absolutely!"

"What about oral sex? 'Cause he loves it but I never much cared for that, either."

Good lord, what is wrong with you, woman?? Journey began to wonder what it was Clyde had seen in Molly in the first place all those years ago.

"Well...if I were you, I'd just stick with the feet for right now," Journey advised. "Anybody can do oral sex. Show him how much you've *really* changed by inviting him to have his way with your feet."

"Wow, you think so? I've never thought about it like that..."

"I definitely think that's the way to go. Get you a nice pedicure; hell, I'll even do it for you. Then be waiting on him in another one of those new nighties and with some flavored massage oil."

"Oh my gosh, that stuff tastes disgusting."

"I've had some pretty good ones. And you're not going to be the one tasting it, anyway; he'll be licking it off *your* feet."

"True..." Molly chewed her lip, deep in thought. "It's worth a try. Though I still can't imagine how anyone can get aroused by feet."

"You'd be surprised."

"Thanks, Journey. I'm going to take your advice on this and hope to high heaven it works."

Journey left a little while later feeling quite proud of herself. She didn't tell Molly anything wrong. She actually encouraged her to be intimate with Clyde.

Just not in the way that Clyde was now intimate with *her.*

It was just too good. Clyde's oral skills were too exquisite to share, and Journey didn't care if Molly *was* his wife, she didn't want her getting the same thing Clyde was giving her. Molly could have the foot stuff, as great as it was. Journey couldn't imagine how in the world Molly didn't like receiving oral sex, especially if Clyde was the one giving it, but whatever.

More for Journey.

• • • •

"I THINK WE SHOULD GO out to dinner. It's about time, don't you think?"

Journey looked at her phone in surprise. This was certainly an invitation she wasn't expecting.

"Umm...this is a little out of the blue. I mean, we don't really...do that."

"No reason we can't, though."

"Okay, what's up with you?"

"Why does something have to be up?"

"Mama."

"Do you want to go to dinner or not, dammit?"

"Fine, yeah, I guess. When?"

"Tonight. I don't think this needs to wait."

"And what about Theo?"

"He can stay with Mama. He doesn't need to be around this conversation."

Journey didn't know what was going on with Clarice, but she couldn't deny that her curiosity was piqued a little bit. She and Clarice didn't spend much one-on-one time together at all so Journey couldn't help but wonder what they could possibly have to talk about.

When they finally met up at Clarice's favorite spot, Waffle House, Clarice wasted no time getting to the point of her invitation.

"So I see you took my advice."

"What?"

"How long have you had a sugar daddy?"

Journey was glad that her skin was dark because she felt all of the color drain from it just like that. Still, she tried to keep her composure.

"I don't know what you're talking about," she asserted, straightening her back.

"Don't try that. You're talking to the OG, here."

"What makes you think I have...one of those?"

"You went from struggling to pay your bills with a full-time job to *just* going to school and no money worries at all. It doesn't take a genius. And don't waste your time telling me that crap about having a temporary job 'cause it's an insult."

"It's funny that you assume it's a sugar daddy. For all you know, I could just be selling drugs."

"Ha! I *know* you don't have the spine for *that*."

"You're way off base here, Mama."

"Am I?" Clarice glanced out the window towards the parking lot. "I see you got a new car, there."

Journey's face flamed. She didn't expect Clarice to notice that. "It's not *new*; it's used..."

"It's a luxury vehicle compared to that junkpile on wheels you were driving. But no sugar daddy, huh?"

"Haven't you ever heard of saving money for a rainy day?"

"Didn't you lose your job like six or seven months ago? You trying to tell me you had *that* much saved up to carry you that long?"

"That's not impossible."

"No, it ain't. But I'd be willing to bet my G-spot that you didn't do that."

"I'd rather not talk about your G-spot in any capacity, thank you."

"Whatever. Be real with me, daughter. What's the deal?"

Journey started to deny it again, but realized she wanted to come clean to someone. She was keeping what she was doing with Clyde from everyone, and holding it inside was very binding, regardless of how much she tried to act like it wasn't. Clarice might not usually have been at the top of her list of confidants, but when Journey really thought about it, she was pretty ideal for this situation.

"Okay, fine," Journey finally admitted, lowering her voice to a hush. "Fine, I *do* have one. But I can't tell you who it is."

"I don't need to know who it is. I'm just glad you're finally admitting it. Don't know what you're hiding it for."

"It's not exactly something I'm proud of."

"Hell, why not? You're not ashamed of it, are you?"

"Can't say I want to shout it from the rooftops."

"You don't have anything to be ashamed of. It's not like you're a lazy-ass who didn't even try to find a real job. You're doing what you need to do to support your child."

"I guess that's a way to look at it, but-"

"Does this man make you do things you don't want to do? Does he hurt you in any way?"

"No. Not at all."

"You doing anything illegal with him?"

"No. Immoral, maybe, but not illegal."

"He must be married."

Journey glanced around them, hoping no one was listening to their conversation. She lowered her voice again. "Yeah."

Clarice shrugged, swirling her straw around her orange juice. "So was Senior, when I met him."

"And that didn't bother you at all?"

"She was Senior's problem, not mine. He *chose* to be with me."

Journey shook her head. "Yeah, well this isn't gonna end like that over here. I don't want him to leave her or anything. He's a means to an end."

"Yeah, okay. But what *is* the end?"

"Huh?"

"How long are you gonna keep this up? Until you get your bank account fattened up enough? Or are you waiting on *him* to end it?"

"I...I don't know. Haven't really thought about all that."

"You should."

"He actually suggested we stop with the...*physical* part of things a while ago and he just keep supporting me financially, if I wanted."

"And you didn't do it?? Hell, I *wish* Senior had offered me something like that, 'cause sex with him is like washing the dishes."

"At first I thought it was a good idea. Then I realized that's not what I really wanted."

Clarice sat back in her seat, eyes brightening in realization. "Sounds like somebody's getting caught up."

"What? No I'm not!"

"He gave you an out and you didn't take it. You're *enjoying* it."

"I...well, I can't help it. The man has *skills*. And it's hard to give that up when I haven't had anything nearly as good in years, if ever."

"You in love with him?"

"Absolutely not."

"You sure?"

"I'm positive."

"Do you contact him to meet up more than he contacts you?"

"Not at first, but now..." Journey couldn't believe she was admitting all this.

"Well, whether you're in love with him or not, you're clearly sprung. You've got the sugar daddy sweet tooth."

"And what is that, Mother?"

"You've gotten to where this is more than just about the money for you. I'd be willing to bet you've probably started getting selfish with it, too, not even wanting him to give the dick to his own wife."

"Just the tongue," Journey corrected, her face flaming in disbelief. She could not believe she was having this conversation with her mother. "We've only had oral sex. Well, he's only done it to me. I haven't gotten the...any of that you just said."

"Hmph. Got you hooked just with that, huh? Let me guess; you fantasize. Neglect shit you're supposed to do. The more time goes on, the more you want. How close am I?"

Journey averted her eyes, not wanting to admit that Clarice was pretty much spot-on.

"You ain't gotta admit it; I already know," Clarice assured, her brown eyes roaming her daughter's flushed face. "The man has you rotten. And I'm gonna tell ya; I don't think you're cut out for this kind of thing. Not really."

Journey jutted a defiant chin. "What makes you say that?"

"You can't even say *dick*, let alone tell me who it is. I bet if someone found out his identity tomorrow, you'd want to go hide under a rock. You're too worried about what folks are gonna say."

"It's not anybody's business," Journey declared, even though there was some truth to Clarice's words. If Roz or Molly or Olivia found out about her and Clyde, Journey wouldn't know what to do with herself.

"Yeah, all right." Clarice pulled the plate of waffles and eggs that the server had just sat in front of her closer. "If you say so. Just warning you, daughter; everybody can't handle this kind of thing. That sweet tooth could leave you with a stomachache that might just do you in, if you're not careful."

"You are killing that metaphor. And thanks for the concern and the advice, but I think I've got it."

Clarice just chewed her food, looking at Journey knowingly. Journey began digging into her own meal, trying to look as self-assured as she sounded.

. . . .

TO JOURNEY'S DELIGHT, Clyde let her know he was available for her to come over. She'd sent him a few messages, throwing some very heavy hints, before he finally invited her.

Clarice agreed to watch Theo while Journey went to see Clyde, thankfully not mentioning anything about their Waffle House conversation. Journey practically itched from excitement as she got ready, anticipating the orgasms and wondering if he could possibly top what he'd done the last time, as usual.

They'd been *doing their thing* for months now and amazingly, there had been no ruts. No time when Journey was bored or felt like fulfilling her part of their arrangement was a chore. Clyde didn't start out strong and then fade out or slack off. If anything, he only gave her tastes and nibbles at first, as if to test her. Or to see how much she would allow him to do. And probably to both of their surprise, she kept letting him go a little further over time.

Now, they had done just about everything but the main thing. Part of Journey was fine with that; the other part was curious. And she knew he wanted to go there with her, but his allegiance to Molly wouldn't let him. Journey began getting the prickles of thoughts; wonderings about what might happen if she tried to take things further this time. Would he *really* resist her if she put it all the way out there?

This, among other things, was on her mind when she arrived at Clyde's apartment. She grinned when he opened the door.

"Hey," she greeted, her tone flirtatious. She stepped inside without invitation.

"Hey, yourself." Clyde closed the door behind her, then slid a hand in his pocket. His white work shirt was partially unbuttoned and his shoes were off.

She stepped forward to give him a hug, squeezing him tight. "It's good to see you. I missed you."

Clyde hugged her back, though he was caught a little off guard. Journey had never initiated such a hug with him before, or held him this tightly. "It's always good to see you." He stepped back with a smile, his hands still on her waist. "I'll get you your drink."

"Ahh, you know what? I don't need one tonight."

He looked at her, eyebrows raised. "No? That's a first."

"Maybe that won't be the last first of the evening."

Looking at her curiously, Clyde cocked his head slightly. "You all right?"

"I'm great." Journey grabbed his hand and led him to the couch, smiling at him as she pulled him down next to her. "I'm *really* great."

"You seem different this evening."

"Maybe I'm just finally comfortable with you."

"That would be wonderful, but I get the sense that there's something else on your mind."

"Oh, I have a *lot* on my mind," she purred, leaning towards him.

"Something to do with Theo? Is he all right?"

"Yeah, he's fine," Journey waved a dismissive hand. "I'd much rather talk about *you*."

"What about me?"

"Well...I hear you have an anniversary coming up."

Clyde eyed her. "Yeah...yeah, I do."

"Oh, so you remember it?"

"Of course I remember it. Journey, what's going on?"

"I'm just curious...do you have any plans or anything?"

"I'm actually not sure yet. We haven't really done much these past few years because Molly never wanted to leave the house. But now that she's trimmed down considerably and getting her confidence back, she's more open to it, so maybe I can take her to a nice dinner."

"Hmm. Dinner, huh?" She inhaled his cologne. "Damn, you smell amazing..."

"So do you. As always."

She placed a hand on his thigh. "So...all y'all are gonna do is have dinner?"

"Most likely. I told you I wasn't sure."

"Right, but..." Her hand inched farther up his thigh. "I can't imagine she's gonna be satisfied with just going out to eat and that's it. What about when you get home?"

Clyde looked at her intently. He knew something was up. "You've never wanted to talk about Molly during your time here before. Why the change?"

"It was just a question. Curious, you know."

He gently placed his hand over hers right before it reached his crotch. "Why don't you just say what's on your mind. Ask me what you really want to ask."

Journey bit her lip. She had hoped to get him worked up a little first. He was too clear-headed for her to come out with what she really wanted to say. As comfortable as she now was around Clyde, she didn't know how he would receive it.

"How come you've never kissed me, Clyde?" she finally asked. "Is it for the same reason you won't have sex with me?"

"I didn't think you'd be interested in that, honestly."

"Why?"

Clyde shrugged. "I know what this is. It's not anything romantic. I pleasure you...you *let* me pleasure you..."

"What about *your* pleasure?"

"I get plenty of that, believe me. I enjoy what we do as much as you."

"So...you don't want me to do anything back to you?" Journey placed her hand back on his leg, this time skipping the slow trail to his dick and going straight for it. She smirked at Clyde's sharp intake of breath, and also at finally realizing just how much he was working with. She slowly massaged him through his pants, loving the sight of him going slack-jawed at her manipulations. "I think it's time I started returning the favor some, don't you think?"

Clyde bit his lip, his posture sagging in pleasure. "Journey..."

She leaned forward and lightly grazed her tongue along his jawline. "Do I need to stop?"

"No. Hell no."

"Good." She continued massaging him for several more moments, enjoying his increasing moans. "'Cause I don't want to stop. Not with this."

He looked at her. "What do you mean?"

Releasing him, she stood. Boldly looking right into his eyes, she lowered the straps of her tank dress, shimmying it down her body. Clyde's eyebrows shot straight up upon seeing she was wearing nothing underneath.

"What's going on?" he asked, his eyes roaming her body.

"What, you don't like what you see?"

"That's not it at all." He eyed her 38Ds. "Not at *all*. But...you've never done anything like this before."

"No time like the present, right?"

"One of my favorite mantras. You look absolutely delicious..."

"Why don't you taste me and see?"

With an eager groan, Clyde sat forward and pulled Journey closer to him. Easing her left leg over his shoulder and keeping his grip on her hips, he proceeded to follow her suggestion. Journey gripped his shoulder with one hand and his head with the other, throwing her head back and trying to keep her knee from buckling.

"Oooh, Clyde...oh baby, yessss..."

He feasted on her until she was screaming his name over and over, using his tongue like the master he'd proven himself to be. Journey finally looked down at him, somehow even more turned on than when she arrived.

When she caught her breath, she smiled at him devilishly. "Your turn."

"Journey-"

"Shhh." She kneeled in front of him, boldly pushing him against the back of the couch. She unbuckled his belt. "Just let me do this."

"You don't have to-"

"I *want* to." She yanked his pants down and took his shaft in her hand, stroking it, ignoring how hairy his thighs were. "I *really* want to."

Clyde started to protest again but she placed a finger to his lips. "I got this, baby."

She slid her mouth over him, and his hips lifted off the couch slightly. He shuddered, the pleasure ripping through him immediately. His hand gripped her hair.

"It's been so long," he whispered, already slowly pumping into her mouth. His head rolled along the back of the couch, eyes closed in ecstasy. "*Fuck*, it's been so long..."

Journey's vigor increased upon hearing this. It did something to her, knowing she was giving him something no one else had in who knew how long. His wife was probably too much of a square to give him any head, even before she gained all that weight. "You just remember who's giving this to you. Whose making you feel like this. I don't want you to forget."

"Oh I won't," Clyde quickly assured, biting his lip. His hands were sliding through her hair and around her shoulders and neck as if he couldn't control them. "I absolutely won't."

"You like this, don't you?" Journey taunted in between slurps and slobs.

"Mmm-*hmm*..."

"You ain't *never* had head this good, have you, baby?"

"Nooo..."

"That's right..."

"Please don't stop, sweetheart. You have *no* idea how much I needed this, Journey; please *please* don't stop..."

"I'm not, baby. I'm here to please you tonight."

Journey continued working her mouth and hands up and down his manhood, taking an immense amount of pleasure in how much he was enjoying what she was doing to him. Maybe this was why Clyde liked doing things to her so much. Journey couldn't deny she was feeling pretty powerful and sexy right then.

He was starting to shudder and Journey knew he was getting close. She pulled him in deeper, totally filling her mouth with him. His grip on her hair tightened almost to the point Journey thought he would tear it out by the roots.

When he finally exploded, Journey made sure she sucked out every drop. Clyde whispered obscenities as he came down from the orgasm, his grip on Journey's hair loosening as he sank against the couch. Journey smiled triumphantly as she rubbed his thighs and stood.

"Feeling good, baby?" she asked him.

"I'm feeling *great*," Clyde verified. He was wearing a goofy smile Journey had never seen and almost looked like a different person.

"I'm glad to hear it."

"Journey... sweetheart, you are *incredible*."

"I aim to please. I'm curious, though; what did you mean when you said 'it's been so long' and that you 'really needed this'?"

Clyde grunted and ran a hand down his face, looking away momentarily. "Intimacy isn't something I've gotten much of at all in a long while. I haven't had sex in years, for various reasons, since before everything took a turn for the worse in my house."

"Wow...you seriously have gone without all this time?"

"Yes. As hard as I'm sure it is to believe, I haven't touched another woman, though I've admittedly been tempted. The last time I've had sex was with my wife and that's been several years ago now. I've buried myself in work and kicked up my workouts to try to suppress it, but I've been sexually frustrated for too long. It's part of the reason I got this apartment; being at home gets overwhelming at times. And in case you were wondering, no other woman has been here." He grabbed her hand, biting his lip as his eyes floated up to her face. "That's another reason why I love my time with you so much...especially since it's better than I could've imagined it would be."

Grinning, Journey processed this information. So Clyde had been abstaining all this time, even though Molly and Roz were so sure he'd been stepping out. Journey was mildly surprised herself; that was a long time to go without, especially when your spouse was right there in the same house. Journey felt privileged that he shared such an admission with her, she empathized with him...and she wanted to help make up for lost time.

"Well," she eased down onto his lap, straddling him and nibbling on his earlobe. "You definitely deserve this, then."

She tore open his shirt, sending buttons flying, before sliding her arms around his neck. Being flesh-to-flesh with his dick like this revved her up immediately and she began to move, unable to help herself. "You feel *so* good, Clyde. I love this..."

His eyes opened and she could see the battle of reluctance and pleasure on his face. He bit his lip. "We shouldn't…" His arms encircled her, despite his words. "This is dangerous."

"Why?"

"Because it's too tempting to slide inside of you when we're like this."

"Is it?" Journey grinded on him harder, wishing with everything in her that Clyde would just say to hell with it and take her like she wanted him to; like she knew he wanted to. She put her lips close to his ear. "You feel how wet I am for you?"

He groaned loudly, his dick twitching between her legs. "Journey, please…we're playing with fire. I'm not a machine. Don't do this to me."

"Move me off of you, then."

"I…" His hands slid to her hips and tensed, and Journey feared he was going to do exactly as she dared. He didn't. "I can't. *Fuck*, I can't. You feel too amazing."

Journey sucked on his neck as she continued to grind on him, loving how he held onto her. His resistance seemed to be weakening with every minute that passed, as his movements and intensity were slowly increasing to her level. Journey prayed he didn't come to his senses and put a stop to things; she knew his guard was finally lowering. If she could just get him to the point of no return…

They hadn't been in this position since the night he revealed when his attraction towards her started, because Journey hadn't wanted to tempt herself. She'd been determined to be satisfied with the amazing oral sex and fingering and breast action Clyde blessed her with. But that was out the window now. She didn't know when she'd gotten to the point where she was ready to just say *fuck it* and give Clyde all of her, but she was there. And she wanted to get him there, too.

"You gonna come for me again, baby?" she panted.

"If you keep doing what you're doing, I am."

"That's what I wanna hear." She grabbed his hand and forcefully put it on her bouncing breast. He immediately began squeezing and kneading it, making her moan loudly. "Suck it."

Immediately obliging, Clyde's moans matched hers as he greedily enjoyed her breast. Journey wanted to scream; the headiness overtaking her in that moment was the most overwhelming thing she'd ever experienced. She almost felt high. They kept going, each working up a sweat, taunting each other to release. Journey *ached* for him to fuck her, and was getting frustrated at the self-control he was apparently able to hold onto despite her being naked and willing on his lap.

"I want you," she whispered, her tongue trailing his ear as her hand gripped the other side of his face, their bodies sliding against each other. "I'll say yes to whatever you want."

"Shit..." Clyde muttered. His thumb found her clit and mouth fell open slightly when she screamed and threw her head back in pleasure. His movements started becoming erratic.

"Clyde, please..."

"I wanna fuck you so bad, Journey. You have no *fucking* idea."

"I'd let you."

A hard shudder ripped through him at her words. "Why'd you have to tell me that, sweetheart? I can't resist..."

Journey lifted slightly, shifting so she could feel the tip of Clyde against her opening. Clyde's eyes widened slightly before sliding closed, and the anguish on his face slowly melted into conceding pleasure. Journey felt she might finally get what she wanted, but she wanted him to be the one to finally press the accelerator and take it all the way. All he had to do was lift his hips.

She slid the head of his dick against her wetness, teasing him. "You want it? It's yours, baby...take it, Clyde."

"I can't resist you," he whispered again, looking into her eyes. "I'm about to lose it..."

She felt him just start to slide inside of her before he suddenly forcibly readjusted himself, as if realizing what he'd been about to do. In the next second, he was shuddering and calling out Journey's name louder than ever before, his arms crushing her to him as he was hit with the hardest and most intense orgasm he'd experienced with her. Journey held him just as tightly, still moving against him. She felt his warm release between their bodies, but she was in no hurry to move. As good as that had felt, she was still frustrated.

*Damn, I was **so** close!!*

Finally, Clyde gently eased her off of him so he could go clean himself up and change his shirt. Journey waited, still buzzed and even more determined, and eyed him lustfully when he strolled back into the room holding a wet cloth. He cleaned her stomach and returned the cloth to the bathroom before rejoining her on the couch. Journey immediately cuddled up to him. His hand gripped her thigh.

"That was intense," she purred.

"It was. Intense and amazing. I think you've become my one weakness, sweetheart."

Hearing that gave her a bolt of confidence. She began sucking his neck and he groaned, leaning his head back and closing his eyes. "I love that I can please you as much as you please me."

"You absolutely do that."

"And I can please you in other ways, too, you know."

He opened his eyes. "Really?"

"Any way you want." She looked at him pointedly as she eased her leg over his lap. "And I mean *any* way."

"I'm certainly pleased. Make no mistake about that." He slid off the couch and knelt between her legs, licking his lips. Journey grinned devilishly.

"Another round?" he offered.

"I told you I'd say yes to anything."

Clyde moaned as he began pleasing her in her favorite way, and Journey grabbed his head with both hands. Her hips moved against his mouth, and she gasped when his tongue slid inside of her. She lifted her head and watched him, biting her lip as she worked up the nerve to finally say what she wanted to say. But his tongue and lips were rendering her speechless, and it didn't take long for another orgasm to overtake her body. She whimpered a string of obscenities as she continued to hold the back of his head, riding the ecstasy.

"I still can't believe what you do to me, Clyde," she panted as he leisurely licked her inner thighs.

He just moaned, continuing to lick on her.

"Just think how much better it would be, though, if this was just between us."

The licking stopped and he looked up at her, confused. "I thought it was. I certainly haven't told anyone about our arrangement."

"That's not what I'm saying. I mean you doing what you do to me...*only* to me."

The rest of his dreamy look fading, Clyde sat up a little straighter, easing away from her slightly. "What?"

"Call me selfish, but I don't want anybody else getting what I'm getting."

Standing, Clyde quickly stepped away from her, looking troubled as he finally zipped and buttoned his pants as he hadn't bothered before. After buckling his belt, he ran a hand down his face and braced his fists against his hips, shifting his weight from leg to leg.

"I was afraid this might happen."

"You were afraid *what* might happen?"

"You're getting attached."

Journey frowned. "What? No, I'm not!"

"Then what is this?" Clyde motioned towards her naked body. "You being so aggressive, seducing me like you did, now telling me you want us to be exclusive-"

"Whoa, whoa, hold up!" Journey stood, holding up her hands. "I don't think we're on the same page, here. I don't want a relationship with you. Is that what you think?"

"Well, you just said-"

"All I meant was that I only want you going down on me and me only. That's *all*."

Realization crossed Clyde's face. "Are you serious?"

Journey held her arms out. "Don't I seem serious?"

"So that's what all of this is about? Journey, I can't promise you that. You know I'm married."

"I'm well aware of that. But your wife doesn't even *like* oral sex, remember?"

Frowning, Clyde folded his arms. "And how do you know that?"

"She told me. During one of our workouts."

"I see. What, she confided in you and now you're using it against her? Is that why you offered to train her?"

"Wow, really?? You think I was scheming this whole time? You stepped to *me*, remember?"

"I thought we had an understanding."

"Our understanding was that I wouldn't do anything I don't want to do. That's it."

"This is completely out of the blue."

"I can't help it if I love what you do so much that I don't want to share it."

"You kind of already are, Journey. Don't you know that? Every time I leave from here with you, I go home to her."

"You go to the same *house* as her, but you and I both know that you spend more time in your office than in your bedroom with her. I don't care if you sleep with her. All I'm asking is for this *one* thing to be exclusive to me. Something she doesn't even like. That's not too much to ask, is it?"

"Journey," Clyde's brow was furrowed. "Do you hear yourself? Do you *see* yourself?"

As if having forgotten that she was standing there naked, Journey looked down at her body and then at Clyde, who was clothed. Sudden shame washed over her and she hurried over to get her dress, trying to cover her breasts with her arm. She couldn't look at him.

"I'll just go, then," she muttered.

"You don't have to go-"

"No, you've made things perfectly clear. I get it." Journey's cheeks were flaming.

"Journey, I just don't want to mislead you about anything. Nothing has to change."

"Things already *have* changed." Hands shaking, Journey slipped her dress over her head and grabbed her purse. As bold as she had been just moments before, now she felt nothing but increasing embarrassment. What had she been thinking?

"Journey-"

"Can you please...*please* just let me get up outta here with just a *little* bit of dignity? I've already humiliated myself enough."

"If you were starting to feel differently about things, I wish you would've just talked to me about it."

"Instead of sucking your dick, right?" Journey stalked to the door, yanking it open. "My mistake."

"Journey! That's not what I meant!"

She slammed the door and ran down the hallway towards the elevator, praying he didn't follow her. Tears of humiliation were stinging her eyes but she fought to not let them fall. At least not until she got to her car.

She was outside and almost home free when she heard her name being called. But it wasn't Clyde's voice.

"Dino??" Journey looked around, pulling her camisole tighter around her to cover the fact that she was braless under her thin dress. "What are you doing over here?"

"Shelly lives over here." He pointed to the apartment building next to Clyde's before he looked her up and down. "What are *you* doing?"

"I'm not doing anything!"

"I've never seen you over this way."

"Yeah, well...I have a...a friend in the area." Journey hated that she sounded so flustered, and tried to continue to her car. "Well, good night."

"You okay?"

"I'm fine. Bye."

"What's up with you?" Dino asked, looking at her suspiciously. "You're looking real..."

Journey's eyes snapped to him. "Real what?"

"I don't know. Suspect."

"*Suspect*? Please. I don't know *what* you're talking ab-"

"Journey!"

Her eyes closed and she cursed under her breath. Dino looked over her shoulder at Clyde trotting towards them, then at Journey, his eyes brightening in realization.

"I see," he smirked.

"Shut up, Dino," Journey hissed. "Why don't you mind your own damn business?"

"Journey," Clyde caught up to her, looking concerned. He only briefly glanced at Dino. "Can we talk, please?"

His smirk widening, Dino just folded his arms, looking like the definition of smug.

Shooting a glare at her ex-husband, Journey turned to Clyde and snipped, "No, sir. I don't think we have anything to talk about. Maybe this man here would be willing to buy your insurance."

She got into her car and sped out of the parking lot, feeling like the biggest fool.

Chapter 16

. . . .

JOURNEY KNEW DINO WOULD show up at her door sooner rather than later. The very next day, he was in her doorway with the same smug expression from the previous night.

"What do you want?" Journey snapped, still on edge.

"So how long have you been creepin' with Roz's dad?"

"Shhh! Theo is back there!" Journey glanced towards the back of the apartment.

"Where was he last night? Who watches him while you're bangin' Pops?"

Journey actually lifted her hand to slap him, but stopped herself. Taking a breath, she tried to get him back out the door. "You need to go."

"Why? Mad 'cause your spot got blown up? I guess you didn't expect me to recognize him, huh?"

"Dino, I guess you forgot; you and I are divorced. That means I don't have to answer to you. What I do, and with whom I do it, is *my* business. Not yours."

"Is it *Roz's* business? I bet she doesn't know anything about this, does she?"

Journey glared at him. "Stay in your lane, Dino."

"You've been judging me, not letting me see my own son. You always got something to say about what *I'm* doing. Yet you're messing around with a married man. *Your homegirls' daddy.* And I'm supposed to just sit idly by and act like it's nothing, huh?"

"Actually yes, that's exactly what you're supposed to do. What I get onto you about is in relation to our son and that's it; I don't care *what* you do outside of that."

"Still, though. You ain't right."

"You don't know what you're talking about, Dino. Unless you saw me riding him into the sunset, you have no proof of anything. So, like I said..." She tried to push him out again.

"Nah, I'm not going for that," Dino persisted, sidestepping her and advancing further into the apartment. He rubbed his thin beard, looking Journey up and down with a mischievous grin on his face. "You were looking too guilty for it not to be anything. And you're a little too eager to get rid of me now."

"There's an easy explanation for that. I don't like you."

"Whatever. I know guilt when I see it."

"I bet you do."

"What's it worth to you for me to keep this to myself?"

Journey recoiled. "Are you really trying to blackmail me?"

"We don't have to call it that. How 'bout you just do to me whatever you were doing to old man? We'll call it even."

Journey looked at him, disgusted. In that moment, she didn't know what she ever saw in Dino. He was enjoying this way too much.

"Don't you still have a girlfriend?"

"That clearly doesn't mean anything to you. At least I ain't married."

"Would she like to know that you seduced me recently?"

His eyed darkened. "If you tell, I'll tell."

"Tell *what*, exactly? Like I said, you don't know anything."

"Right." Dino folded his arms. "So Roz wouldn't care if she knew about this? That I saw you running out of that building in the cut in a flimsy dress looking like you were trying to get away from the man? And that her dad just happened to come running after you, wanting to talk? What, lovers' quarrel?"

"I so, *so* hate you."

"You wanna go in the kitchen? That time up against the counter was hot."

"I'd rather fuck the cucumbers in the refrigerator."

Dino's face hardened. "So you wanna be like that? Fine. Call off the child support or I'll tell Roz what I saw. And whatever other stuff I feel like making up."

"Like she'd believe you," Journey retorted, trying to keep her voice strong. Part of her didn't put it past Dino to do exactly that. He could be extremely petty when he wanted to be. "She doesn't like you either, remember? There's no way she'd buy such a story coming from you."

"Only one way to find out."

"You're just trying to rattle me and I'm not falling for it. So you might as well quit wasting your time. And mine."

Dino scratched his head. Journey could tell he recently got his locs retwisted. They were elegantly styled into a bun, which only happened when he went to the salon. Most of the time, he wore the locs down.

"Nice pictures you've been posting on IG lately," he commented. "Been doing a lot of hair, I see."

Her eyes narrowed. "Yeah. So?"

"I know you're not doing all that for free. Are you *supposed* to be charging people to do their hair when you don't have a license?"

"I'm in school for that, Dino."

"But you don't have your license yet," he reiterated. "And you have pictures of it all over social media."

"If you notice, *asshole*, I don't post anything about prices. I'm not calling myself anything I'm not. Most people don't care if you're licensed or not, as long as you know what you're doing. And I know what I'm doing."

"Yeah, but still. All I'm saying is, I have some good stuff on you. And if you want me to chill with this Clyde thing and keep what I saw to myself, you'll go back to letting me get my son whenever I want and call off the child support. And I won't put you on blast about your little side hustle."

Journey got in his face. "Get. OUT."

"Fine, have it your way," Dino threw his hands up. He smacked his lips at her as he stepped around her towards the door. "Don't say I didn't try to warn you."

Journey just scowled at him, but as soon as he was gone, her strong stance faltered. As much as she wanted to brush off Dino's threats, she couldn't. He could very well do everything he threatened to do. He might even go so far as to tell Olivia, if he felt like going the extra mile with it. And if Olivia ever learned about her and Clyde, Journey wanted it to come from her.

She plopped onto the couch and put her face in her hands. Clyde had left her several messages since she ran out of his apartment the night before, but she hadn't been able to bring herself to respond to any of them. She felt like an idiot. What had she been thinking, going up in there and requesting such a thing of him? Even tried to purposely lower his resistance with sex, despite his telling her he couldn't go there with her more than once. She couldn't blame it on the cognac, because she hadn't had any. That was all her.

Groaning at the memory, Journey's head snapped up when her phone chimed again. Part of her expected it to be Roz, confronting her. Or Olivia, confronting her. She had managed to put the guilt about her arrangement with Clyde to the side over the past couple of months, but now it was starting to creep back in. Before too long, she was kicking herself for ever getting involved with Clyde at all.

Her thoughts continued to haunt her as she went about her day, only managing to partially concentrate when Theo asked for help with his homework and when they had dinner together. The thought of Roz finding out about her and Clyde made her itch. If Dino kept his word and blabbed, Journey knew her friendship with Roz could be in serious jeopardy. Even if Journey told her herself, it could be in jeopardy, anyway. She couldn't imagine Roz taking the news well at all, no matter how much explanation and justification came with it.

Regardless, though, Journey knew she had to tell Roz about everything. Several times over the next couple of days, she picked up the phone to tell her they needed to talk, but she chickened out.

"This is gonna be harder than I thought," she muttered, dropping her cell onto her bed and burying her face in her hands. "Why didn't I consider all of this before??"

She knew why. She was desperate for money and Clyde provided her an out. And then when he started giving her pleasure that *way* exceeded anything she could have expected, she got hooked. At times, she didn't even care about the money; she just wanted his tongue between her legs.

Journey was glad that she was nearing the end of her schooling and that her bills were paid up, because she knew she'd had her last tryst with Clyde. There was no way she could face him after making such a fool of herself. When she thought about how she acted, it actually made her cringe.

"'Yeah Clyde, your wife can have your dick as long as your tongue is reserved for me,'" she mimicked, wagging her head from side to side. "Though, hell, it's not like I didn't want the dick, too, if I'm being real about it. Idiot!"

Several more days passed without any confessions to Roz. Journey kept punking out, making more and more excuses to herself why it wasn't the right time. The couple of times she talked to Roz during those days, either Roz vented about Cooper or about one of her diva clients, and Journey gladly let her monopolize the conversation. In the back of her mind, Journey knew that with every day that passed without coming clean she was only digging her hole deeper, but it was just way easier said than done to tell her best friend she'd been intimate with her dad. *And* that she'd gotten money from him in exchange.

And since Dino apparently hadn't said anything yet, Journey ventured to believe his threats were nothing but bluffs. What was he waiting on? For her to let her guard down? Journey had to admit that she didn't know *what* Dino was going to do; he could have forgotten about it already or he could be tracking Roz down right then. Maybe he was too occupied with his pyramid schemes or his girlfriend to worry about tattling on Journey.

She could only hope. Journey wanted to call Dino and try to reason with him, but that would be all but admitting she had something to feel guilty about. Dino didn't have any concrete proof of anything; all he saw was her coming out of Clyde's building. He was just speculating, glad to finally have something to hold over her head for once. Well, Journey wasn't going to give him the satisfaction.

· · · ·

MOLLY INVITED JOURNEY and Roz with her to shop for something to wear for her and Clyde's anniversary. Journey feebly claimed to be busy, but Roz and Molly double-teamed her and she relented. She could only hope Molly's anxiety about being out in public would kick in and she'd just stay home and order something online.

"This feels strange, being at the mall," Molly mused as they eased through the front entrance. "I haven't been to a mall in years."

"You haven't missed much," Roz informed her. "Just more people, more stores, and higher prices."

"Has it always been this big?"

"Well, things *have* changed in all these years, Mom. Plus, it's not that big, really."

"It seems huge to me."

"Okay, are you gonna freak out? We can always go back home."

If only, Journey thought to herself.

"No, no...I *want* to do this," Molly stated, determined. "So where are the big girl stores?"

"Mom, you've lost enough weight where you don't have to *only* shop at plus-sized places. But I think Ashley Stewart is on the second floor."

"I'm still overweight, Roz, let's not kid ourselves. Just not as grossly obese. But Ashley Stewart sounds good. Where's the escalator? No, wait; I should take the stairs, huh? Get some more steps in on the new Fitbit?"

Roz shook her head. "Just come on."

They headed towards the escalator, Journey silently tagging along. She glanced at her phone, hoping they wouldn't be there too long.

Thankfully, Molly found a black dress that she didn't hate her own reflection in pretty quickly. Journey breathed a sigh of relief.

"Where has shapewear *been* all my life?" Molly gushed as they left the store, bags in hand. "It makes all my bumps and lumps look so much smoother."

"Yeah, it's amazing like that," Roz chuckled. "I've even worn those when I'm bloated."

"I cannot *wait* to see Clyde's face when he sees me in this!" Molly exclaimed with a grin. Her blonde hair fell over her face. "It's been years since I've gotten dressed up. And I can wear these heels you talked me into since we'll be sitting down most of the time, anyway."

"I kinda want to see his face, too. You're gonna knock his socks off. Don't you think so, Journey? You've been really quiet today."

"Hmm? What?" Journey blinked, embarrassed. Her mind had drifted off to different scenarios of how things would go when Roz found out about her and Clyde.

"I said Dad is gonna be blown away when he sees Mom in her new outfit."

"Oh...yeah, he definitely will."

Roz eyed her strangely. "You all right?"

"Yeah, you seem like your mind is somewhere else," Molly chimed in. "Is everything okay with school? Theo?"

"Yeah, everything is good with that. And Theo is fine. I guess..." Journey looked back and forth between Roz and Molly, noting their concerned expressions. "I just had a blowup with Dino, that's all. It's kinda bugging me."

"Oh hell, what did he do this time?" Roz asked, sucking her teeth. "Is he bitching 'cause he has to pay child support now?"

"Child support is...definitely part of the argument, yeah."

"That's a damn shame. Fussing about having to do what he's supposed to do for his own child. I just can't with men, sometimes."

"That's one thing I'm so thankful I never had to worry about with Clyde," Molly added. "Even with everything we've dealt with over the years, he was always a wonderful provider. I never had to worry about him not taking care of me and Roz."

"Yeah, I can give the old man credit for that," Roz grudgingly admitted. "Never had time for any father-daughter dances but he always made sure I was laid when I went by myself."

"Roz."

"Just saying."

"Maybe you can ask Clyde for some advice, Journey," Molly suggested. "I know you've never been very close to your stepfather; maybe some positive male influence would be helpful."

"Uhh, I don't know," Journey tried not to stammer. She fought not to avert her eyes. "I'm not sure he can help with this particular issue. Plus, I'm sure he has plenty of other stuff to worry about. Being a lawyer takes up a lot of his time. I figure."

"You're right about that," Molly mused, absently kicking at a gum wrapper on the ground. "Clyde *is* a very busy man. Sometimes I can't help but wonder..."

Roz looked at her. "Wonder what?"

"Exactly what he's always so busy *doing*. I know his career is very demanding, but...there *have* been times when I've been curious about...oh, I can't even say it."

"You think Dad is cheating, don't you?"

Uh-oh, Journey thought. *Let's not go here again...*

Molly looked guiltily at her daughter. "It's crossed my mind, especially over the past few months. There are so many times when I call and can't reach him and it didn't used to be like that. And I know that can happen if he's in court or with a client or something, but...still. When he gets home late, or doesn't acknowledge my texts, I just can't help but imagine that he's with another woman."

Journey's face was on fire. Keeping her expression even was taking every ounce of strength she had.

"Well it makes sense, Mom. You two haven't exactly been close these past few years. It's only natural that you'd have these suspicions."

"So you think he's cheating?" Molly quickly asked, clutching Roz's arm. "You think he's been unfaithful, don't you? I'm *right*!"

"Mom, calm down! I'm not saying he did anything. I'm just saying I can understand why you think he would."

"Of *course* he would! I've been a cow and he couldn't stand the sight of me, so he went out and got someone sexier. Clyde loves sex too much to go without it this long...he *has* to be seeing someone else. Oh god...where's the food court??"

"Mom!" Roz clutched her shoulders. "I need you to calm down, all right? Look, Dad is totally devoted to you. If he stayed with you through everything you two went through, he can hold out on any...*primal* desires he may have. In fact, I think that's *why* he buries himself in work so much; to have an outlet for that frustration."

Molly looked at her hopefully, and Journey had to turn her eyes away. Clyde's admission of his abstinence over the years ran through her head, but she couldn't share that with Molly without revealing how she found out. As far as Molly or Roz knew, she and Clyde weren't close enough for him to tell her such a thing.

The guilt was becoming too much. It mortified Journey to imagine how Molly would react if she ever found out about her and Clyde.

"You really think so?" Molly asked her daughter.

"I *do* think so. Now, I need you to chill, okay? All you need to worry about is your anniversary and how good you're going to look when you go out with Dad. Don't stress yourself out letting your imagination go off a tangent."

Molly eyed her for a moment before she finally sighed. "Okay. Okay, you're right. I'm just being paranoid, as usual. Clyde would never do such a thing to me."

"Of course not."

They left the mall a little while later. After dropping off Molly at home, Roz went back to Journey's apartment with her, although Journey would have preferred she didn't. It was enough of a struggle not blowing her own cover at the mall. She didn't know how she was going to manage to keep it together one-on-one with Roz, feeling like she was.

Just chill out, she told herself. *This isn't the first time I've hung out with Roz since this thing with Clyde started. She has no idea what I did; if I just act normal, I can keep it that way.*

"You want anything to drink?" she offered her friend. "I think I have some Moscato in here."

"No, thanks. I wouldn't enjoy it."

Journey looked at her, eyebrows raised. "Why wouldn't you?"

"Because I'm still wrapped up in what Mom said about Dad at the mall. That she thinks he's cheating."

We're back on that? "What's the problem? You said he was probably just working a lot. It makes sense. A lot of people bury themselves in their work when they have issues at home."

"Yeah, true, but still," Roz dropped onto the couch, then looked around her. "Where's my godbaby?"

"He's with Mama. They've been spending a good amount of time together lately."

"Really? That's surprising. You used to say you wouldn't trust Ms. Clarice with your pet rock."

"They've been getting along. I think she likes him being there so much 'cause he's a buffer between her and Senior. And Senior actually likes kids, so it's like they're a little family in there."

"Well that's nice, I guess."

"It is. Plus, I get a little time to myself."

"Hmph. Sometimes that can lead to bad shit."

"What?"

"Folks tend to do stuff they regret when they have too much time on their hands."

"Please don't tell me you're still talking about your dad."

"Well, I can't help it."

"Why? You've never been so consumed with what he does before. And this doesn't apply, anyway, since we were *just* talking about how busy he is."

"I know he's busy, but he doesn't work twenty-four-seven. You can't tell me that *all* the time he's away from Mom, he's working."

Journey felt pricked. "Roz..."

"Yeah, I know you have no way of knowing that," Roz forged ahead with a distracted wave. "And I know we've talked about this before. I just know in my gut that he's doing something foul. If not now, he has in the past."

"I think you're obsessing a little bit."

"So what if I am? You think I shouldn't be upset that my dad is cheating on my mother?"

"Roz, no offense, but you're not exactly the embodiment of fidelity, yourself. You've been cheating on Cooper the entire time you've been together, practically. And anyway, you and Mr. C. aren't even all that close. I'm surprised you even care."

"Damn, what do you think I am, heartless? I love my dad just fine. And anyway, I'm more worried about how it would affect Mom if she were to find out about it."

"Find out about *what*, Roz? You don't know that he's done anything."

"I know that he has another apartment, though."

Feeling like she'd just had the wind knocked out of her, Journey slowly lowered herself to the couch. Did Roz know? Was this her way of trying to goad Journey into a confession? Why else would she keep harping on this?

"Oh really?" Journey asked with a churning stomach. "And...how do you know that?"

"I followed him one time."

Oh no. What if Roz was staked out in the parking lot one of the times I went over there?? No, she would've surely said something to me about it by now.

"Roz...why would you feel the need to do that?"

"I was suspicious of where he was going. One night after Mom called me crying about how lonely she was, I went to his office, waited for him to come out, and followed him. He went to this apartment building damn near twenty miles away."

"How do you know he wasn't just visiting somebody? Did you follow him inside the building, too?"

"If I could have without him noticing, I would have. But he has an assigned space. And after he left, I went inside and looked at the mailboxes. There was one labeled McMillan."

"Right, 'cause y'all are the *only* family with that last name."

"It's too much of a coincidence. Plus, I followed him one other time. I saw him check the mailbox through the window."

"I guess you're wasting your time doing makeup; maybe you need to be a P.I.," Journey quipped, trying to lighten the mood. Her head was starting to hurt.

"Funny."

"Okay, so if you saw this, why didn't you confront him about it?"

"Why, so he can tell me to mind my own business? I saw all I needed to see. He wouldn't need another apartment if he wasn't creepin'."

Journey rubbed her temples. "Maybe he has it so he'll have a place to get away. It could be nothing but a reprieve from when things get too heavy at home."

"I don't buy that."

"Well..." Journey squeezed her eyes shut. "Whether you *buy it* or not, you don't know anything for sure, so...why don't you just let it go?"

"What's wrong with you?"

"Nothing, I just...I've had a long day and I'd rather talk about something else."

"Well hell, if I can't vent to my best friend, who can I vent to?"

Journey sighed. This was torture.

"It would just be nice to focus on something a little less dramatic."

"What fun is that?"

"Damn it..."

"Come on, girl, help me figure this out."

"Figure *what* out??"

"Figure out what my dad might be doing."

"And what makes you think *I'm* supposed to know?"

"If we put our heads together-"

"Roz, what is even the point? We could sit here all night pondering this and still not know anything for sure. And really, there are better ways I can think of to spend my evening."

"Fine." Roz tossed her hands up. "I don't see what the big deal is, but whatever."

"Thank you."

"I just know if there was something that was bothering *you* this much, I wouldn't trip if you wanted to talk about it whether it made sense or not."

"Roz!"

"Well, it's true!"

"Actually, it's *not*! You would tell me to either go right to the source or get over it. And you *know* you would!"

"I'm just trying to figure this out so I'll know how to deal with Mom if he slips up!"

"Why don't you just tell her that he was at his other apartment with *me*, then!" Journey exploded, shooting off the couch. She couldn't take it anymore.

"You?" Roz looked up at her, frowning in confusion. "Why would I tell her *that*?"

"Because it's true!" Journey gripped her pounding head. "I've been to his apartment...several times."

Roz stood slowly, her frown deepening. "Look at me, Journey."

"I can't."

"Why not? Are you telling me this just to get me to shut up? 'Cause it's a little over the top, if you are."

"I wish that was the reason," Journey sighed, dropping her hands. "But it's not. I was there to see Clyde."

Roz's head jerked back. "Clyde? Since when do you call him *Clyde*??"

"Since...oh god..."

"You cannot *possibly* be telling me what I think you're telling me. *Please* tell me you're not trying to say you...you had an *affair* with my *father*??"

Journey made herself turn and face her friend. Roz's face was reddening by the second and Journey felt the tears coming full force. "I'm so sorry..."

"You're sorry?" Roz stepped back. "*You're sorry??* That's all you have to say??"

"I can explain, Roz!"

"So you've been up in my mama's face pretending to be her friend and trying to help her while you've been banging her husband the whole time??"

"No! Roz, it's not like that! I mean, it wasn't! Look, this wasn't about sex...we never even took it there. We never even kissed! It was just-"

"Save it! If you did *anything* with him, it was too much!" Roz looked at Journey as if she'd never seen her before, and

Journey knew things would never be the same between them. The disgust in Roz's eyes was evident.

"I was desperate! I got laid off at Metro, couldn't find anything else that paid worth a damn, I was starting school, bills were coming in left and right, things around here were breaking, Theo was always needing something, I couldn't get any help from Dino...look, I know there's no excuse. But Roz, you *know* me...you know the kind of person I am. I just...at the time I was just doing what I had to do!"

"So that's why you were asking me all that shit about sugar daddies? 'Cause you were scheming?"

"I was *not* scheming! He came at *me*! And at first I turned him down, I swear I did. But when things kept going downhill, I just..." Journey's hands fell again, emotions drained and exhausted. "Roz..."

"I can't believe what I'm hearing! Are you serious with this, Journey??"

"I'm sorry!"

"Fuck your *sorry*! Were you 'sorry' when you were messing around with my dad while smiling in me and my mama's faces?? She *trusted* you, Journey!"

"Roz, you have no idea how hard this has been for me. *Please* try to understand-"

"*Understand*? Are you serious??"

"Roz-"

"I-I can't even *look* at you right now!" Roz sputtered, storming out and slamming the door behind her.

Journey grabbed her pounding head again, tears streaming down her face, hoping her friend would come back but knowing she wouldn't.

Chapter 17

. . . .

JOURNEY LOCKED HERSELF in her apartment after blabbing her confession to Roz. She was glad to finally get it off her chest, but she worried about what affect it would have on their friendship.

She tried to call Roz but of course got nowhere. Roz wouldn't take any of her calls. Journey began to really consider the weight of what she'd done and how it could change so much, namely people's opinion of her, and she sunk deeper and deeper into a self-pitying funk. She asked Clarice to keep Theo, who thankfully agreed without issue, sensing that things had hit the fan as predicted. Journey only bothered to leave the house to load up on alcohol. After that, she just sequestered herself in and got really, really drunk.

Clyde tried to call several times, but he was the last person she wanted to talk to. Seeing his name on her phone only reminded her of how stupid she'd been. Not only for agreeing to his semi-indecent proposal in the first place, but for allowing herself to get so caught up in it. What started off as just some toe-sucking slowly escalated to her propositioning him naked and asking him not to go down on his own wife. Every time she thought about it, she felt more ridiculous.

She could only imagine what Roz thought of her. A practically lifelong friendship was probably ruined, and no alcohol was strong enough to numb the pain of that. Even though Roz had insisted she would never judge Journey for doing what she had to do, Journey knew better than to think she could pull that card. There was no way Roz would consider that Journey would ever even *think* of fooling around with Clyde like that. As free-spirited as Roz was most of the time, even Journey knew this was a stretch.

"I am such an idiot," she groaned as she laid across her bed. "Why did I let things get this far? Why did I even *start* this??"

Journey knew why. But all of the reasons she used to justify her arrangement with Clyde in the past just seemed flimsy now. Even if all of her bills were now paid, it just didn't seem worth it if Roz hated her for it.

Her phone rang, and Journey eagerly grabbed for it, hoping it was Roz, and deflated when she saw it wasn't. Sucking her teeth, she just shoved the phone away, already forgetting who it was that was actually calling. She didn't want to talk to anyone else.

This went on for a couple of days. Journey didn't even bother going to school; she just sent a quick email to the main office saying she was sick. The last thing she cared about was learning about hair and nails right then. All she wanted was to turn back time and figure out some other way to solve her money problems instead of ever starting anything with Clyde. Or at least, not be stupid enough to admit it to Roz. It might've been the right thing to do, but that didn't mean she felt good about it.

• • • •

THERE WAS LOUD BANGING on the front door. Journey slowly untangled herself from the covers, squinting her eyes to the light. She couldn't even remember what day it was.

Her phone started ringing, and Journey ignored it. She buried her face back into her pillow, hoping whoever was bothering her would get the hint and go away. But the banging and the ringing continued. And when her phone started chiming with text messages, Journey groaned loudly and snatched up her phone. Her eyebrows lifted slightly seeing the messages from Dino.

Open the door, J. I'm worried.

What's up with you? Why haven't you been answering your phone?

If you don't answer the door in the next two minutes, I'm getting the landlord.

"Oh hell," Journey muttered, throwing back the covers. Wobbling slightly, she stomped towards the door and yanked it open. Dino was standing there with his phone in his hand, typing another message with his other fist in the air preparing to bang on the door again. Journey glared at him.

"What the hell do you want??"

"What's going on, J.? I've been blowing you up since yesterday."

"Some might take the fact that I didn't answer as a hint that I don't want to be bothered."

Dino glanced inside the apartment. "Where's Theo?"

"Theo is being taken care of. Now go away."

"Are you okay? Have you been drinking?"

"So what if I have? I'm grown."

"J...can I come in?"

"I wish you wouldn't but whatever."

Dino had a concerned look on his face as he stepped inside the apartment. He'd never seen Journey like this before; her hair was all over the place, her eyes were red, and her face was smudged with days-old makeup. She looked like she'd been sleeping in her clothes for days, they were so wrinkled.

"What's wrong, Journey? I'm kinda trippin', seeing you like this."

"Why do you care? Weren't you just over here the other day trying to blackmail me? You can't be *too* worried about how I'm doing, after that bullshit."

"Look, about that-"

"Dino, we really don't have anything to talk about. Unless you're trying to fuck."

"What?"

"That's what you do, right? That's what we do? We don't get along except when we're getting busy. And I don't have the energy to fight with you, so..." Journey lifted her shirt over her head.

"Whoa, whoa!" Dino gently grabbed her wrists as she began to pull down her pants. "That's not what I came over here for, J."

"Sure it's not. That's what it always comes down to with you. Even when we're fighting, you're trying to get in my damn pants. So I'm making it easy for you this time. Maybe you can bang out this headache."

"Journey!" Dino stopped her again from pulling down her pants, then retrieved her shirt from the floor and covered her chest with it. He knew for sure something was up with her; she wasn't even acting like herself. There was an empty look in her eyes he didn't recognize.

"Let's just get this over with, Dino-"

"Come on, stop, stop," he whispered. Dino gathered her in his arms, holding her to him. He could feel her trembling and moments later, sobbing. He just held her, noting how she clung to him, and let her get it out.

When she finally calmed down, she hastily pushed away from him, wiping her eyes. She wordlessly put her shirt back on, keeping her face turned away.

Dino eyed her. "You want some water or something?"

"No."

"Talk to me, J. What's going on?"

"I don't want to get into any details. I'm just going through it right now."

"Well, if I've added to that, I apologize."

"Why? You meant everything you said."

"At the time, yeah, but when I thought about it later, I realized how wrong I was. It just felt good to have something to hang over your head for once, as petty as that sounds. Truth be told, I was never gonna say anything to Roz."

Journey glanced at him as she dropped onto the couch. "Oh, really?"

Dino nodded, joining her. "I just wanted to mess with your head. But at the end of the day, whatever you did or didn't do with Roz's ol' man isn't any of my business. Like you said, we're divorced and I'm in a whole other relationship."

"Uh-huh."

"I'm serious, J. I know my word hasn't meant much to you lately, and I get why, but regardless of anything, I *do* care about you. Straight up. I don't like seeing you like this."

"Yeah, well. Thanks. Though it's too bad that it takes me looking and feeling like shit to get some respect from you."

"Journey...look, I was missing you. I *still* miss you. But I know trying to blackmail you was jacked up."

"Very."

"Well, I'm sorry, again."

Journey looked at him, noting how contrite he seemed. Sighing, she rubbed the back of her neck.

"Dino, it's nice of you to say all this. But frankly, I need more than that. I need to be able to depend on you. I'm sick of us butting heads like we're still in high school or something. We have to deal with each other; why make it more unpleasant than it needs to be?"

Dino nodded again. "You're right."

"A lot of things are about to change for me soon and it would be nice if you *weren't* on my list of issues. And Theo needs to see us getting along instead of just tolerating each other."

"True."

"And, you don't need to be doing more for Shelly's child than you're doing for your own."

"I get it. I guess I did all that stuff 'cause, on some level, I was trying to get back at you. But I didn't consider that I was hurting Theo, too. When he gets older, I don't want him thinking that I'm some bum that didn't step up to the plate when he was supposed to."

"Well," Journey sighed, pushing her hair out of her face. "I guess we'll see if you mean all this."

"I *do* mean it, Journey. And you might not care about this, but I told Shelly I stepped out on her."

Journey's eyebrows shot up in surprise. "You did? You told her it was with me?"

"No. She didn't even ask who it was with; she was upset enough that I did it."

"What made you tell her?"

"Felt bad. I might be a lot of things but I'm usually not a cheater, and I knew I'd want to know if the shoe was on the other foot."

"Did she dump you?"

"Surprisingly, she didn't. She cussed my ass out and didn't talk to me for a few days, but she eventually forgave me. She appreciated my honesty. I know I'm still on thin ice with her, though, and if I fuck up again, that's it. But I don't regret admitting it. Keeping that from her was eating at me."

"Hmm." Journey could surely relate to that part. "Well, I'm proud of you for that, Dino. And I'm glad y'all are trying to work things out."

"Me, too." He gently nudged her with his shoulder, waiting for her to look at him. "Are you sure you don't want to talk about what's going on with you?"

"I'm very sure."

"Aight, I'll respect that. But I'm here if you change your mind."

Journey knew that Dino would be last on the list of people she would call to confide in, despite all the years of history they had. But she appreciated his concern, nonetheless. And she knew she wasn't in the best position to judge anybody, anyway.

"Thanks, Dino," she finally replied. "That's really nice of you. But I'll be all right. I hope."

. . . .

AFTER DINO LEFT, JOURNEY tried to call Roz again, and again her call went right to voicemail. Journey tried to tell herself that Roz just needed some time to process everything and calm down; surely she'd talk to her eventually. She had to believe that.

She trudged to the kitchen to get some more wine, cursing loudly when she realized she was all out. Deciding against going out looking the way she did, she wandered back into her room, phone in hand, and plopped onto the bed. She scrolled mindlessly through Facebook, half expecting some kind of subliminal post from Roz about their situation, but there wasn't one. Her feed was full of the usual musings, check-ins, pseudo-political experts, and memes. Nothing special.

Without thinking about it too much, Journey typed her own post:

Sometimes desperation makes you do crazy things. And not everybody will understand it.

It wasn't subliminal; it was Journey's truth. She didn't even expect Roz to see it. It was just something she needed to get off her chest.

Journey started to crawl back underneath the covers, wanting to go back to sleep and drown everything out for another few hours. When there was another urgent knock on her door, she almost screamed.

"Funny how I get so popular when I don't want to be bothered," she muttered, throwing the covers off of her and stomping towards the door. Part of her expected it to be Dino again, but when she peeked through the peephole, it was Olivia standing there.

"Wonderful," she muttered, even though her attitude dissipated slightly upon seeing her grandmother. She wasn't quite ready to face her, but knew there was no way to avoid it. Olivia wasn't going away.

After a few nerve-steeling moments, Journey opened the door, plastering what she hoped was a pleasant-enough smile on her face.

"Grandmama...what brings you by?"

"You know full well what brings me by here," Olivia replied, the stern edge already peppering her voice. "It's time to end this foolishness."

Journey started to act oblivious, but realized she was tired of doing that. What was the point, anyway? She'd already made a fool of herself.

"Come on in," she offered softly, stepping aside.

Olivia eyed her granddaughter as she stepped inside the apartment. Journey motioned towards the couch, wishing she could go and fix herself up a little bit, because she still looked a mess.

"So," Olivia began, putting her purse beside her on the couch. "You've made quite a mess for yourself, huh?"

Journey sighed. "Mama told you?"

"Not really. I did ask her what was going on with you and why she was watching Theo so much, but she just told me I needed to talk to you. Said it wasn't her business to tell."

That surprised Journey. Discretion wasn't exactly one of Clarice's strong suits.

"So are you gonna finally tell me the truth?" Olivia asked her. "Or are you gonna keep trying to act like you have everything under control?"

"I think it's obvious that ship has sailed," Journey retorted dryly. "I mean, look at me."

"Oh, I see you. I'm just too much of a lady to comment on it. Now what's going on?"

Journey really wished she had some alcohol to fuel herself. This wasn't something she wanted to admit to her grandmother, but she was out of energy to build any more walls.

"I got a sugar daddy," she finally admitted. "After I got laid off from Metro and couldn't find anything else...it was something that was offered to me and I turned it down at first, but I eventually accepted. And then...ended up enjoying a little too much."

Only looking mildly surprised, Olivia nodded. "I see. And is this the same man you came to talk to me about some months ago? The one that was making you feel things you didn't want to feel?"

"Yes ma'am."

"And this man is married?"

Journey looked at her hands. "Yes, ma'am."

"Hold your head up. No need in being 'shamed now. You were grown enough to do it, be grown enough to take it when being questioned about it."

Journey looked at Olivia, trying to detect the judgment in her expression but finding none.

"It was stupid, but I admit I was desperate," Journey admitted. "With everything that was going on, it just seemed like the only way out at the time. I realize it was dumb, but I just…" She sniffled. "He was offering me relief and I took it."

"I see."

"I know you're probably ashamed of me. Especially since this is how Mama and Senior got together. Not exactly something I wanted to have in common with her."

Olivia actually chuckled. "Well, you're right about that. But one big difference is that Clarice never showed any remorse for what she was doing. You clearly don't look very proud of yourself."

"Oh, I'm not. I feel like an idiot."

"Why? Did you do something with him that you didn't want to do?"

"No, it's nothing like that. He always insisted that I set the limits and he never tried to push me into anything. We never even…went all the way…"

"Child, just say it. You never had sex. I'm not a dinosaur."

Blushing, Journey continued. "Okay, we never had sex. I think for him it was more about fulfilling a fantasy and for me, well, I needed to get my bills paid. I didn't fall for him, didn't want him to leave his wife."

"I thought you said you enjoyed it too much."

"Yeah, I enjoyed what he did to me and wanted more of it," Journey verified, her face flaming. She couldn't believe she was discussing this with her grandmother. "Wanted it all to myself. But that's all."

"So what brought it to this point? Something must have happened to make you send your child away and shut yourself in your apartment. Clearly punishing yourself," Olivia added, noting all of the empty wine bottles that littered the living room.

"I just got too deep into it. Asked things of him I shouldn't have and he denied me. I immediately realized how foolish I was. That was the last time I saw him."

"I'm not going to ask you who this man is because I can tell you're humiliated enough already, and that's not what I'm trying to do to you. I'm not trying to make you feel bad, child, but I'm not gonna baby you, either. You knew what you were doing when you did it. And now you just have to deal with whatever fallout comes from that."

Immediately thinking of Roz, who still hadn't acknowledged any of her calls or messages, Journey just nodded in agreement.

Several quiet moments passed before Olivia spoke again. "Not too long after I had Clarice, your grandfather - God rest his soul - lost his job. He started trying to sell things door-to-door, and you can just imagine how that went back then; a big ol' Black man showing up on people's porches uninvited. He got chased by dogs, guns pulled on him; a couple of times, the police were called. It wasn't pretty."

"Wow...and he couldn't just find anything else?"

"He tried, but it was slow-movin', and Clarice needed things then. So I resorted to stealing diapers and formula from the corner store. Felt like I had no choice."

Journey looked incredulous. "You?"

"Yes, me. My baby needed them. I couldn't work myself 'cause we couldn't afford a babysitter. I was willing to do anything I needed to do for my child."

"I can understand that."

"My reasons might have been understandable, but I was still wrong," Olivia continued. "And what you did isn't all that different, when it comes right down to it. I get that sometimes, especially as mothers, we just have to do what we have to do, even if it's something we're not proud of."

"True."

Olivia reached for her hand. "You don't ever have to be ashamed to tell me anything, baby. You don't have to keep secrets from me or hide things. I'm not a saint; I've been where you are. I *know* it gets hard sometimes. But things only stay in the dark for so long. At some point or another, that light is gonna come on and you're gonna have to face whatever you did."

"You're right. If I didn't know that before, I surely know it now. I doubt anything will be the same after this."

"Maybe it won't. But that's not always a bad thing."

"But what if the people I've...*affected* by this, never forgive me for it?"

"Then that's on them," Olivia immediately replied. "All you can do is own what you did and apologize; you can't control their reaction."

"You're right."

"Let 'em be mad at you for a while, if that's what they need to do. They'll come to you when they're ready. You just focus on improving yourself and your situation from here. How's school going?"

"Haven't been in a couple days."

"Girl, you better get your behind back over to that school. You've waited too long and did too much to start letting your emotions stop your progress. I get that you're upset. But you still gotta handle your business. It's time to woman-up, baby."

Journey didn't really want to hear that, but she knew her grandmother was right. She had waited years to go to cosmetology school, not to mention resorting to sharing herself with Clyde to afford paying for it. It would be stupid to let herself get behind when she was this close to finishing.

"I appreciate the advice, Grandmama," she finally said with a small smile. "As hard as it is to admit, I needed that kick in the ass right now."

"Sometimes we all do." Olivia smiled at her. "I'm gonna be here for you as long as the good Lord keeps me on this earth. Don't forget that, okay?"

Journey leaned over and hugged Olivia, feeling some of the weight on her shoulders being lifted. She suddenly felt better about everything, if only slightly. Olivia always did have a way of clearing out the gunk and getting right to the root of things.

After Olivia left, Journey began cleaning up her messy apartment, getting rid of all of the wine bottles and food wrappers. Then she hopped in the shower, something she hadn't bothered to do in a couple of days, giving her hair a much-needed washing while she was in there. She turned her face to the water, trying to will any residual tension to disappear down the drain along with the shampoo.

Journey knew that school wasn't the only area she needed to get back on track. She'd also been semi-neglecting her child. With everything that had been going on, Theo practically became an afterthought, and the realization burned her. If nothing else, she always prided herself on being a good mother, but she didn't even have *that* to hang her hat on at the moment.

Eager to see her son, she quickly got dressed, slathered her hair in deep conditioner before slicking it into a bun, covering it with a plastic cap and a scarf, and slapping on a hat. She called Clarice and let her know that she was coming to get Theo.

"I thought you wanted him to spend the night over here, since you were all depressed and stuff," Clarice said.

"I never said I was *depressed*. I just needed some time, that's all."

"Uhh-huh. So you're feeling better now, I guess."

"I am, yeah."

"I told you that sugar daddy life ain't for everybody. What, did the wife catch you or somethin'?"

"No, nothing like that. Let's just say I made a fool of myself without anybody's help."

"Hmm."

"But it's for the best. I needed to get off that roller coaster."

"Those are my favorite kinds of rides; I've got the stomach for it, though. You don't. Anyway, the boy will be ready when you get here."

Shaking her head, Journey hung up the phone. She was glad that she didn't share Clarice's pride about such a thing.

When Theo came running out to the car, all smiles, Journey felt herself getting emotional; she realized how much she'd missed him even though they'd been living under the same roof the whole time. She quickly got out of the car so she could give him a hug.

"Hey Mama!" Theo greeted her, throwing his arms around her waist, as usual. He seemed a little taller to Journey. "I thought I was spending the night over here."

"You were, but I just missed you so much I had to come get you." She leaned down and kissed his forehead, giving him another squeeze.

"We going back home?"

"Not unless you want to go get some...*pizza*!"

"Yeah! Pizza, pizza, pizza!" Theo yelled, jumping up and down. Journey just laughed, glad that she could make him so happy so easily.

As they went on their pizza date and then to a movie, Journey put everything out of her mind and just enjoyed her time with her son. She was reminded of how happy she was before she started letting bills stress her out. She always managed to figure things out before. But she'd let herself get caught up with the whole Clyde mess.

Regardless, Journey knew she couldn't waste any more time kicking herself. What's done was done. She had a son to raise and business to handle. And that's exactly what she intended to focus on.

Still, she hoped that Roz would reach out to her eventually.

Chapter 18

• • • •

"JOURNEY, HOW ARE YOU? I bet you're a little surprised to hear from me."

"Yeah, I must say I am," Journey agreed, putting down the rag she'd been using to dust the furniture. "You're kinda the last person I expected to get a call from."

"I'm not surprised. I know we didn't exactly part ways on the best of terms."

"Water under the bridge."

"I'm glad to hear you say that. I have some news that I hope will make you very happy."

"Okay..."

"We've merged with another company and things are looking up around here; there are several positions that we need filled, including some in management," Owen revealed. "You were the first person I thought of."

"Wow, really? That's flattering, Owen, thank you."

"Don't mention it. I'd love to have you come back, if you haven't found anything else. Hell, even if you have. You'd definitely be making more than you were before. And I can throw in a few more perks, too."

Journey might have jumped at Owen's offer a few months earlier, but now, she had no interest. Metro Service Group, or whatever they were called now, was in her past.

"Thanks so much for thinking of me, Owen, but I'm actually good. I'm about to finish cosmetology school and I'm working as a salon apprentice. And I'm loving it. The extra money and perks sound nice, but I'm going to have to decline."

"Well, that's disappointing. But I get it. Can't fault you for wanting to do what you enjoy."

"I appreciate it."

"Well, if you ever change your mind, you know how to reach me," Owen said. "You were one of my best employees so if there's ever anything I can do for you, just let me know."

"I will. And thanks again, Owen."

Journey hung up the phone with a smile. *Well, how about that*, she mused. Even though she had no desire whatsoever to go back to Metro, it was nice to know they appreciated her so much.

She resumed her dusting, humming to herself. Theo was back in his room, working on a school project. Journey hadn't felt this kind of peace in a while. After her talk with Olivia and resolving to stop feeling sorry for herself, she dove back into school full-force, catching up on any work she missed. One of the teachers, who also owned a salon, let her know she was looking for an apprentice, and Journey jumped at it. Now when school let out, she went and spent a few hours at the salon, doing shampoos, blow-outs, and roller sets. It was heaven, and Journey couldn't wait to graduate so she could do this all day every day.

Then she'd pick up Theo from Olivia's and they'd spend the evening together, doing crafts or playing games, or watching movies. She'd resumed letting Dino come get him on the weekends, and that was when she spent time with Hunter.

Hunter was a student at BSC, but he attended nights and weekends, after his full-time job. He had stopped by the school to pick up some paperwork when he and Journey crossed paths. Journey was immediately drawn to his easygoing demeanor, bright smile, and skin the color of roasted peanuts. When he asked her for her number, she started to automatically make up some excuse, but realized she didn't want to do that. She had no *reason* to do that. Why was she depriving herself?

So while Theo was with his dad, Journey met up with Hunter.

"I'm glad you could make it out today," he said to her as they waited in line at Bruster's. "You seem to have a lot going on."

"I kinda do, but Sundays are the one day I don't really have to go anywhere, thankfully. I'm glad we're finally meeting up."

"You and me both. Talking on the phone is all good but there's nothing like getting to look into those eyes in person."

"Stop that," Journey blushed, smiling. She loved how he flirted with her. "You're always making me blush."

"That's what I'm supposed to do, right?"

Journey just smiled harder as they ordered their ice cream. After getting their treats, they took a seat on a nearby bench, sitting close but not touching.

"I've been enjoying getting to know you, Journey," Hunter revealed. "I probably shouldn't tell you how much you've been on my mind since we met."

"Yeah?" Journey was blushing again, rather stumped on what to say. She hadn't been on a real date in years. "I...I guess I can admit that you've been on my mind a lot, too."

"I'm glad to hear it. So does that mean I'll get to see more of you? I have every intention of taking you on a better date than this."

Chuckling, Journey nudged him with her shoulder. "You don't hear me complaining."

"I'm certainly not, either," he replied, gazing at her tenderly before quickly dropping his eyes back to his butter pecan.

When Hunter saw Journey home later, he didn't try to come into her apartment, which she appreciated. He just walked her to the door, hugged her, and with her silent permission, gave her a gentle kiss on the lips. Journey felt tiny explosions go off all over her body, and she pulled him to her to deepen the kiss, which he gladly accepted. They just stood at her door, getting acquainted with each other's lips, letting their hands roam but not too much. When he finally left, Journey was already looking forward to the next time.

• • • •

JOURNEY KNEW SHE'D have to face him sooner or later, but that didn't mean she didn't feel a shot of uneasiness when Clyde showed up at her door.

"Are you ready to talk to me now?"

Stepping aside, Journey waved him into the apartment. "Come in."

Obliging, Clyde glanced around him, never having been inside Journey's place before. "It's nice in here."

"It's nothing special."

"You should've seen my first apartment. This is a palace compared to that." He turned to her, hands in his pockets. "Is Theo here?"

"No, he's with his dad."

Clyde nodded, looking down at his shoes. Journey eyed him, wondering how she ever got caught up with this man. Yes, he was still attractive, but she was back to seeing him as her friend's father, not the deceptively sexy man whose every touch made her shudder and who could suck orgasms out through her feet.

"Journey, I just...I want to apologize if I've caused you any pain, in any way," Clyde finally said. "I'd hate to be the reason your friendship with Roz ended."

"Oh...she confronted you?"

"No, but she hasn't been talking to me at all. It was so out of the blue that I just put two and two together."

"Yeah; she hasn't had anything to say to me, either. Which I get."

"What made you tell her?"

"I just didn't want to keep that secret. And she was going on and on about how she felt you were cheating on Ms. Molly with someone; part of me wondered if she already knew. I just couldn't keep it from her anymore."

"I can understand that."

"I thought you'd be upset with me for telling her."

"No, that was your decision. And truthfully, I should have considered that Roz might find out about it eventually, anyway, and what the fallout would be if she did. But when you want something as badly as I wanted you, rational thinking tends to fall by the wayside."

Journey nodded. "I can certainly relate to that."

"I'm just so sorry for causing such a mess for you."

"You don't owe me any apology. I'm the one that agreed to it; you didn't force me to do anything. And at the end of the day, you helped me out big-time, and I appreciate it. For the first time in years, I'm back on my feet financially and that wouldn't have happened if it weren't for you."

"So...you're still doing well, then? Where are you working now?"

"I'm a salon apprentice. It doesn't pay a ton, but the owner has already promised me a booth when I graduate next month. And I've already been doing hair as a side hustle for a while now, so I'm doing okay."

"I'm glad to hear that, Journey. I truly am."

"If anything, I owe *you* an apology, Mr. C."

Clyde chuckled. "We're back to Mr. C., huh?"

Grinning, Journey nodded. "Yeah, I think we need to be."

"Fair enough."

"But the way I acted the last time we were together...I'm so embarrassed. I shouldn't have come at you like that-"

"Please," Clyde dismissed with a wave of his hand. "No need for any apologies. I think we *both* got a little too caught up in things. I looked forward to seeing you more than I did my wife, and that's never a good thing. And if I'm honest, too big a part of me wanted what you were offering, and I knew I was in too deep, myself. So let's just say we both learned a lesson and leave it at that, all right?"

Rubbing her arms, Journey smiled appreciatively. "How *is* Ms. Molly doing? How did your anniversary turn out?"

"It went really well, actually. We had an evening out on the town, which is something we hadn't done in years. And since then, we've been talking more, about all the things that were said and done after her parents were killed, and even some issues we were having prior to that. We're both at fault for the state our marriage is in and we're finally going to get some counseling."

"Wow, that's *great* news, Mr. C. For real. I can just imagine how happy Ms. Molly is about all that."

"The happiest she's been in years. She's even joined a gym and found a personal trainer that she's comfortable with, although she does sometimes mention missing the workouts you two used to have."

"Between Theo, school, the salon, and my side clients, I had to take something off my plate. Not to mention, it was getting too hard being around her knowing what you and I were doing."

Nodding, Clyde heaved a heavy sigh. "Understandable. I can't say I always felt great about it, myself."

"Really?"

"Yes. Believe it or not, Journey, I've never stopped loving Molly. My attraction to you was something totally separate. And right or wrong, I enjoyed every minute we spent together."

Journey felt the same way, but didn't want to admit it out loud.

Sensing as much, Clyde smiled to himself. "If you ever need anything, Journey, I hope you know you can call me.

I'm more than happy to help you out still, if you need it. No strings attached."

"That's really sweet of you, Mr. C. But I think we should leave well enough alone. And my ex-husband is finally stepping up with the child support, so I'm doing all right."

"Well, good." He eyed her for a moment before looking away. "I'll go ahead and get out of your hair, then. Hopefully this won't be the last time I ever see you."

"Yeah, hopefully," Journey sincerely concurred. "Take care of yourself, Mr. C."

"You, too, Journey."

When Clyde opened the door, both he and Journey were surprised to see Roz standing there. Her face reddened upon seeing Clyde.

"Are y'all kidding me?" she exclaimed. "Y'all are *still* messing around??"

"Calm down, Roz," Clyde coolly instructed. "That is not why I'm here."

"Yeah, Roz, nothing happened," Journey quickly added. She was thrilled that Roz had showed up and didn't want her to run away again. "We were just talking, that's *all*."

Roz eyed them both warily for a moment before stomping into Journey's apartment in a huff. Clyde just mouthed 'good luck' to Journey and walked away, hands in his pockets.

Journey was nervous as she closed the door and turned to face her friend. Roz was standing there, looking at her accusingly.

"Are you sure y'all were *just* talking?"

"Yes, Roz. That's all it was."

"About when your next tryst is gonna be?"

Journey sighed and rubbed her face with her hands. "Roz, look...I love you and I'm glad you're here. And I understand that you're upset with me. But this is a waste of time if you're just going to hurl accusations and not give me the benefit of the doubt. Remember, I *chose* to tell you about me and Clyde; I could have very well kept it to myself, as hard as it would have been. So if we're gonna talk, I need you to put the claws away."

Roz glared at her for a moment before releasing a sigh of her own, shaking her head.

"You're right," she admitted. "I didn't want to come over here until I had cooled off, and then when I get here and see him leaving-"

"I get it," Journey insisted. "I can understand the reaction. But just know that whatever I tell you is gonna be the truth, 'cause I don't have the energy to hide stuff anymore. All right?"

"All right."

"You want something to drink?"

"I'm okay. Where's Theo?"

"Dino has him. Look, Roz," Journey sat on the couch, tucking a leg underneath her. "Let me go ahead and say this. I'm sorry for what I did. At the time I didn't think about how it would affect you or our friendship; I just needed some relief. I was sinking and Clyde provided me a way out. That was my only motivation."

"I know," Roz softly replied, joining her on the couch. She turned to face her friend. "I thought a lot about what you said that night, about why you did it. And I truly get it. You were struggling. And I certainly don't know anything about what it's like to be a single mother; I can't even say I know what it's like to struggle *at all*. You just did what you felt you had to do."

"So...you forgive me?"

"I do, but really, Journey, I don't know if there's anything for me to forgive. Yes, he's my dad and it's weird, but at the end of the day, y'all are both grown. And I *was* the main one saying that you should do what you needed to and not worry about me judging you."

"But you didn't think that would involve your dad, and I know that," Journey quickly countered. "Plus, there's your allegiance to Ms. Molly..."

"Yeah. And I'm not crazy about it from that aspect. But as strange as it sounds, if Dad was gonna fool around with anybody, I'm kinda glad it was with you and not some random chick off the street who only wanted him for his money and didn't give a damn about anything else."

"I wanted the money, but honestly, it was *tough* being around you and Ms. Molly, knowing what I was doing. That's why I started distancing myself."

"Makes sense." Roz reached for Journey's hand. "Look, girl...I love you way too much to end our friendship over this. As weird as it is to think about the two of you doing anything together, I can get past it. But at least, *please* tell me y'all are done."

Journey chuckled. "Yeah, it's over. I'm actually seeing someone else now. A guy named Hunter from my school."

"Yeah? That's great news. At least *one* of us is in a relationship. Cooper dumped me."

"What? When??"

"A few days ago. I had actually planned on coming to talk to you before that, but then he found out about Dick and we had this big fight...it kinda messed me up. I needed some time to recover from that."

"Oh, Roz, I'm sorry..."

"Nobody to blame but myself. I'm the one that chose to cheat and tried to justify it by saying Cooper was probably cheating, too. I just had no business trying to be in a long distance relationship knowing I have the libido of a jackrabbit."

Journey couldn't help throwing her head back and laughing. She surely missed her friend. "Are you gonna be okay, though?"

"Oh yeah, I'll be fine."

"Are you still seeing Dick, at least?"

"Girl, believe it or not, he caught a case of the morals and wanted to focus on his wife. So I'm assed out either way. Which is another reason why I had to check myself about all this; I've made some questionable decisions and done some stuff that I knew was wrong. Cheating with a married man doesn't exactly give me a lot of moral high ground to stand on."

"I've never judged you for that."

"I know. And I'm not gonna judge you for *this*. I can't. So let's just let the past stay in the past, okay? We don't ever have to mention it again 'cause Lord knows I don't want any details."

Laughing, Journey leaned over to hug her friend. She was so relieved that Roz was forgiving her and willing to move past this. The last thing she wanted was to lose her best friend.

When they separated, Journey looked at Roz thoughtfully. "Do you think I should tell Ms. Molly what I did? I still feel guilty, knowing she's still in the dark about everything."

"No," Roz quickly retorted. "Let her stay in the dark."

"Really?"

"She won't be able to handle that, Journey. I *know* she won't. Her imagination will go off on a tangent, she'll start questioning everything and everybody, and slip right back into that funk that it's taken her months to get out of. It's best to just leave well enough alone and let her think Dad has been faithful this whole time."

"But she doesn't seem to think he has, though."

"She has occasional suspicions but knows she has no proof. Besides, from what she's told me, the two of them are getting closer, talking more; even going to counseling soon. So let's just leave it at that."

"Okay. 'Nuf said." Journey wasn't exactly looking forward to confessing to Molly, anyway. "What about you and Clyde? Are y'all gonna be all right?"

"I'm sure we will. It'll take me a minute to deal with the fact that he propositioned you, but he and I will hash that out. If I angle it towards the fact that he was helping you out and not that he was lusting after my best friend, I can handle it better. I still love him, at the end of the day. Even if he is a dumb ass sometimes."

Journey just grinned and grabbed Roz for another hug. Everything was all right again now.

• • • •

"CONGRATULATIONS, JOURNEY!"

Journey's cheeks were hurting, she was smiling so much. She had just graduated from BSC, and at the top of her class. Everyone was there; Olivia, Theo, Roz, Clyde, Molly, Clarice, and (to Journey's surprise) Senior. Even Dino showed up with Shelly and her daughter. Hunter was there, armed with two dozen roses; he was the first one to her when the ceremony ended, laying a big kiss on her in front of everyone. Roz was standing behind him, grinning and giving her an approving thumbs up.

"Thank y'all so much for coming," Journey gushed, looking at everyone with glassy eyes. She rubbed Theo's black wavy hair as he hugged her waist. "It really means a lot to me."

"Wouldn't have missed it for the world," Olivia assured her, giving her a tight squeeze. "I am *so* proud of my grandbaby!"

"When you gon' start doing *my* hair, now that you're official and everything?" Clarice asked Journey. "I'm sick of wearin' wigs."

Journey just shook her head and laughed, giving her mother a kiss on the cheek. "I love you, Mama. With your crazy self."

"Mmm-hmm."

Clyde kept his distance, even after Molly rushed over to give Journey a big hug. Journey almost didn't recognize her, she looked so different. She was down to a curvy size fourteen, her skin was tanned, and her hair was longer and slightly darker than before. She was practically glowing, and Journey knew Roz had been right about not telling her anything about what went down with Clyde.

"Journey," Molly pulled her aside. "I just wanted to thank you again."

"For what?"

"For being so sweet and patient, and taking the time to work out with me. You got me back on the horse, and there's no doubt in my mind that if it weren't for you, I'd still be obese and stuck to my bed. Or dead."

"That's...quite a leap."

"I'm just saying; I was going nowhere fast and you saved me. You probably even saved my marriage. I feel better than I have in years."

Journey swallowed, forcing herself to ignore the tiny prickles of guilt she would probably always feel in Molly's presence. "It was my pleasure. I heard you got a new trainer."

"Yeah, I finally found someone that I like. She's tough and kicks my ass in the gym but she's compassionate, too. And Clyde and I are closer than we've been in forever." Molly leaned in, a mischievous grin on her face. "And we finally *did it.*"

Journey couldn't help but giggle. Molly could come across as very inexperienced for someone in their late fifties.

"Good for you!" Journey exclaimed. Truth be told, she was hoping that she and Hunter would finally *do it* later on that evening, themselves. It had been too long and he was driving her crazy with his amazing kisses and light petting they'd been doing. Journey had been horny during her entire graduation ceremony.

After things started to die down, Olivia, Clarice, and Senior left, and Dino and Shelly took Theo with them, as he was going to be staying with Dino for most of his summer vacation. Journey had been surprised when Shelly came over to her to make sure Dino was still paying his child support like he should, offering to double-team him, if necessary. Apparently she had the same issue with her child's father. Journey realized she actually liked this woman.

"Well, I'm about to head on back to my side of town," Roz announced, stretching. She glanced around. "Where's Hunter?"

"He went to get the car."

"Y'all going out?"

"He's taking me to dinner. Then hopefully back to his place."

"Ahh, sounds like somebody wants some celebration sex," Roz grinned, nudging her playfully. "I ain't mad at ya, girl. He's a cutie."

"Yes, he is." Journey blushed, returning her friend's grin. "I like him a lot. Last night he asked me to be his woman."

"If you said anything other than yes, I'll slap you right now."

"Of *course* I said yes! He makes me feel all giddy and tingly and bubbly, and I haven't felt that for anyone in years. I want to see where this will go."

"Girl..." Roz looked at her, smiling and shaking her head slightly. "I am *so* happy for you. Got your shit together; everything you wanted is happening. You deserve it."

Feeling herself tearing up, Journey gave Roz a tight hug. The truth was, Journey *did* finally feel like she was getting everything she wanted. She wasn't hurting for money, Theo was thriving, she and Dino weren't at each other's throats, she was finally doing something she loved for a living, she had a wonderful new man, and Roz was still her best friend. She had absolutely nothing to complain about.

When Roz left, Journey chatted with some of her classmates as she waited for Hunter to navigate through the congested parking lot. Her phone chimed, and Journey's jaw dropped when she saw that she had just been sent a thousand dollars. A text soon followed.

Just a graduation gift. Enjoy, beautiful. And congratulations.

Journey looked up and scanned the full parking lot. She thought Clyde and Molly had left already but they were still standing off to the side, Clyde on his phone and Molly talking excitedly to someone. As if sensing her, Clyde looked up directly at Journey, then back down to his phone.

I hate to admit it, but I still think about you. And I doubt it's going to stop. But you look very happy with that young man, and I wish you all the happiness you deserve. He better treat you right.

Journey blushed and looked around her, as if anyone could have read the message. Hunter finally pulled up and honked, smiling at her.

"You ready, babe?" he asked, getting out of the car.

"Absolutely," Journey replied, quickly deleting both messages from Clyde. She grinned at Hunter as he took her hand, lead her to the passenger's side, and opened the door for her.

Right before she lowered herself into the car, Journey glanced back over at Clyde. He was eyeing her intently as he held his car door open for Molly. Journey averted her eyes, got into Hunter's car, and let him take her away.

Thank you for reading *Sugar Daddy Sweet Tooth*! This was a fun one to write; misbehaving characters are a hoot. LOL

Fun fact: I started writing this story years and years ago; I don't even know how many. It's been on and off the shelf and many books have been completed since I began writing this. So it feels good to finally get it out to y'all!

Please consider leaving a review; they're so, so vital to us indies. And if you want to show *extra* love, share that you read it on social media! ☺

You can find me on Instagram and TikTok at @authorjessicaterry and on Twitter at @itsJessicaTerry. I'm on Facebook under AuthorJessicaTerry, as well. And don't forget to subscribe to my email list at jessicaterry.com.

Also by Jessica Terry

Some Like 'em Thick

It's All Right...Now

Not By a Long Shot

Get Right

Decisions and Consequences

Take One For the Team

When You Share Too Much

Backtalk

Emasculated

Restless

The Beginning of Again

Always and Nevers

She is Me

Split By the Bell

The Karma Call

Forehead Kiss

All Because of Ava

Love Intolerant

Mr. Time Waster

The Stubborn Kind

From Meltdown to Mistletoe

Mrs. Soul Crusher

I Want Us

Trade Rumors

<u>The Introvert Series</u>

An Introvert's Christmas

Wooing the Introvert

The Introvert Roast
I, Take Thee Introvert
The Introvert Series Compilation (paperback only)

Discussion Questions

1. Was Journey's situation understandable?
2. Do you feel there was something else Journey could have done instead of accepting Clyde's offer?
3. Was Olivia intrusive or just concerned?
4. Roz and Clyde weren't terribly close. Do you think that's because Roz was more like Clyde than she'd be willing to admit?
5. If Molly wasn't in the picture, would there have been anything wrong with Journey and Clyde's arrangement?
6. Did you agree with Roz's advice not to tell Molly about what happened?
7. What did you think about Journey's relationship with Dino?
8. Journey got more and more caught up with Clyde as the story progressed. Do you feel that Clyde led her on in any way? Or did she delude herself?
9. Do you feel that Clyde started making the effort with Molly because he wanted to or because things ended with Journey? Did you feel his love for Molly was just obligatory?
10. Has desperation ever made *you* do something out of character?

Did you love *Sugar Daddy Sweet Tooth*? Then you should read *Trade Rumors*[1] by Jessica Terry!

Van thought she was doing the right thing by leaving the wonderful but financially-lacking Joe for millionaire Grant, but given the fallout from her decision, she's beginning to have second thoughts. She didn't count on the effect it would have on her twins, on her relationship with her cousin (and Grant's ex) Raven, or the fact that it would leave Joe hating her.

Joe is angry and bitter over giving all his heart and devotion to Van only to be left high and dry. He and Raven

1. https://books2read.com/u/3GlNZL

2. https://books2read.com/u/3GlNZL

consoling each other might make them both feel better but it brings out the green-eyed monster in Van. And Grant can't help but notice that his fiancée is a little too consumed with what her ex is doing.

Van and Grant aren't exactly swimming in bliss, and it doesn't help that Joe and Raven continue to get closer. And when Van crosses the line one too many times, she might just be left with nothing.

Read more at https://www.jessicaterry.com/.

Also by Jessica Terry

Restless
The Beginning of Again
Split By the Bell
The Karma Call
Forehead Kiss
Backtalk
She is Me
All Because of Ava
The Introvert Series Compilation
Love Intolerant
Mr. Time Waster
The Stubborn Kind
Mrs. Soul Crusher
From Meltdown to Mistletoe
I Want Us
Trade Rumors
Sugar Daddy Sweet Tooth

Watch for more at https://www.jessicaterry.com/.

About the Author

Jessica Terry caught the writing bug at a young age and loves little more than holing up at home in Douglasville, GA, cranking out contemporary novels. And eating. www.jessicaterry.com

Read more at https://www.jessicaterry.com/.

www.ingramcontent.com/pod-product-compliance
Lightning Source LLC
Chambersburg PA
CBHW020600260626
47157CB00003B/788